ALSO BY JENNIFER LYNN BARNES

The Naturals

All In

KILLER INSTINCT

JENNIFER LYNN BARNES

A **NATURALS** NOVEL

LITTLE, BROWN AND COMPANY
New York   Boston

Copyright © 2014 by Jennifer Lynn Barnes
Excerpt from *All In* copyright © 2015 by Jennifer Lynn Barnes

Cover photos by Shutterstock.com. Cover design by Marci Senders.
Cover copyright © 2014 by Hachette Book Group, Inc.

Little, Brown and Company
Hachette Book Group
1290 Avenue of the Americas, New York, NY 10104
Visit us at LBYR.com

Originally published in hardcover and ebook by Hyperion, an imprint of Disney Book Group, in November 2014
First Trade Paperback Edition: November 2015

Little, Brown and Company is a division of Hachette Book Group, Inc.
The Little, Brown name and logo are trademarks of Hachette Book Group, Inc.

The publisher is not responsible for websites (or their content) that are not owned by the publisher.

Library of Congress Control Number for the Hardcover Edition: 2014001038

ISBNs: 978-1-4231-7182-9 (pbk.), 978-1-4231-9512-2 (ebook)

Printed in the United States of America

CW

10 9 8 7 6 5

For "Special Agent" Elizabeth Harding.
Thanks for everything.

CHAPTER 1

The majority of children who are kidnapped and killed are dead within three hours of the abduction. Thanks to my roommate, the walking encyclopedia of probabilities and statistics, I knew the exact numbers. I knew that when you went from discussing *hours* to *days* and *days* to *weeks*, the likelihood of recovery dropped so far that the FBI couldn't justify the manpower necessary to keep the case active.

I knew that by the time a case was classified "cold" and found its way to us, we were probably looking for a body—not a little girl.

But . . .

But Mackenzie McBride was six years old.

But her favorite color was purple.

But she wanted to be a "veterinarian pop star."

You couldn't stop looking for a kid like that. You couldn't stop *hoping*, even if you tried.

"You look like a woman in need of amusement. Or possibly libation." Michael Townsend eased himself down onto the sofa next to me, stretching his bad leg out to the side.

"I'm fine," I said.

Michael snorted. "The corners of your mouth are turned upward. The rest of your face is fighting it, like if your lips parted into even a tiny smile, it might clear the way for a sob."

That was the downside to joining the Naturals program. We were all here because we saw things that other people didn't. Michael read facial expressions as easily as other people read words.

He leaned toward me. "Say the word, Colorado, and I will selflessly provide you with a much-needed distraction."

The last time Michael had offered to distract me, we'd spent half an hour blowing things up and then hacked our way into a secure FBI drive.

Well, technically, *Sloane* had hacked our way into a secure FBI drive, but the end result had been the same.

"No distractions," I said firmly.

"Are you sure?" Michael asked. "Because this distraction involves Lia, Jell-O, and a vendetta that begs to be paid."

I didn't want to know what our resident lie detector had done to provoke the kind of vengeance that came laden with Jell-O. Given Lia's personality and her history with Michael, the possibilities were endless.

"You do realize that starting a prank war with Lia would be a very bad idea," I said.

"Without question," Michael replied. "If only I weren't so overly burdened with good sense and a need for self-preservation."

Michael drove like a maniac and had a general disdain for authority. Two months earlier, he'd followed me out of the house *knowing* that I was the subject of a serial killer's obsession, and he'd gotten shot for his trouble.

Twice.

Self-preservation was not Michael's strong suit.

"What if we're wrong about this case?" I asked. My thoughts had looped right back around: from Michael to Mackenzie, from what had happened six weeks ago to what Agent Briggs and his team were out there doing right now.

"We're not wrong," Michael said softly.

Let the phone ring, I thought. *Let it be Briggs, calling to tell me that this time—*this time—*my instincts were right.*

The first thing I'd done when Agent Briggs had handed over the Mackenzie McBride file was profile the suspect: a parolee who'd disappeared around the same time Mackenzie had. Unlike Michael's ability, my skill set wasn't limited to facial expressions or posture. Given a handful of details, I could crawl into another person's skull and imagine what it would be like to be them, to want what they wanted, to do the things that they did.

Behavior. Personality. Environment.

The suspect in Mackenzie's case had no focus. The abduction was too well planned. It didn't add up.

I'd combed through the files, looking for someone who

seemed like a possible fit. *Young. Male. Intelligent. Precise.* I'd half begged, half coerced Lia into going through witness testimony, interrogations, interviews—any and every recording related to the case, hoping she'd catch someone in a revealing lie. And finally, she had. The McBride family's attorney had issued a statement to the press on behalf of his clients. It had seemed standard to me, but to Lia, lies were as jarring as off-key singing was to a person with perfect pitch.

"No one can make sense of a tragedy like this."

The lawyer was young, male, intelligent, precise—and when he'd said those words, he'd been lying. There was one person who could make sense of what had happened, a person who *didn't* think it was a tragedy.

The person who'd taken Mackenzie.

According to Michael, the McBrides' lawyer had felt a thrill just mentioning the little girl's name. I was hoping that meant there was a chance—however small—that the man had kept her alive: a living, breathing reminder that he was bigger, better, smarter than the FBI.

"Cassie." Dean Redding burst into the room, and my chest constricted. Dean was quiet and self-contained. He almost never raised his voice.

"Dean?"

"They found her," Dean said. "Cassie, they found her on his property, exactly where Sloane's schematics said they would. She's alive."

I jumped up, my heart pounding in my ears, unsure if I

was going to cry or throw up or shriek. Dean smiled. Not a half smile. Not a grin. He beamed, and the expression transformed him. Chocolate-brown eyes sparkled underneath the blond hair that hung perpetually in his face. A dimple I'd never seen appeared in one cheek.

I threw my arms around Dean. A moment later, I bounced out of his grip and launched myself at Michael.

Michael caught me and let out a whoop. Dean sat down on the arm of the couch, and there I was, wedged in between them, feeling the heat from both of their bodies, and all I could think was that Mackenzie was going to get to go home.

"Is this a private party, or can anyone join?"

The three of us turned to see Lia in the doorway. She was dressed from head to toe in black, a white silk scarf tied neatly around her neck. She arched an eyebrow at us: cool and calm and just a little bit mocking.

"Admit it, Lia," Michael said. "You're just as happy as we are."

Lia eyed me. She eyed Michael. She eyed Dean. "Honestly," she said, "I doubt that anyone is as happy as Cassie is at this exact moment."

I was getting better at ignoring Lia's suggestive little digs, but this one hit its target, dead center. Squished in between Michael and Dean, I blushed. I was *not* going to go there—and I wasn't going to let Lia ruin this.

A grim expression on his face, Dean stood and marched toward Lia. For a moment, I thought he might say something to her about spoiling the moment, but he didn't. He just picked her up and tossed her over his shoulder.

"Hey!" Lia protested.

Dean grinned and threw her onto the sofa with Michael and me and then resumed his perch on the edge of the couch like nothing had happened. Lia scowled, and Michael poked her cheek.

"Admit it," he said again. "You're just as happy as we are."

Lia tossed her hair over her shoulder and stared straight ahead, refusing to look any of us in the eye. "A little girl is going home," she said. "Because of us. Of course I'm as happy as you are."

"Given individual differences in serotonin levels, the probability that any four people would be experiencing identical levels of happiness simultaneously is quite—"

"Sloane," Michael said, without bothering to turn around. "If you don't finish that sentence, there's a cup of fresh ground coffee in your future."

"My immediate future?" Sloane asked suspiciously. Michael had a long history of blocking her consumption of caffeine.

Without a word, Michael, Lia, and I all turned to look at Dean. He got the message, stood up, and strode toward Sloane, giving her the exact same treatment he'd given Lia. When Dean tossed Sloane gently on top of me, I giggled and almost toppled onto the floor, but Lia grabbed hold of my collar.

We did it, I thought, as Michael, Lia, Sloane, and I elbowed for room and Dean stared on from his position, just outside the fray. *Mackenzie McBride isn't going to be some statistic. She's not going to be forgotten.*

Mackenzie McBride was going to grow up, because of us.

"So," Lia said, a decidedly wicked glint in her eyes. "Who thinks this calls for a celebration?"

CHAPTER 2

t was late September, the time of year when you could practically feel the last, labored breaths of summer as it gave way to fall. A slight chill settled over the backyard as the sun went down, but the five of us barely felt it, drunk on power and the unfathomable thing we'd just managed to do. Lia chose the music. The steady beat of the bass line drowned out the sounds of the tiny town of Quantico, Virginia.

I'd never really belonged anywhere before I joined the Naturals program, but for this instant, this moment, this one night, nothing else mattered.

Not my mother's disappearance and presumed murder.

Not the corpses that had started piling up once I had agreed to work for the FBI.

For this instant, this moment, this one night, I was invincible and powerful and part of something.

Lia took my hand in hers and led me from the back porch onto the lawn. Her body moved with perfect, fluid grace, like she'd been born dancing. "For once in your life," she ordered, "just let go."

I wasn't much of a dancer, but somehow, my hips began to keep time to the music.

"Sloane," Lia yelled. "Get your butt out here."

Sloane, who'd already had her promised cup of coffee, bounded out to join us. It became quickly apparent that her version of dancing involved a great deal of bouncing and occasional spirit fingers. With a grin, I gave up trying to mimic Lia's liquid, sensuous movements and adopted Sloane's. *Bounce. Wiggly fingers. Bounce.*

Lia gave the two of us a look of consternation and turned to the boys for backup.

"No," Dean said curtly. "Absolutely not." It was getting dark enough that I couldn't make out the exact expression on his face from across the lawn, but I could imagine the stubborn set of his jaw. "I don't dance."

Michael was not so inhibited. He walked to join us, his gait marked by a noticeable limp, but he managed some one-legged bouncing just fine.

Lia cast her eyes heavenward. "You're hopeless," she told us.

Michael shrugged, then threw in some jazz hands. "It's one of my many charms."

Lia looped her arms around the back of his neck and

pressed her body close to his, still dancing. He raised an eyebrow at her, but didn't push her away. If anything, he looked amused.

On again, off again. My stomach twisted sharply. Lia and Michael had been *off* the entire time I'd known them. *It's none of my business.* I had to remind myself of that. *Lia and Michael can do whatever they want to do.*

Michael caught me staring at them. He scanned my face, like a person skimming a book. Then he smiled, and slowly, deliberately, he winked.

Beside me, Sloane looked at Lia, then at Michael, then at Dean. Then she bounced closer to me. "There's a forty percent chance this ends with someone getting punched in the face," she whispered.

"Come on, Dean-o," Lia called. "Join us." Those words were part invitation, part challenge. Michael's body moved to Lia's beat, and I realized suddenly that Lia wasn't putting on a show for my benefit—or for Michael's. She was getting up close and personal with Michael solely to get a rise out of Dean.

Based on the mutinous expression on Dean's face, it was working.

"You know you want to," Lia taunted, turning as she danced so her back was up against Michael. Dean and Lia had been the program's first recruits. For years, it had been just the two of them. Lia had told me once that she and Dean were like siblings—and right now, Dean looked every inch the overprotective big brother.

Michael likes pissing Dean off. That much went without saying. *Lia lives to pull Dean off the sidelines. And Dean . . .*

A muscle in Dean's jaw ticked as Michael trailed a hand down Lia's arm. Sloane was right. *We were one wrong move away from a fistfight.* Knowing Michael, he'd probably consider it a bonding activity.

"Come on, Dean," I said, intervening before Lia could say something inflammatory. "You don't have to dance. Just brood in beat to the music."

That surprised a laugh out of Dean. I grinned. Beside me, Michael eased back, putting space between his body and Lia's.

"Care to dance, Colorado?" Michael grabbed my hand and twirled me. Lia narrowed her eyes at us, but rebounded quickly, wrapping an arm around Sloane's waist, attempting to coerce her into something that resembled actual dancing.

"You're not happy with me," Michael said once I was facing him again.

"I don't like games."

"I wasn't playing with *you*," Michael told me, twirling me around a second time. "And for the record, I wasn't playing with Lia, either."

I gave him a look. "You *were* messing with Dean."

Michael shrugged. "One does need hobbies."

Dean stayed at the edge of the lawn, but I could feel his eyes on me.

"Your lips are turning upward." Michael cocked his head to one side. "But there's a wrinkle in your brow."

I looked away. Six weeks ago, Michael had told me to figure out how I felt about him—and about Dean. I'd been doing my best not to think about it, not to let myself feel anything about *either* of them, because the moment I felt something—anything—Michael would know. I'd gone my whole life without romance. I didn't need it, not the way I needed *this*: being part of something, caring about people in a way that I hadn't realized I still could. Not just Michael and Dean, but Sloane and even Lia. I *fit* here. I hadn't fit anywhere in a very long time.

Maybe ever.

I couldn't screw that up.

"You sure we can't talk you into dancing?" Lia called out to Dean.

"Positive."

"Well, in that case . . . ." Lia cut in between Michael and me, and the next thing I knew, I was dancing with Sloane and Lia was back with Michael. She looked up at him through heavily lashed eyes and put her hands flat on his chest.

"Tell me, Townsend," she said, practically purring. "Do you feel lucky?"

This did not bode well.

was dead. Outmanned, outgunned, seconds away from disaster—and there was absolutely nothing I could do about it.

"I'll see your three and raise you two." Michael smirked. If I'd been an emotion reader, I could have determined if it was an *I have an incredible hand and I'm spoon-feeding you your own doom* smirk or an *it's smirk-worthy that you can't tell I'm bluffing* smirk. Unfortunately, I was better at figuring out people's personalities and motivations than the exact meaning of each of their facial expressions.

Note to self, I thought. *Never play poker with Naturals.*

"I'm in." Lia twirled her gleaming black ponytail around her index finger before sliding the requisite number of Oreos to the center of the coffee table. Given that her expertise was spotting lies, I took that to mean that there was a very good chance that Michael was bluffing.

The only problem was that now I had no idea if *Lia* was bluffing.

Sloane looked on from behind a veritable mountain of Oreos. "I'll sit this one out," she said. "Also, I'm entertaining the idea of eating some of my poker chips. Can we agree that an Oreo missing its frosting is worth two-thirds of its normal amount?"

"Just eat the cookies," I told her, eyeing her pile mournfully—and only partially joking. "You have plenty to spare."

Before joining the Naturals program, Sloane had been Las Vegas born and raised. She'd been counting cards since she'd learned to count. She sat out about a third of the hands, but won every single hand she played.

"Somebody's a bad sport," Lia said, waggling a finger at me. I stuck my tongue out at her.

Somebody only had two Oreos left.

"I'm in," I sighed, pushing them into the pot. There was no point in delaying the inevitable. If I'd been playing with strangers, I would have had the advantage. I could have looked at a person's clothes and posture and known instantly how much of a risk taker they were and whether they'd bluff quietly or put on a show. Unfortunately, I wasn't playing with strangers, and the ability to get a read on other people's personalities wasn't nearly as useful in a group of people you already knew.

"What about you, Redding? Are you in or are you out?" Michael issued the words as a challenge.

So maybe Lia misread him, I thought, turning that idea over in my head. *Maybe he's not bluffing.* I doubted Michael would have challenged Dean unless he was certain he was going to win.

"I'm in," Dean said. "All in." He pushed five cookies into the pot and raised an eyebrow at Michael, mimicking the other boy's facial expression almost exactly.

Michael matched Dean's bet. Lia matched Michael's. My turn.

"I'm out of cookies," I said.

"I'd be open to discussing a modest interest rate," Sloane told me before returning her attention to divesting an Oreo of its frosting.

"I have an idea," Lia said in an overly innocent tone that I recognized immediately as trouble. "We could always take things to the next level." She unknotted the white kerchief around her neck and tossed it to me. Her fingers played with the bottom of her tank top, raising it up just enough to make it crystal clear what the "next level" was.

"It is my understanding that the rules of strip poker specify that only the loser is required to disrobe," Sloane interjected. "No one has lost yet, ergo—"

"Call it a show of solidarity," Lia said, inching her shirt up farther. "Cassie's almost out of chips. I'm just trying to even the playing field."

"Lia." Dean was not amused.

"Come on, Dean," Lia said, her bottom lip jutting out in an exaggerated pout. "Loosen up. We're all friends here."

With those words, Lia pulled off her tank top. She was wearing a bikini top underneath. Clearly, she'd dressed for the occasion.

"Ante up," she told me.

I wasn't wearing a bathing suit under *my* top, so there was no way it was coming off. Slowly, I took off my belt.

"Sloane?" Lia turned to her next. Sloane stared at Lia, a blush spreading over her cheeks.

"I'm not undressing until we establish a conversion rate," she informed us tartly, gesturing toward her mountain of chips.

"Sloane," Michael said.

"Yes?"

"How would you feel about a second cup of coffee?"

Forty-five seconds later, Sloane was in the kitchen, and neither of the boys was wearing a shirt. Dean's stomach was tanned, a shade or two darker than Michael's. Michael's skin was like marble, but for the bullet scar, pink and puckered where his shoulder met his chest. Dean had a scar, too—older, thinner, like someone had drawn the tip of a knife slowly down his torso in a jagged line from the base of his collarbone to his navel.

"I call," Lia said.

One by one, we flipped over our cards.

Three of a kind.

Flush.

Full house, queens and eights. The last was from Michael.

I knew it, I thought. *He wasn't bluffing.*

"Your turn," Lia told me.

I flipped my own cards over, and my brain cataloged the result. "Full house," I said, grinning. "Kings and twos. Guess that means I win, huh?"

"How did you . . . ?" Michael sputtered.

"Are you telling me the pity party was an act?" Lia sounded impressed despite herself.

"It wasn't an act," I told her. "I fully expected to lose. I just hadn't actually looked at my final cards yet."

I'd figured that if *I* didn't know what my hand held, there was no way for Michael or Lia to figure it out, either.

Dean was the first one to start laughing.

"Hail Cassie," Michael said. "Queen of loopholes."

Lia huffed.

"Does this mean I get to keep your shirts?" I asked, reaching for my belt and snagging an Oreo while I was at it.

"I think it would be best if everyone maintained possession of their own shirts. And put them on. *Now.*"

I froze. The voice that issued that command was female and crisp. For a split second, I was taken back to my first weeks in the program, to our supervisor, my mentor. Special Agent Lacey Locke. She'd trained me. I'd idolized her. I'd trusted her.

"Who are you?" I forced myself back to the present. I couldn't let myself think about Agent Locke—once I went down that rabbit hole, it would be hard to fight my way out. Instead, I focused on the person barking out orders. She was tall and thin, but nothing about her seemed slight. Her dark brown hair was pulled into a tight French knot at the nape of her neck, and she held her head with her chin thrust slightly forward. Her eyes were gray, a shade lighter than her suit. Her clothes were expensive; she wore them like they weren't.

There was a gun holstered to her side.

Gun. This time, I couldn't cut the memories off at the knees. *Locke. The gun.* It was all coming back. *The knife.*

Dean laid a hand on my shoulder. "Cassie." I felt the warmth of his hand through my shirt. I heard him say my name. "It's okay. I know her."

One shot. Two. Michael goes down. Locke—she's holding a gun—

I concentrated on breathing and fought back the memories. I wasn't the one who'd gotten shot. This wasn't *my* trauma. I was the reason Michael had been there in the first place.

I was the one that, in her own twisted way, the monster had loved.

"Who are you?" I asked again, clawing my way back to the here and now, my voice crisp and pointed. "And what are you doing in our house?"

The woman in gray raked her eyes over my face, leaving me with the uncomfortable feeling that she knew exactly what was going on in my head, exactly where I'd been a moment before.

"My name is Special Agent Veronica Sterling," she said finally. "And as of right now, I live here."

"Well, she's not lying." Lia broke the silence. "She's really a special agent, her name really is Veronica Sterling, and for some reason, she's operating under the misguided belief that she resides under our roof."

"Lia, I presume?" Agent Sterling said. "The one who specializes in lies."

"Telling them, spotting them—it's all the same." Lia executed a graceful little shrug, but her eyes were hard.

"And yet," Agent Sterling continued, ignoring both the shrug and the intensity of Lia's gaze, "you interacted on a daily basis with an FBI agent who was moonlighting as a serial killer. She was one of your supervisors, a constant presence in this house for *years*, and no alarm bells went off." Agent Sterling's tone was clinical—just stating the facts.

Locke had fooled us all.

"And you," Agent Sterling said, her eyes lighting on mine,

"must be Cassandra Hobbes. I hadn't pegged you for the type to play strip poker. And no, you don't get credit for being the only person in this room besides me who's still wearing a shirt."

Agent Sterling pointedly turned her attention from me to the pile of clothes on the coffee table. She folded her arms over her chest and waited. Dean reached for his shirt and tossed Lia's to her. Michael didn't appear overly bothered by the crossed arms, nor did he seem at all compelled to get dressed. Agent Sterling stared down the length of her nose at him, her gaze settling on the bullet scar on his chest.

"I take it you're Michael," she said. "The emotion reader with the attitude problem who's continually doing stupid things for girls."

"That's hardly a fair assessment," Michael replied. "I do plenty of stupid things that aren't for girls, too."

Special Agent Veronica Sterling didn't show even the slightest inclination to smile. Turning back to the rest of us, she finished her introduction. "This program has a vacancy for a supervisor. I'm here to fill it."

"True," Lia said, drawing out the word, "but not the whole story." When Agent Sterling didn't rise to the bait, Lia continued. "It's been six weeks since Locke went off the deep end. We were starting to wonder if the FBI would ever send a replacement." She raked her eyes over Agent Sterling. "Where did they find you, central casting? One young female agent swapped in for another?"

Trust Lia to cut through the niceties.

"Let's just say I'm uniquely qualified for the position," Agent Sterling replied. Her no-nonsense tone reminded me of something. Of someone. For the first time, her last name sank in, and I realized where I'd heard it before.

"Agent Sterling," I said. "As in Director Sterling?"

I'd only met the FBI director once. He'd gotten involved when the serial killer Locke and Briggs were hunting had kidnapped a senator's daughter. At the time, none of us had known that the UNSUB—or *Unknown Subject*—was Locke.

"Director Sterling is my father." Agent Sterling's voice was neutral—too neutral, and I wondered what daddy issues she had. "He sent me here to do damage control."

Director Sterling had chosen his own daughter as Locke's replacement. She'd arrived when Agent Briggs was out of town on a case. I doubted the timing was accidental.

"Briggs told me you left the FBI," Dean said quietly, addressing the words to Agent Sterling. "I heard you transferred to Homeland Security."

"I did."

I tried to pinpoint the expression on Agent Sterling's face, the tone of her voice. She and Dean knew each other— that much was clear, both from Dean's earlier statement and from the way her face softened, almost imperceptibly, when she looked at him.

A maternal streak? I wondered. That didn't fit with the way she was dressed, her super-erect posture, the way she talked *about* the rest of us rather than *to* us. My first impression of Agent Sterling was that she was hypercontrolled, professional, and kept other people at a distance. She either didn't like teenagers, or she disliked us specifically.

But the way she'd looked at Dean, even if it was only for a second . . .

You weren't always this way, I thought, slipping into her head. *Tying your hair back in French knots, keeping your every statement clinical and detached. Something happened to send you into hyperprofessional mode.*

"Is there something you'd care to share with the class, Cassandra?"

Whatever sliver of softness had crept into Agent Sterling's expression disappeared now. She'd caught me profiling her and called me out. That told me two things. First, based on the way she'd chosen to do so, I sensed a hint of sarcasm buried beneath her humorless exterior. At some point in her life, she would have said those words with a grin instead of a grimace.

And second . . .

"You're a profiler," I said out loud. She'd caught me profiling her, and I couldn't keep from thinking, *It takes one to know one.*

"What makes you think that?"

"They sent you here to replace Agent Locke." Saying those words—seeing her as a replacement—hurt more than it should have.

"And?" Agent Sterling's voice was high and clear, but her

eyes were hard. This was a challenge, as clear as the earlier subtext between Michael and Dean.

"Profilers put people in boxes," I said, meeting Agent Sterling's eyes and refusing to look away first. "We take in an assortment of random details, and we use those details to construct the big picture, to figure out what *kind* of person we're dealing with. It's there in the way you talk: Michael's 'the emotion reader with the attitude problem,' you didn't 'peg me' for being the type to play strip poker."

I paused, and when she didn't reply, I continued, "You read our files, and you profiled us before you ever stepped foot in this house, which means you know exactly how much it *kills us* that we didn't see Agent Locke for what she was, and you either wanted to see how we'd deal with you mentioning it, or you just wanted to pick at the wound for kicks." I paused and raked my eyes over her body, taking in all the tiny details—her fingernail polish, her posture, her shoes. "You seem like more of a masochist than a sadist, so I'm guessing you just wanted to see how we'd respond."

The room fell into an uncomfortable silence, and Agent Sterling wielded that silence like a weapon. "I don't need you to lecture me on what it means to be a profiler," she said finally, her voice soft, her words measured. "I have a bachelor's in criminology. I was the youngest person ever to graduate from the FBI Academy. I clocked more field time during my stint at the FBI than you will see in your entire life, and I've spent the past five years with Homeland

Security, working on domestic terrorism cases. While I am residing in this house, you will address me as Agent Sterling or ma'am, and you will not refer to yourself as a profiler, because at the end of the day, you're just a kid."

There it was again in her voice, the hint of something else beneath her frosty exterior. But like a person staring at an object trapped under several feet of ice, I couldn't make out what that *something* was.

"There is no 'we' here, Cassandra. There's you, and there's me, and there's the evaluation I'm writing of this program. So I suggest that you all clean this mess up, go to bed, and get a good night's sleep." She tossed Michael his shirt. "You're going to need it."

CHAPTER 5

I lay in bed, staring up at the ceiling, unable to shake the fear that if I closed my eyes, there would be nothing to keep the ghosts at bay. When I slept, it all ran together: what had happened to my mother when I was twelve; the women Agent Locke had killed last summer; the gleam in Locke's eyes as she'd held the knife out to me. *The blood*.

Turning over onto my side, I reached toward my nightstand.

"Cassie?" Sloane said from her bed.

"I'm fine," I told her. "Go back to sleep."

My fingers closed around the object I'd been looking for: a tube of Rose Red lipstick, my mother's favorite shade. It had been a gift from Locke to me, part of the sick game she'd played, doling out clues, grooming me in her own image. *You wanted me to know how close you were*. I slipped into Locke's head, profiling her, the way I had on so many other nights

27

just like this one. *You wanted me to find you.* The next part was always the hardest. *You wanted me to be like you.*

She'd offered me the knife. She'd told me to kill the girl. And on some level, she'd believed that I would say yes.

Locke's real name had been Lacey Hobbes. She was the younger sister of Lorelai Hobbes—fake psychic, presumed murder victim. *My mother.* I turned the lipstick over in my hand, staring at it in the dark. No matter how many times I tried to throw it away, I couldn't. It was a masochistic reminder: of the people I'd trusted, the people I'd lost.

Eventually, I forced my fingers to set it back down. I couldn't keep doing this to myself.

I couldn't stop.

Think about something else. Anything else. I thought about Agent Sterling. Locke's replacement. She wore her clothes like armor. They were expensive, freshly pressed. She'd had a coat of clear polish on her nails. Not a French manicure, not a color—clear. Why wear polish at all if it was transparent? Did she enjoy the ritual of applying it, putting a thin layer between her nails and the rest of the world? There was subtext there: protection, distance, strength.

You don't allow yourself weaknesses, I thought, addressing her, the way I'd been taught to address anyone I was profiling. *Why?* I went back over the clues she'd given me about her past. She was the youngest person to graduate from the FBI Academy—and proud of that fact. Once upon a time, she'd probably had a competitive streak. Five years ago, she'd left the FBI. *Why?*

Instead of an answer, my brain latched on to the fact that sometime before she'd left, she'd met Dean. *He couldn't have been more than twelve when you met him.* That set off an alarm in my head. *The only way an FBI agent would have interacted with Dean that long ago was if she was part of the team that took down his father.*

Agent Briggs had led that team. Shortly thereafter, he'd started using Dean—the son of a notorious serial killer—to get inside the head of other killers. Eventually, the FBI had discovered what Briggs was doing and, instead of firing him, they'd made it official. Dean had been moved into an old house in the town outside of Marine Corps Base Quantico. Briggs had hired a man named Judd to act as Dean's guardian. Over time, Briggs had begun recruiting other teenagers with savant-like skills. First Lia, with her uncanny ability to lie and to spot lies when they exited the mouths of others. Then Sloane and Michael, and finally me.

You used to work with Agent Briggs, I thought, picturing Veronica Sterling in my mind. *You were on his team. Maybe you were even his partner.* When I'd joined the program, Agent Locke had been Briggs's partner. Maybe she'd been Agent Sterling's replacement, before the situation was reversed.

You don't like being replaceable, and you don't like being replaced. You're not just here as a favor to your father, I told Agent Sterling silently. *You know Briggs. You didn't like Locke. And once upon a time, you cared about Dean. This is personal.*

"Did you know that the average life span of the hairy-nosed wombat is ten to twelve years?" Apparently, Sloane had decided that when I said I was fine, I was lying. The more coffee my roommate ingested, the lower her threshold for keeping random statistics to herself—especially if she thought someone needed a distraction.

"The longest-living wombat in captivity lived thirty-four years," Sloane continued, propping herself up on her elbows to look at me. Given that we shared a bedroom, I probably should have objected more strenuously to cup of coffee number two. Tonight, though, I found Sloane's high-speed statistical babbling to be strangely soothing. Profiling Sterling hadn't kept me from thinking about Locke.

Maybe this would.

"Tell me more about wombats," I said.

With the look of a small child awaking to a miracle on Christmas morning, Sloane beamed at me and complied.

YOU

You were nervous the first time you saw her, standing beside the big oak tree, long hair shining to halfway down her back. You asked what her name was. You memorized everything about her.

But none of that matters now. Not her name. Not the tree. Not your nerves.

You've come too far. You've waited too long.

"She'll fight you if you let her," a voice whispers from somewhere in your mind.

"I won't let her," you whisper back. Your throat is dry. You're ready. You've been ready. "I'll tie her up."

"Bind her," the voice whispers.

Bind her. Brand her. Cut her. Hang her.

That's the way this has to be done. That's what awaits this girl. She shouldn't have parked so far away from the man's building. She shouldn't have slept with him in the first place.

Shouldn't.

Shouldn't.

Shouldn't.

You're waiting for her in the car when she climbs in. You're prepared. She has a test today, but so do you.

She shuts the car door. Her eyes flit toward the rearview mirror, and for a split second, they meet yours.

She sees you.

You lunge forward. Her mouth opens to scream, but you slam the damp cloth over her mouth, her nose. "She'll fight you if you let her," you say, whispering the words like sweet nothings in her ear.

Her body goes slack. You pull her into the backseat and reach for the ties.

Bind them. Brand them. Cut them. Hang them.

It has begun.

slept until noon and woke up feeling like I hadn't slept at all. My head ached. I needed food. And caffeine. And possibly some Tylenol.

"Rough night?" Judd asked the second I stepped foot in the kitchen. He had a sharpened number two pencil in his hand and filled in a line on his crossword puzzle without ever looking up at me.

"You could say that," I replied. "Have you met Agent Sterling?"

Judd's lips twitched slightly. "You could say that," he said, parroting my own words back at me.

Judd Hawkins was in his sixties. His official job description involved both looking after the house and looking after us. The house was in excellent condition. As for the five teenagers who lived here . . . well, other than making sure we were fed and our limbs were kept relatively intact, Judd was pretty hands-off.

"Agent Sterling seems to think she's moving in," I commented. Judd filled in another line on his crossword. If he was bothered by the fact that an FBI agent had shown up, more or less unannounced, he didn't show it. "Can she even do that?" I asked.

Judd finally looked up from his puzzle. "If she were anyone else," he said, "the answer would be no."

Given that Agent Sterling had come here at her father's request, I understood that there probably wasn't anything Judd could do about it. What I didn't understand was why Judd didn't seem to *want* to do anything about it. She was here to write an evaluation of the program. She'd called it damage control, but from where I was sitting, it seemed more like an invasion.

"Good. You're up."

Speak of the devil, and she appears, I thought. Then I stopped myself. I wasn't being objective—or fair. I was judging Agent Sterling based more on what I thought she *would* do than anything she'd done already. Deep down, I knew that no matter who they'd sent to replace Locke, I wouldn't have been ready. Every similarity was salt in an open wound. Every difference was, too.

"Do you always make it a practice to sleep until noon?" Agent Sterling asked, cocking her head to the side and giving me the once-over. Since I couldn't make her stop studying me, I returned the favor. She was wearing makeup, but didn't look made up. Like the clear coat of polish on her nails, the colors she'd chosen for her eyes and lips looked almost natural.

I wondered how much effort it took her to look that effortlessly perfect.

If you want to get close to an UNSUB, I could practically hear Locke telling me, *don't say* she *or* her. *Say* you.

"You spent the night here?" I asked Sterling, rolling that over in my mind. *Locke never slept here. Briggs doesn't. You don't do things halfway.*

"There's a pullout sofa in the study," Judd told me, sounding mildly disgruntled. "I offered her my room, but Miss Stubborn refused to take it."

Miss Stubborn? Before working for the Naturals program, Judd had been career military. I'd never heard him refer to any FBI agent by anything other than their title or last name. So why was he referring to Agent Sterling in the exact same tone I would have expected him to use with Lia?

"I'm not kicking you out of your own bed, Judd." The twinge of exasperation in Agent Sterling's voice told me they'd already had this argument at least twice.

"Sit down," Judd grunted in return. "Both of you. Cassie hasn't had anything to eat today, and I can make two sandwiches as easy as one."

"I can make my own sandwich," I said. Judd gave me a look. I sat. This was a side of him I hadn't seen before. In a strange way, he almost reminded me of my very Italian grandmother, who thought I was off at some kind of progressive, government-sponsored gifted program. Nonna considered the putting of food in bellies one of her major missions in life, and woe be to the unfortunate soul who stood in her way.

"I already made myself a sandwich," Agent Sterling said stiffly.

Judd made two sandwiches anyway. He slid one in front of me and put the other in front of an empty spot at the table before sitting down and resuming his crossword. He didn't say a word, and after a long moment, Agent Sterling sat.

"Where are the others?" I asked Judd. Usually, I couldn't spend five minutes in the kitchen without Lia coming in to swipe some ice cream, or Michael helping himself to food off my plate.

Agent Sterling was the one who answered. "Michael hasn't made an appearance yet. Dean, Lia, and Sloane are in the living room, taking a practice GED."

I almost choked on a bite of ham. "A what?"

"It's September," Agent Sterling replied, in that too-calm tone that I imagined made her very good at interrogating suspects. "If you weren't a part of this program, you'd be in school. In fact, I'm fairly certain your family was told that you would be receiving schooling here. Some people might be willing to let that slide. I'm not."

I got the distinct feeling that when Agent Sterling said "some people" she was talking about Agent Briggs, not Judd.

"You're lucky enough to have a family who might actually check up on your schooling someday," she continued. "Not everyone in this house is so fortunate, but you will *all* receive the education you were promised." Her eyes flicked over to Judd, then back to me. "Dean and Lia have been homeschooled here for years. If Judd's done his job right, they should be able to pass the GED. I'm not concerned about Sloane."

That just left Michael and me. If it hadn't been for the program, I would have started my senior year in high school this month.

"Take the practice test," Sterling ordered in an offhand way that told me she was used to being obeyed. "If you need a tutor, we'll get you a tutor, but either way, the other aspects of your . . . *education* can wait."

In the time since I'd joined the program, I'd forgotten that there was a type of learning that didn't involve the ins and outs of the criminal brain.

"Can I be excused?" I pushed back from the table.

Judd gave me an amused look. "You ever asked me that before?"

I took that as an answer and started for the door. Judd finished his crossword and turned his attention to Agent Sterling. "You going to eat your sandwich, Ronnie?"

Ronnie? My eyebrows shot into my hairline, and I slowed my exit. Out of the corner of my eye, I saw Agent Sterling stiffen slightly at the nickname.

"It's Veronica," she said. "Or it's Agent Sterling. In this house, it has to be."

They know each other, I thought. *They've known each other for a very long time.*

It occurred to me then that Director Sterling might have chosen his daughter for this assignment for reasons other than the fact that she shared his blood.

I made it to the kitchen door just as it swung inward, nearly knocking me off my feet. Agent Briggs stood on the other side, looking like he'd just stepped off a plane. He reached out to steady me, but his gaze was directed elsewhere.

"Ronnie."

"Briggs," Agent Sterling returned, very pointedly not using his first name or any abbreviation thereof. "I assume the director briefed you."

Briggs inclined his head slightly. "You could have called."

I was right, I thought. *They've definitely worked together before.*

"Cassie." Agent Briggs seemed to remember that his hands were on my shoulders, and he dropped them. "I see you've met Agent Sterling."

"We met last night." I studied Briggs, looking for some hint that he resented the intrusion this woman represented. "How's Mackenzie?" I asked.

Briggs smiled—a rare enough event in itself. "She's home. She'll need a lot of support going forward, but she'll make it. The kid's a survivor." He turned his attention back to Agent Sterling. "The Naturals program just closed its second cold case this month," he told her. "A child abduction."

There it was—the hint that Agent Briggs had no intention of ceding his authority to the newcomer. His words were designed to communicate one message, very clearly: He didn't *need* to feel threatened. The Naturals program was working. We were saving lives.

"Impressive," Agent Sterling said, her tone making it clear

that she thought it was anything but. "Especially considering that only two children have been hospitalized because of this program and, really, only one of them was actually shot, so clearly, that all just comes out in the wash."

Two children—Michael and Dean. I opened my mouth to tell Agent Sterling that we weren't *children*, but Briggs shot me a warning look. "Cassie, why don't you go see what the others are doing?"

He might as well have said "Why don't you run outside and play?" Annoyed, I obeyed. When I made it to the living room, I wasn't surprised to see that the only one actually taking a practice GED was Dean. Lia was filing her nails. Sloane appeared to be constructing some kind of catapult out of pencils and rubber bands.

Lia caught sight of me first. "Good morning, sunshine," she said. "I'm no Michael, but based on the expression on your face, I'm guessing you've been spending some quality time with the lovely Agent Sterling." Lia beamed at me. "Isn't she the best?"

The eerie thing about Lia was that she could make anything sound genuine. Lia wasn't fond of the FBI in general, and she was the type to flout rules based on principle alone, but even knowing her enthusiasm was feigned, I couldn't see through it.

"There's something about that Agent Sterling that just makes me want to listen to what she has to say," Lia continued earnestly. "I think we might be soul mates."

Dean snorted, but didn't look up from his practice test.

Sloane set off her catapult, and I had to duck to keep from taking a pencil to the forehead.

"Agent Briggs is back," I said once I'd straightened.

"Thank God." Lia dropped the act and slumped back against the sofa. "Though if anyone tells him I said that, I'll be forced to take drastic measures."

I truly did not want to know what Lia's idea of "drastic measures" entailed.

"Briggs knows Agent Sterling," I announced. "So does Judd. They call her Ronnie."

"Dean," Lia said, drawing out his name in a way specifically designed to annoy him. "Stop pretending to work and tell us what you know."

Dean ignored her. Lia raised an eyebrow at me. Clearly, she thought I'd have better luck at getting him to talk than she would.

"Agent Sterling was a part of the team that took down your dad, wasn't she?" I said, testing out my theory. "She was Briggs's partner."

At first, I thought Dean might ignore me, the same way he'd ignored Lia. But eventually, he put down his pencil. He lifted his brown eyes to meet mine. "She was his partner," he confirmed. Dean's voice was low-pitched and pleasant, with a hint of Southern twang. Usually, he was a man of few words, but today, he had five more for us. "She was also his wife."

he was his wife, I thought. *Past tense—meaning that she's not his wife anymore.*

"She's Briggs's ex-wife?" I said incredulously. "And the director sent her *here*? That can't be ethical."

Lia rolled her eyes. "Any more unethical than an off-the-books FBI program that uses underage prodigies to catch serial killers?" She smirked. "Or what about sending his own daughter to replace Agent Locke? Clearly, nepotism and shadiness are alive and well at FBI headquarters."

Sloane looked up from making some adjustments to her catapult. "As of 1999, the FBI had no written policies on interoffice dating," she rattled off. "Intercompany marriages between supervisors, agents, and support staff aren't uncommon, though they constitute a minority of employee marital unions."

Lia gave me a look and flipped her hair over her shoulder. "If the FBI doesn't have an official dating policy, I doubt they have one for divorce. Besides, we're talking about Director Sterling here. The man who basically bought Michael from his father by promising to make the IRS look the other way." She paused. "The man who had the FBI haul me in off the streets and told me my other option was juvie."

This was the first time I'd ever heard Lia mention her past before the program. *Juvie?*

"Briggs and Sterling both worked my father's case." Dean volunteered that information, using his own past to change the subject from Lia's, which told me that she'd been telling the truth and he wanted to protect her from questions. "Briggs was the strategist," Dean continued. "He was driven, competitive—not with her, but with any UNSUB they hunted. Briggs didn't just want to catch killers. He wanted to win."

It was easy to forget, when Dean said the word *UNSUB*, that his father had never been an Unknown Subject to him. Dean had lived with a killer—a true psychopath—day in, day out, for years.

"Sterling was impulsive." Dean stuck to describing the agents. I doubted he would mention his father again. "Fearless. She had a hot temper, and she followed her gut, even when that wasn't the smart thing to do."

I'd suspected that Agent Sterling's personality had undergone some major changes in the past five years, but even so, it was hard to see the connection between the short-tempered, instinct-driven woman Dean was describing and the Agent Sterling in the kitchen now. The additional data sent my brain into overdrive, connecting the dots, looking at the trajectory between past and present.

"Briggs has a case." Michael liked to make an entrance. "He just got the call."

"But his team just got back." Sloane loaded her catapult again. "The FBI has fifty-six field offices, and the DC field office is the second-largest in the country. There are dozens of teams who could take this case. Why assign it to Briggs?"

"Because I'm the most qualified for the job," Briggs said, coming into the room. "And," he added under his breath, "because somewhere along the way, the universe decided I needed to suffer."

I wondered if that last bit was about the case—or about the fact that Agent Sterling was on his heels. Now that I knew they'd been married, I doubted his irritation with her when he'd sent me out of the room had been entirely professional. She was playing in his sandbox—and they clearly had *issues.*

"I'm going with Agent Briggs." Sterling pointedly ignored her ex-husband and addressed those words to us. "If any of you hope to come within ten feet of a training exercise or cold case this month, you'll have those practice GEDs finished when I get back."

Lia threw her head back and laughed.

"You think I'm joking, Ms. Zhang?" Agent Sterling asked. It was the first time I'd ever heard Lia's last name, but Lia didn't bat an eye.

"I don't *think* anything," Lia said. "I *know* that you're

telling the truth. But I also know that the FBI brass isn't going to let you ground their secret assets from doing their jobs. They didn't bring us here to take the GED. They brought us here because we're useful. I've met your daddy dearest, Agent Sterling. He only plays by the rules when it's useful for him to do so, and he definitely didn't go to the trouble of blackmailing me into this program to let you clip my wings." Lia leaned back against the sofa and stretched out her legs. "If you think otherwise," she added, her lips parting in a slow, deliberate smile, "you're lying to yourself."

Agent Sterling waited to reply until she was certain she had Lia's full attention. "You're only useful as long as you aren't a liability," she said calmly. "And given your individual histories—some of them *criminal*—it wouldn't take much for me to convince the director that one or two of you might be a bigger risk than you're worth."

Dean was the son of a serial killer. Michael had anger management issues and a father who'd traded him to the FBI for immunity from prosecution on white-collar crimes. Lia was a compulsive liar—and apparently had some kind of juvie record. Sloane had her catapult aimed at Agent Sterling's head.

And then there was me.

"Lia, just humor her and take the test." Agent Briggs sounded very much like someone whose head was beginning to pound.

"Humor me?" Agent Sterling repeated. "You're telling her to *humor me*?" Sterling's voice went up a decibel.

"Lia already took the test." Dean spoke up before Agent Briggs had a chance to reply. Everyone in the room turned to look at him. "She's a human lie detector. She can do multiple choice questions in her sleep."

Detecting lies was as much about the words people used as the way they said them. If there was a pattern to the way the test makers wrote the questions, a subtle difference between the true answers and the false ones, a deception detector would find it.

Lia shot Dean a dirty look. "You never let me have any fun," she muttered.

Dean ignored her and directed his next words at Agent Sterling. "You have a case? Work your case. Don't worry about us. We'll be fine."

I got the feeling that what he was really saying was *I'll be fine*. For all her talk about liabilities, Agent Sterling seemed to need to hear that.

You and Briggs caught Daniel Redding, I thought, watching Agent Sterling carefully. *You saved Dean*. Maybe Briggs's ex wasn't okay with the idea that she'd saved Dean for *this*. We lived in a house where serial killers' pictures dotted the walls. There was an outline of a dead body sketched on the bottom of our pool. We lived and breathed death and destruction, Dean and I even more than the others.

If she's got something against this program, why would the director draft her as Locke's replacement? Something about this entire situation just didn't add up.

Briggs's phone vibrated. He looked to Sterling. "If you're

done here, the local PD is contaminating our crime scene as we speak, and some idiot thought it would be a bright idea to talk to the press."

Agent Sterling cursed viciously under her breath, and I changed my mind about the makeup and the nail polish, the way she was dressed, the way she talked. None of it was about presenting an image of professionalism to the rest of the world. It wasn't a protective layer to keep the rest of the world out.

She did it, all of it, to keep the old Veronica Sterling—the one Dean had described—*in*.

As I turned that thought over in my head, Briggs and Sterling took their leave. The moment the front door closed behind them, Lia, Michael, and Sloane bolted for the TV control. Sloane got there first. She flipped the television on to a local news channel. It took me a moment to realize why.

Some idiot thought it would be a bright idea to talk to the press.

Agent Briggs wouldn't tell us anything about an active case. The Naturals program was only authorized to work on cold cases. But if the press had gotten wind of whatever it was that had sent Briggs's team out on a new assignment, we wouldn't *have* to rely on Briggs for information.

"Let's see what Mommy and Daddy are up to, shall we?" Lia said, eyeing the TV greedily and waiting for the fireworks to commence.

"Lia, I will give you one thousand dollars to never refer to Sterling and Briggs as Mommy and Daddy again."

Lia gave Michael a speculative look. "Technically true," she said, assessing his promise. "But you don't come into your trust fund until you turn twenty-five, and I'm not much of a believer in delayed gratification."

I hadn't even known that Michael *had* a trust fund.

"Breaking news." All conversation in the room ceased as a female reporter came onto the screen. She was standing in front of a building with a Gothic spire. Her hair was wind-whipped, her expression serious. There was an odd energy to the moment, something that would have made me stop and watch even if I didn't already have some idea of what was coming.

"I'm standing here outside of Colonial University in northern Virginia, where today, the sixty-eight hundred students who comprise the Colonial student body saw one of their own brutally murdered—and gruesomely displayed on the university president's lawn."

The screen flashed to a picture of a plantation-style house.

"Sources say that the girl was bound and tortured before being strangled with the antenna of her own car and displayed on the hood. The car and the body were found parked on Colonial president Larry Vernon's front lawn early this morning. The police are currently investigating every lead, but a source within the police department has been quoted as saying that this man, Professor George Fogle, is a person of interest."

Another picture flashed briefly onto the screen: a man in

his late thirties, with thick, dark hair and an intense gaze.

"Professor Fogle's courses include the popular Monsters or Men: The Psychology of Serial Murder, the syllabus for which promises that students will become 'intimately familiar with the men behind the legends of the most horrific crimes ever committed.'"

The reporter held her hand to her ear and stopped reading from the teleprompter. "I've gotten word that a video of the body, taken from a student phone shortly after the police arrived at the scene, has been leaked online. The footage is said to be graphic. We're awaiting a statement from local police on both the crime itself and the lack of security that allowed such footage to be taken. This is Maria Vincent, for Channel Nine News."

Within seconds, the television was muted and Sloane had located the leaked footage on her laptop. She positioned the screen so that we could see it and hit play. A hand-held camera zoomed in on the crime scene. *Graphic* was an understatement.

Not one of the five of us looked away. For Lia and Michael, it might have been morbid curiosity. For Sloane, crime scenes were data: angles to be examined, numbers to be crunched. But for Dean and for me, it wasn't about the scene.

It was about the body.

There was an intimate connection between a killer and the person they'd killed. Bodies were like messages, full of symbolic meanings that only a person who understood the *needs* and *desires* and *rage* that went into snuffing out another life could fully decode.

This isn't a language anyone should want to speak. Dean was the one who'd told me that, but beside me, I could feel his eyes locked on to the screen, the same as mine.

The corpse had long blond hair. Whoever had taken the video hadn't been able to get close, but even from a distance, her body looked broken, her skin lifeless. Her hands appeared to be bound behind her back, and based on the fact that her legs weren't splayed apart, I was guessing her feet had been bound as well. The bottom half of her body was hanging off the front of the car. Her shirt was covered in blood. Even with the questionable camera work, I could make out a noose around her neck. Black rope stood out against the white car, going all the way up to the sunroof.

"Hey!" On the video, a police officer noticed the student holding the phone. The student cursed and ran, and the footage cut out.

Sloane closed the laptop. The room went silent.

"If it's just one murder," Michael said finally, "that means it's not serial. Why call in the FBI?"

"The person of interest teaches a class on serial killers," I replied, thinking out loud. "If the professor's involved, you might want someone with expertise in the field." I looked to Dean to see if he agreed, but he was just sitting there, staring at the silent TV screen. Somehow, I doubted he was enthralled by the weather report.

"Dean?" I said. He didn't respond.

"Dean." Lia reached her foot out and shoved him with her heel. "Earth to Redding."

Dean looked up. Blond hair hung in his face. Brown eyes stared through us. He said something, but the words were garbled in his throat, caught halfway between a grunt and a whisper.

"What did you say?" Sloane asked.

"Bind them," Dean said, his voice still rough, but louder this time. "Brand them. Cut them. Hang them." He shut his eyes, and his hands curled into fists.

"Hey." Lia was beside him in a second. "Hey, Dean." She didn't touch him, but she stayed by his side. The look on her face was fiercely protective—and terrified.

Do something, I thought.

Taking my cue from Lia, I crouched by Dean's other side. I reached a hand out to touch the back of his neck. He'd done the same for me, more than once, when I'd first started learning to climb into the minds of killers.

The second my hand made contact, he flinched. His arm shot out, and my wrist was suddenly caught in a painfully tight grip. Michael jumped to his feet, his eyes flashing. With a jerk of my head, I told him to stay put. I could take care of myself.

"Hey," I said, repeating Lia's words. "Hey, Dean."

Dean blinked rapidly, three or four times. I tried to concentrate on the details of his face and not the death grip he had on my wrist. His eyelashes weren't black. They were brown, lighter than his eyes. Those eyes stared at me now, round and dark. He let go of my wrist.

"Are you okay?" he said.

"She's fine," Lia answered for me, her eyes narrowed to slits, daring me to disagree with her.

Dean ignored Lia and fixed his eyes on me. "Cassie?"

"I'm fine," I said. I was. I could feel the place where his hand had been a moment before, but it didn't hurt anymore. My heart was pounding. I refused to let my hands shake. "Are you okay?"

I expected Dean to shut me down, to refuse to answer, to walk away. When he responded, I saw it for what it was—penance. He'd force himself to say more than he was comfortable saying to punish himself for losing control.

To make it up to me.

"I've been better." Dean could have stopped there, but he didn't. Each syllable was hard-won, and my gut twisted as I realized just how much it was costing him to form these words. "The professor they're looking for, the one who teaches the Monsters or Men class? I'd bet a lot of money that the reason he's a person of interest is that one of the killers he lectures about in his class is my father." Dean swallowed and stared holes into the carpet. "The reason Briggs and Sterling were called in is that they were the original agents on my father's case."

I remembered what it had felt like to walk through a crime scene, knowing it had been patterned after my mother's murder. Dean had been there with me. He'd been there *for* me.

"Bind them. Brand them. Cut them. Hang them," I said softly. "That was how your father killed his victims." I didn't phrase it as a question, because I knew. Just by looking at Dean, I knew.

"Yes," Dean said, before lifting his eyes to look at the still-muted TV. "And I'm almost certain that's what was done to this girl."

YOU

The president's lawn was a nice touch. You could have dumped her anywhere. You didn't have to risk being seen.

"No one saw me." You murmur the words with a self-satisfied hum. "But they saw her."

They saw the lines you carved into her body. They saw the noose you slipped around her neck. Just thinking about it, about the way her eyes bulged as the life drained out of her, fragile little arms tensing against the restraints, pale skin dyed with dainty rivulets of red . . .

Your lips curve into a smile. The moment has passed, but the game—the game is long. Next time, you won't be so eager. Next time, you'll have nothing to prove. Next time, you'll take it slow.

ean left the room right after dropping the bombshell about his father's MO. The rest of us sat there in silence, the minutes ticking by, each more saturated than the last with all the things we *weren't* saying.

There was no point in trying to take a practice GED. The only thing I could think about was the girl in the video, her body dangling off the front of the car, black noose fitted tightly around her lifeless neck. Dean hadn't said what it was about the video that had convinced him that the UNSUB was mimicking his father's crimes.

The fact that her arms and her legs were bound?

The way she was hung from the car?

Logically, those could have been coincidences. But Dean had sounded so sure, and he had believed me at a time when I'd had a theory that sounded just as crazy. Crazier, even.

"You're thinking about last summer." Michael was the one who broke the silence as he directed those words to me.

"Your whole body is hunched with the effort of holding it in."

"Don't you think it's weird?" I said, my eyes darting from Michael to the others. "Six weeks ago, Locke was reenacting my mother's murder, and now someone's out there playing copycat to Dean's dad?"

"News flash, Cassie." Lia stood up, her eyes flashing. "Not everything is about *you*." I was taken aback by the venom in her voice. Lia and I might not have been friends—exactly— but she didn't usually see me as the enemy, either.

"Lia—"

"*This. Is. Not. About. You.*" She turned on her heels and stalked toward the door. Halfway there, she stopped and turned back, her eyes boring through mine. "You think you know what this is doing to Dean? You think you *relate*? You don't have any idea what he's going through. *None.*"

"You're not angry at Cassie, Lia," Michael cut in. "You're angry at the situation and the fact that Dean's off some- where, dealing with this *alone.*"

"Screw you, Michael," Lia spat back. She let the words hang in the air, her fury a palpable thing, and then she left. A few seconds later, I heard the front door open and slam shut. Sloane, Michael, and I stared at one another in stunned silence.

"It's possible I was mistaken," Michael said finally. "Maybe she's not *just* angry at the situation."

Michael could diagnose the precise mix of emotions a per- son was feeling. He could pinpoint the difference between annoyance and simmering fury and fight-or-flight rage. But the whys of emotions . . . That fell somewhere in between his skill and mine. The things that mattered to people, the things that hurt them, the things that made them the people they were—that was all me.

"Lia's known Dean longer than any of us," I said, mentally going through the details of the situation and the personalities involved. "No matter how many people come into this house, to Lia, they'll always be a unit of two. But Dean . . ."

"Unit of one," Michael finished for me. "He's Mr. Lone Wolf."

When things got bad, Dean's impulse was to put up walls, to push other people away. But I'd never seen him shut Lia out before. She was his *family*. And this time, he'd left her on the outside—with us.

"Dean likes Cassie," Sloane announced, completely oblivious to the fact that perhaps now was not the time for a conversation about any fondness Dean might feel for me. Michael, ever a master of masking his own emotions, didn't show any discernable reaction as she continued. "Lia knows Dean likes Cassie. I don't think she minds. Mostly, I think she just thinks it's funny. But right now . . . it's not funny."

Sloane's grasp of human psychology was tenuous at best, but at the same time, I could see the kernel of truth in what she was saying. Lia had zero romantic interest in Dean. That didn't mean she liked that when he'd dealt us in on the situation, he'd been answering *my* questions. I'd been the one to break through to him. Lia wasn't okay with that. *She* was supposed to be the person he leaned on, not me.

Then I'd gone and compounded my sins by highlighting the similarities—such as they were—between Dean's situation and what I'd gone through with Locke.

"I wasn't trying to say that I know exactly how he feels." I felt like I had to justify myself, even though Sloane and Michael probably weren't expecting me to. "I just meant that it seems like this truly horrific twist of fate that we were all brought here to solve *cold* cases, and yet Briggs's active cases keep tying back to us." I glanced from Michael to Sloane. "Seriously, what are the chances?"

Sloane pressed her lips together.

"You want to tell us what the chances are, don't you?" Michael asked her.

"It's not that simple." Sloane shook her head, then pushed white-blond hair out of her face with the heel of her palm. "You're not dealing with separate variables. Dean is a part of the program because he understands killers, and Dean understands killers because his father is a killer." Sloane gestured with her hands out in front of her, like she was trying to grab hold of something that wasn't there. "It's all connected. Our families. The things that have happened to us. The things we can do."

I glanced over at Michael. He wouldn't meet my eyes.

"Being a Natural isn't just about being born with an incredible aptitude for something. You have to hone it. Your whole *life* has to hone it." Sloane's voice got softer. "Did you know they've done studies about people like Lia? I've read them. All of them."

I understood, the way I always did, without even having to think about it, that Sloane reading articles about lie detection was her way of trying to connect with Lia. The rest of us inherently understood people. Sloane was better with objects. With numbers. With *facts*.

"For adults, an enhanced ability to detect lies mostly seems dependent on a combination of innate ability and explicit training. But with kids, it's different." She swallowed hard. "There's a specific subset who excel at spotting lies."

"And what subset is that?" I asked.

Sloane's fingertips worried at the edge of her sleeve. "The subset that have been exposed to highs and lows. Changing environments. Abuse." Sloane paused, and when she started talking again, the words came out faster. "There's an interaction effect—statistically, the best deception detectors are the kids who aren't submissive, the ones who grow up in abusive environments, but somehow fight to maintain some sense of control."

When Briggs talked about what it meant to be a Natural, he tended to use words like *potential* or *gift*. But Sloane was saying that raw talent alone wasn't enough. We hadn't been born Naturals. Something about Lia's childhood had turned her into the kind of person who could lie effortlessly, the kind who *knew* when someone else was lying to her.

Something had made Michael zero in on emotions.

My mother had taught me to read people so I could help her con them out of money. We were constantly on the move, sometimes a new city every week. I hadn't had a home. Or friends. Getting inside people's heads, understanding them, even if they didn't know I was alive—growing up, that was the closest to friendship I'd been able to come.

"None of us had normal childhoods," Sloane said quietly. "If we had, we wouldn't be Naturals."

"And on that note, I take my leave." Michael stood up. He kept his voice casual, but I knew he didn't like talking about his home life. He'd told me once that his father had an explosive temper. I tried not to think about the reasons a little boy might need to become an expert at reading other people's emotions, growing up with a father like that.

Michael paused next to Sloane on his way out. "Hey," he said softly. She peered up at him. "I'm not mad at you," he told her. "You didn't do anything wrong."

Sloane smiled, but it didn't quite reach her eyes. "I've got a lot of data to suggest I do or say the wrong thing at least eighty-six-point-five percent of the time."

"Spoken like someone who wants to get tossed in the pool," Michael countered. Sloane managed a genuine smile this time, and with one last glance back at me, Michael was gone.

"Do you think Dean went out to the garage?" Sloane asked after the two of us had been alone for several minutes. "When he's upset, he usually goes out to the garage."

Dean wasn't just *upset*. I didn't know the exact details of what he'd been through growing up, but the one time I'd asked Dean if he'd known what his father was doing to those women, Dean's response had been *not at first*.

"Dean needs space," I told Sloane, laying it out for her in case she couldn't see it for herself. "Some people like having their friends around when things get tough, and some people need to be alone. When Dean's ready to talk, he'll talk."

Even as I said the words, I knew I wouldn't be able to just sit here, doing nothing. Waiting. I needed to do *something*—I just didn't know what.

"Is he going to be okay?" Sloane asked me, her voice barely audible.

I couldn't lie to her. "I don't know."

CHAPTER 9

I ended up in the library. Wall-to-wall, ceiling-to-floor shelves held more books than I could read in two lifetimes. I hovered in the doorway. I wasn't here for a book. *Third shelf from the left, two up from the bottom.* I swallowed hard, then walked over to the correct shelf. *Interview twenty-eight, binder twelve.*

My fingers closed around the correct binder, and I forced myself to pick it up. The last time I'd tried reading interview twenty-eight, I'd stopped when I'd registered the interviewee's last name.

Lia was right. I didn't fully understand what Dean was going through—but I wanted to. I needed to, because if it had been me spiraling into the abyss, Dean would have understood.

Dean always understood.

I sat down on the floor, propping the binder up on my thighs and opening to the page I'd left off on weeks before.

Briggs was the agent conducting the prison interview. He'd just asked Dean's father to verify the identity of one of his victims.

> Redding: You're asking the wrong questions, son. It's not who they are, it's what they are.
>
> Briggs: And what are they?
>
> Redding: They're mine.
>
> Briggs: Is that why you bound them with zip ties? Because they were yours?
>
> Redding: You want me to say that I bound them so they'd stay. Your fancy FBI psychologists would salivate to hear me talk about all the women who've left me. About my mother and the mother of my son. But did you ever think that maybe I just like the way a woman's skin looks when she struggles against the hold of the plastic? Maybe I liked watching white lines appear on their wrists and ankles, watching their hands and feet go numb. Maybe the way their muscles tensed and some of them fought themselves bloody while I sat there and watched . . . Can you imagine, Agent Briggs? Can you?
>
> Briggs: And branding them? Are you going to tell me that wasn't a mark of ownership? That owning them, dominating them, controlling them—that wasn't the point?
>
> Redding: The point? Who says there's a point? Growing up, people never took to me. Teachers said I was

sullen. My grandfather raised me, and he was always telling me not to look at him like that, not to look at my grandmother like that. There was just something about me, two shades off. I had to learn how to hide it, but my son? Dean? He was born smiling. People would take one look at him and they'd smile, too. Everybody loved that boy. My boy.

Briggs: Did you? Love him?

Redding: I made him. He was mine, and if it was in him to charm, to put people at ease, it was in me.

Briggs: Your son taught you how to blend in, how to be liked, how to be trusted. What did you teach your son?

Redding: Why don't you ask your wife? Pretty little thing, isn't she? But the mouth on that one . . . mmmm, mmm, mmmmm.

"Good reading?"

A voice snapped me back to the present. "Lia."

"You just can't help yourself, can you?" There was an edge to Lia's voice, but she didn't sound as blindly furious with me as she had before.

"I'm sorry about earlier." I took my life in my own hands and risked apologizing, knowing it might set her off. "You're right. I don't know what Dean's going through. The situation with Locke and me—it wasn't the same."

"Always so genuine," Lia said, a hint of sharpness to her singsong tone. "Always willing to own up to her mistakes."

Her gaze locked on to the binder in my lap, and her voice went flat. "Yet always so very ready to make the same mistakes, all over again."

"Lia," I said. "I'm not trying to get between the two of you—"

"God, Cassie. I told you this wasn't about you. Do you really think it's about *me*?"

I wasn't sure what to think. Lia went out of her way to be difficult to profile. The one thing I was sure of was her loyalty to Dean.

"He wouldn't want you reading those." She sounded certain—but then again, Lia always sounded certain.

"I thought it might help," I said. "If I *understood*, then I could—"

"Help?" Lia repeated, biting out the word. "That's the problem with you, Cassie. Your intentions are always *so good*. You always just want to *help*. But at the end of the day, you don't help. Someone gets hurt, and that someone is never you."

"I'm not going to hurt Dean," I said vehemently.

Lia let out a bark of laughter. "It's sweet that you believe that, but of course you are." She slid down the wall until she was sitting on the floor. "Briggs made me listen to an audio recording of Redding's interviews when I was fourteen." She pulled her legs tight to her chest. "I'd been here a year at that point, and Dean didn't want me within a ten-foot pole of anything having to do with his father. But I was like you. I thought it might *help*, but it didn't *help*, Cassie." Each time she said *help*, her expression grew closer to a snarl. "Those interviews are the Daniel Redding show. He's a liar. One of the best I've ever heard. He makes you think he's lying when he's telling the truth, and then he'll say things that can't possibly be true. . . ." Lia shook her head, like she could rid herself of the memory with the motion. "Reading anything Daniel Redding has to say is going to mess with your head, Cassie, and knowing that you've read it is going to mess with Dean's."

She was right. Dean wouldn't want me reading this. His father had described him as a little boy who'd been born smiling, instantly lovable, effortlessly putting other people at ease, but the Dean I knew always had his guard up.

Especially with me.

"Tell me I'm wrong, Cassie, and I'll make you a pretty apology. Tell me that Daniel Redding hasn't already gotten under your skin."

I knew better than to lie to Lia. There was something inside me, the part of me that saw people as puzzles to be solved, that wanted answers, that needed to make things— awful things, *horrible* things, like what had happened to my mother, like what Daniel Redding had done to those women—make sense.

"Dean wouldn't want me doing this," I conceded, catching my bottom lip in between my teeth, before plowing on. "That doesn't mean he's right."

My first week in the program, Dean had tried to send me running. He'd told me that profiling killers would ruin me.

He'd also told me that by the time Agent Briggs had started coming to him for help on cases, there was nothing left to ruin.

If our situations had been reversed, if I'd been the one drowning in all of this, Dean wouldn't have backed off.

"I slept in Michael's room last night." Lia waited for those words to register before giving me a Cheshire cat grin. "I wanted a strip poker rematch, and *Monsieur Townsend* was oh-so-happy to oblige."

I felt like she'd stabbed an icicle straight through my chest. I went very still, trying not to feel anything at all.

Lia reached over and snatched the binder off my lap. She snorted. "Honestly, Cassie, you're too easy. If and when I choose to spend the night with Michael again, you'll know it, because the next morning, you'll be invisible, and Michael won't be looking at anything but me. In the meantime . . ." Lia snapped the binder shut. "You're welcome, because this is officially the second time in the past five minutes that I've saved you from going someplace you really don't want to go." Her eyes bore into mine. "You don't want to crawl into Daniel Redding's mind, Cassie." She flicked her hair over her shoulder. "If you make me go for intervention number three, I'll be forced to get creative."

With those rather concerning words, she left the room—taking the binder and everything it contained with her.

Can she do *that?* I sat there, staring after her. Eventually, I snapped out of it and told myself that she was right, that I didn't need to know the details of Dean's father's case to be there for Dean now, but even knowing that, even *believing* it, I couldn't stop wondering about the parts of the interview I hadn't gotten the chance to read.

What did you teach your son? Agent Briggs had asked.

I'd never even seen a picture of Dean's father, but I could imagine the smile spreading over his face when he'd replied. *Why don't you ask your wife?*

CHAPTER 10

D ean skipped dinner. Judd fixed a plate for him and put it in the refrigerator. I wondered if Judd was used to Dean disappearing for hours on end. Maybe, when Dean had first come here, that had been a normal thing. I found myself thinking more and more about that Dean—the twelve-year-old whose father had been arrested for serial murder.

You knew what he was doing. I slipped into Dean's perspective without even meaning to. *You couldn't stop it.*

Empathizing with Dean: his feelings toward his father, what staring at that girl's corpse must have done to him—I couldn't tuck that away in a separate section of my psyche. I could feel it bleeding over into my own thoughts. Right now, Dean was almost certainly thinking about the fact that he had a killer's blood in his veins. And I had Locke's in mine. Maybe Lia was right. Maybe I couldn't really understand what Dean was going through—but being a profiler meant I couldn't stop trying to. I couldn't keep from feeling his pain and recognizing in it an echo of my own.

After dinner, I meant to go upstairs, but my feet carried me toward the garage. I stopped, just outside the door. I could hear the muted sound of flesh hitting something—over and over, again and again. I brought my hand up to the doorknob, then pulled it back.

He doesn't want you here, I reminded myself. But at the same time, I couldn't keep from thinking that maybe shutting the rest of us out was less about what Dean wanted and more about what he wouldn't let himself want. There was a chance—a good one—that Dean didn't *need* to be alone so much as he thought being alone was what he deserved.

Of its own volition, my hand reached out again. This time, I turned the knob. The door opened a crack, and the sound of heavy breathing added itself to the rhythmic *thwack thwack thwack* I'd heard before. A breath hitching in my throat, I pushed the door open. Dean didn't see me.

His blond hair was beaded with sweat and stuck to his forehead. A thin white undershirt clung to his torso, soaked and nearly transparent. I could make out the lines of his stomach, his chest. His shoulders were bare, the muscles so tense that I thought they might snap like rubber bands or fight their way out from underneath his tanned skin.

Thwack. Thwack. Thwack.

His fists collided with a punching bag. It came back at

him, and he fought harder. The rhythm of hits was getting faster, and with each punch, he put more and more of his body into it. His fists were bare.

I wasn't sure how long I stood there, watching him. There was something animal about the motions, something feral and vicious. My profiler's eye saw each punch layered with meaning. *Losing control, controlled. Punishment, release.* He'd welcome the pain in his knuckles. He wouldn't be able to stop.

I took a few steps closer, but stayed out of range. This time, I didn't make the mistake of trying to touch him. His eyes were locked on the bag, unseeing. I wasn't sure who he was striking out at—his father or himself. All I knew was that if he didn't stop, something was going to give—the bag, his hands, his body, his mind.

He had to snap out of it.

"I kissed you." I wasn't sure what possessed me to say that, but I had to say *something.* I could see the moment the words broke through to him. His movements became slightly more measured; I could feel him regaining aware-ness of the world around him.

"It doesn't matter." He continued punching the bag. "It was just a game."

Truth or Dare. He was right. It was just a game. So why did I feel like someone had slapped me?

Dean finally stopped punching the bag. He was breathing heavily, his whole body moving with each breath. Casting a sideways glance at me, he spoke again. "You deserve better."

"Better than a game?" I asked. *Or better than you?*

Dean didn't reply. I knew, then, that this wasn't really about me. Dean wasn't seeing *me*. This was about some make-believe, idealized Cassie he'd built up in his head, something to torment himself with. A girl who *deserved* things. A girl he could never *deserve*. I hated that he was putting me up on a glass pedestal, fragile and out of reach. Like I didn't get a say in the matter at all.

"I have a tube of lipstick." I threw the words at him. "Locke gave it to me. I tell myself that I keep it as a reminder, but it's not that simple." He didn't reply, so I just kept going. "Locke thought I could be like her." That had been the whole point of her little game. "She wanted it so badly, Dean. I know she was a monster. I know that I should hate her. But sometimes, I wake up in the morning and for just a second, I forget. And for that second, before I remember what she did, I miss her. I didn't even know we were related, but . . ."

I trailed off, and my throat tightened, because I couldn't stop thinking that I should have known. I should have known that she was my last connection to my mother. I should have known that she wasn't what she seemed. I should have known, and I didn't, and people had gotten hurt.

"Don't make yourself say these things because I need to hear them," Dean said hoarsely. "You're nothing like Locke." He wiped his palms on his jeans, and I heard the words he wasn't saying.

You're nothing like me.

"Maybe," I said softly, "to do what you and I do, we have to have a little bit of the monster in us."

A breath caught in Dean's throat, and for the longest time, the two of us stood there in silence: breathing in, breathing out, breathing *through* the truth I'd just uttered.

"Your hands are bleeding," I said finally, my voice as hoarse as his had been a moment before. "You're hurt."

"No, I'm . . ." Dean looked down, caught sight of his bleeding knuckles, and swallowed the rest of his argument.

If I hadn't interrupted, you would have beaten your hands raw. That knowledge spurred me into action. A minute later, I was back with a clean towel and a basin of water.

"Sit," I said. When Dean didn't move, I fixed him with a look and repeated the order. Physically, I resembled my mother, but when given proper motivation, I could do a decent impression of my paternal grandmother. A person butted heads with Nonna at his or her own risk.

Taking in the stubborn set of my jaw, Dean sat down on the workout bench. He held out his hand for the towel. I ignored him and knelt, dipping the towel into the water.

"Hand," I said.

"Cassie—"

"Hand," I repeated. I felt him ready to refuse, but somehow, his hand found its way to mine. Slowly, I turned it over. Carefully, gingerly, I cleaned the blood from his knuckles, coaxing the towel along sinew and bone. The water was lukewarm, but heat spread through my body as my thumb trailed lightly over his skin.

I put down his left hand and started in on the right. Neither of us said anything. I didn't even look at him. I kept my eyes fixed on his fingers, his knuckles, the scar that ran along the length of his thumb.

"I hurt you." Dean broke the silence. I could feel the moment slipping away. I wanted it back, so ferociously it surprised me.

I don't want to want this. I wanted everything to stay the same. I could do this. I'd been doing this. Nothing had to change.

I put Dean's hand down. "You didn't hurt me," I told him firmly. "You grabbed my wrist." I pushed up my sleeve and brandished my right arm as proof. Next to his tan, my skin was almost unbearably fair. "No marks. No bruises. Nothing. I'm fine."

"You were lucky," Dean said. "I was . . . somewhere else."

"I know." The night before, when Agent Sterling's arrival had sent me into a tailspin, he'd been the one to break the hold that *somewhere else* had on me. Dean held my gaze for a moment, and understanding flickered in his eyes.

"You blame yourself for what happened with Agent Locke." Dean was a profiler, the same as me. He could climb into my head as easily as I could climb into his. "To the girls Locke killed, to Michael, to me."

I didn't reply.

"It wasn't your fault, Cassie. You couldn't have known." Opposite me, Dean swallowed hard. My eyes traced the movement of his Adam's apple. His lips parted, and he spoke. "My father made me watch."

Those whispered words carried the power of a gunshot, but I didn't react. If I said anything, if I breathed, if I so much as moved, Dean would clam up again.

"I found out what he was doing, and he made me watch."

What were we doing, trading secrets? Trading guilt? What he'd just told me was so much bigger than anything I could have told him. He was drowning, and I didn't know how to pull him out. The two of us sat there in silence, him on the workout bench, me on the floor. I wanted to touch him, but I didn't. I wanted to tell him it would be okay, but I didn't. I pictured the girl we'd seen on the news.

The dead girl.

Dean could whale away on a punching bag until the skin on his knuckles was gone. We could trade confessions that no one should ever have to make. But none of that could change the fact that Dean wouldn't get a good night's sleep until this case was closed—and neither would I.

CHAPTER 11

The next morning, after tossing and turning most of the night, I woke to find a face hovering three inches above my own. I jerked backward in bed, and Sloane blinked at me.

"Hypothetically speaking," she said, as if it were perfectly normal to bend over a bed and stare at someone until they woke up, "would constructing a model of the crime scene we saw on the video yesterday qualify as intruding on Dean's space?"

I opened my mouth to tell Sloane that she was intruding on *my* space, but then processed her question. "Hypothetically speaking," I said, stifling a yawn and sitting up in bed, "have you already reconstructed the crime scene in question?"

"That is a definite possibility." Her hair was tousled and sticking up at odd angles. There were dark circles under her eyes.

"Did you sleep at all last night?" I asked her.

"I was trying to figure out how the killer managed to pose the girl's body without being seen," Sloane said, which both was and wasn't an answer to my question. When Sloane got absorbed in something, the rest of the world ceased to exist. "I have a theory."

She tugged on the ends of her white-blond hair. I could practically see her waiting for me to snap at her, to tell her that she was handling the situation with Dean *wrong*. She knew she was different from other people, and I was realizing, bit by bit, that somewhere along the line, someone—or maybe multiple someones—had conditioned her to believe that different, her kind of different, was wrong.

"Let me get dressed," I told her. "Then you can tell me your theory."

When Dean was upset, he went to the garage. When Sloane was upset, she went to the basement. I wasn't sure she had another way of coping.

And besides, I thought as I pulled on a T-shirt, *I'm clearly the last person who should be lecturing anyone about giving Dean space.*

The basement ran the length of our Victorian-style house and extended out underneath the front and back yards. Walls that didn't quite reach the ceiling divided the space into distinct sets, each missing a fourth wall.

"I had to make some modifications to the car specs," Sloane said, pulling her hair into a tight ponytail as she stopped in front of a battered car parked on the lawn of a set designed to look like a park. "Briggs had a two-door brought down a couple of weeks ago for a simulation I was running. The hood was two inches too long, and the slope wasn't quite steep enough, but it was nothing a carefully wielded sledgehammer couldn't fix."

Sloane had a willowy build and relatively little regard for recommended safety measures. The idea of her wielding a sledgehammer of any kind was terrifying.

"Cassie, focus," Sloane ordered. "We were somewhat limited on outdoor sets, so I went with the neighborhood park scene. The grass is one and one-quarter inch tall, slightly less uniform than the crime scene lawn. We had a nice arrangement of crash dummies to choose from, so I was able to match the victim's height within two centimeters. The rope is the wrong color, but it's nylon, and the thickness should be a match."

It was easy to forget sometimes that Sloane's gift went far beyond the index of statistics stored in her brain. The video we'd seen of the crime scene had been taken from a distance and lasted less than forty-five seconds, but she'd encoded every last numerical detail: the length and width of the rope tied around the victim's neck; the exact positioning of the body; the height of the grass; the make, model, and specs of the car.

As a result, I was looking at a nearly exact replica of what we'd seen on the film. A faceless, naked dummy was draped across the hood of the car. The dummy's lower extremities dangled over the front; a rope was knotted around its neck. The body was tilted slightly to one side. On the video, we'd only viewed it from the front, but now, I could actually walk around and take in the three-sixty view. The hands were bound at the wrists, unevenly, twisting the upper body slightly to the left. I closed my eyes and pictured the girl.

You fought, didn't you? Fought so hard that the bindings cut into your arms.

"One end of the rope was tied around her neck. The other ran up to the sunroof, down, and was anchored to something inside the car." Sloane's voice brought me back to the present. I stared at the car.

"The UNSUB didn't do all that on the front lawn of the university president's house," I said.

"Correct!" Sloane beamed at me. "Which means that he strung her up and *then* placed the car there. I looked up the topography of the streets surrounding the house. There's a road directly west that curves, but if you don't take the curve, you go off-road and down a forested slope."

"A forest could have provided cover," I said, nibbling at my bottom lip as I tried to picture the UNSUB moving, quickly and quietly, still shrouded in the partial darkness of very early morning. "Assuming he killed her in the car, he could have strung her up in the forest . . ."

Sloane picked up where I left off. ". . . pushed her to the edge of the woods, and the slope of the hill would have done the rest. The only question is how he kept the body from bouncing around on the way down."

I opened my mouth to reply, but someone else beat me to it.

"It was weighted."

Sloane and I turned in unison. Agent Sterling came striding toward us, her long legs making quick work of the space. She'd traded the gray suit for a black one and the pink shirt for a light, silvery gray, a near-perfect match for her eyes. Her hair was in a French braid, and her face was taut, like she'd fixed the braid in place so firmly it pulled her skin tight across her skull.

She stopped, a few feet away from the scene Sloane had rigged up.

"That's an impressive likeness," she said, her clipped words making it clear that the statement wasn't a compliment. "What source material were you using?"

Sloane, completely oblivious to the steely tone in Agent Sterling's voice, replied with a smile. "There was a cell phone video leaked online."

Agent Sterling closed her eyes, bowed her head slightly, and inhaled. I could practically hear her counting silently to ten. When she opened her eyes, they zeroed in on me. "And what was your involvement in all of this, Cassandra?"

I could have told her that Sloane had built the replica completely on her own, but I wasn't about to throw my own roommate to the wolves. Stepping in between Sloane and Sterling, I drew the agent's ire to me.

"My involvement?" I repeated, channeling Lia—or possibly Michael. "Let's go with *moral support*."

Sterling pursed her lips, then turned back to Sloane. "Was there a particular reason you wanted to rebuild this crime scene?" she asked, gentling her voice slightly.

I tried to catch Sloane's eye, telegraphing that she should not, under any circumstances, tell her what Dean had told us about his father.

Sloane met my eyes and nodded. I relaxed slightly, then Sloane turned back to Agent Sterling. "Dean told us this case looks a lot like his father's," she said matter-of-factly.

Clearly, Sloane had misinterpreted my look to mean the exact opposite of what I'd been trying to communicate.

"So you rebuilt the scene to figure out if Dean was right about the similarities?" Agent Sterling asked.

"I rebuilt the scene so Cassie could look at it," Sloane said helpfully. "She said that Dean needed space, so we're giving him space."

"You call this *giving him space*?" Agent Sterling asked, flicking a hand toward the car. "I could kill the kid who leaked that video. Seeing that—it was the very last thing Dean needed. But you know what the second-to-last thing he needs is? Someone re-creating that scene *in his basement*. Did you learn nothing this summer?"

That question was aimed directly at me. Agent Sterling's tone wasn't angry or accusatory. It was incredulous.

"When the director discovered what Briggs was doing with Dean, using him to solve cases, it almost got Briggs fired. It *should* have gotten him fired. But somehow, my father and Briggs reached a compromise. The Bureau would provide Dean with a home, a guardian, and training, and Dean would help them with cold cases. *Not* active cases. Your lives were never supposed to be on the line." Agent Sterling paused, the look in her eye caught somewhere between anger and betrayal. "I looked the other way. Until this summer."

This summer—when we'd been authorized to work on an active case, because the killer had zeroed in on me.

Sloane jumped to my defense. "The killer contacted Cassie, not the other way around."

Sterling's expression softened when she looked at Sloane. "This isn't about what happened this summer. This is about the fact that no one has authorized you to work on *this* case. I need your word the two of you will leave it alone. No modeling it, no profiling it, no hacking."

"No hacking," Sloane agreed. She held out her hand to shake on it, and before Agent Sterling could comment on her selective hearing, she added, "If the entire population of the town of Quantico shook hands with one another, there would be a total of 157,080 possible handshake combinations."

Agent Sterling smiled slightly as she took Sloane's proffered hand. "No hacking *and* no more simulations."

Sloane took her hand back. The dark circles under her eyes made her look younger somehow, fragile—or maybe brittle. "I have to run simulations. It's what I do."

As a profiler, Agent Sterling should have been able to hear what Sloane wasn't saying—that building this model was the only thing she *could* do for Dean. It was also her way of working through her own emotions. It was *what she did*.

"Not on this case," Agent Sterling repeated. She turned from Sloane to me. "No exceptions. No excuses. This program only works if the rules are followed and enforced." Agent Sterling had clearly cast herself in the role of enforcer. "You work on cold cases, and you do so only with the approval of myself and Agent Briggs. If you can't follow these simple instructions, *you're* not just a liability. This whole program is." Agent Sterling met my eyes, and there was no question in my mind that she'd meant me to hear those words as a threat. "Am I clear?"

The only thing clearer was the fact that my earlier impressions of the woman had been right on target. This wasn't just a job to her. This was personal.

CHAPTER 12

"**S**he more or less threatened to shut down the entire program."

Michael leaned back in his chair. "She's a profiler. She knows exactly what threats to issue to keep people in line. She's got your number, Colorado. You're a team player, so she didn't just threaten you. She threatened the rest of us, too."

Michael and I were in the living room. Sloane, Lia, and Dean had passed their practice GEDs the day before with flying colors. Neither Michael nor I had actually taken one, but somehow, answer sheets had been turned in with our names on them. Apparently, Lia had been feeling generous— but not generous enough to ensure that we passed, too. As a result, Michael and I were under strict orders to study.

I was better at following orders than Michael was.

"If you were the one issuing threats," he said, a wicked

grin working its way onto his face, "how would you threaten me?"

I looked up from my work. I was going over the test Lia had filled out for me, correcting the wrong answers. "You want me to threaten you?"

"I want to know how you *would* threaten me," Michael corrected. "Obviously, threatening the program wouldn't be the way to go. I don't exactly have the warm fuzzies for the FBI."

I tapped the edge of my pencil against the practice test. Michael's challenge was a welcome distraction. "I'd start with your Porsche," I said.

"If I'm a bad boy, you'll take away my keys?" Michael wiggled his eyebrows in a way that was both suggestive and ridiculous.

"No," I replied without even thinking about it. "If you're a bad boy, I'll give your car to Dean."

There was a moment of stunned silence, and then Michael put a hand over his heart, like he'd been shot—a gesture that would have been funnier before he'd taken an actual bullet to the chest.

"You're the one who asked," I said. Michael should have known by now not to throw down the gauntlet unless he wanted me picking it up.

"The depravity of you, Cassie Hobbes." He was clearly impressed.

I shrugged. "You and Dean have some kind of pseudo-sworn-enemy, pseudo-sibling-rivalry thing going on. You'd rather I set your car on fire than give it to Dean. It's the perfect threat."

Michael didn't contradict my logic. Instead, he shook his head and smiled. "Anyone ever tell you that you have a sadistic streak?"

I felt the breath whoosh out of my lungs. He couldn't have known the effect those words would have on me. I turned back to the practice test, allowing my hair to fall into my face, but it was too late. Michael had already seen the split second of *horror—loathing—fear—disgust* on my face.

"Cassie—"

"I'm fine."

Locke had been a sadist. Part of the pleasure she'd gotten out of killing had been imagining what her victims were going through. I had no desire to hurt anyone. Ever. But being a Natural profiler meant that I instinctively knew other people's weaknesses. Knowing what people wanted and knowing what they feared were two sides of the same coin.

Michael wasn't really calling me sadistic. I knew that, and he knew that I'd never intentionally hurt anyone. But sometimes, knowing that you *could* do something was almost as bad as having actually done it.

"Hey." Michael tilted his head upside down to get a good look at my face. "I was kidding. No Sad Cassie face, okay?"

"This isn't my sad face," I told him. There was a point in time when he would have pushed the hair out of my face and let his hand linger on my jaw. Not anymore.

The unspoken rules said it had to be my choice. I could feel him, watching me, waiting for me to say something. He stayed there, staring at me upside down, his face just a few inches away from mine.

His mouth just a few inches away from mine.

"I know a Sad Cassie face when I see one," he said. "Even upside down."

I brushed my hair over my shoulders and leaned back. Trying to hide what I was feeling from Michael was impossible. I shouldn't have even tried.

"You and Lia back on speaking terms?" he asked me.

I was grateful for the subject change. "Lia and I are . . . whatever Lia and I normally are. I don't think she's plotting my immediate demise."

Michael nodded sagely. "So she's not going to go for your throat the moment she figures out you broke the holy commandment of *Thou shalt give Dean his space?*"

I'd thought my visit to Dean last night had gone unnoticed. Apparently, I'd thought wrong.

"I wanted to see how he was doing." I felt like I had to explain, even though Michael hadn't asked for an explanation. "I didn't want him to be alone."

Reading emotions made Michael an expert at concealing them, so when I saw a flicker of *something* in his eyes, I knew that he'd chosen not to hide it from me. He liked that I was the kind of person who cared about the people in this house. He just wished that the person I'd spent last night caring about wasn't Dean.

"And how goes Sir Broods-A-Lot's familial angst?" Michael did a good imitation of someone who didn't really care about the answer to that question. He might have even been able to fool another emotion reader—but my ability wasn't just about posture or facial expressions or what a person was feeling at any given moment.

Behavior. Personality. Environment.

Michael was snarking to hide the fact that he *did* care about the answer to that question.

"If you want to know how Dean's holding up, you can just ask."

Michael shrugged noncommittally. He wasn't going to admit that Lia, Sloane, and I weren't the only ones worried about Dean. A noncommittal shrug was as close to an expression of concern as I was going to get.

"He's not okay," I said. "He won't be okay until Briggs and Sterling close this case. If they'd just tell him what's going on, it might help, but that's not going to happen. Sterling won't let it."

Michael shot me a sideways glance. "You really don't like Agent Sterling."

I didn't think that statement merited a reply.

"Cassie, you don't dislike anyone. The only time I've ever seen you get persnickety with someone was when Briggs assigned agents to dog your every move. But you disliked Agent Sterling from the moment she showed up."

I had no intention of replying to that statement, either, but Michael didn't *need* verbal replies. He was perfectly capable of carrying on conversations completely on his own, reading my responses in my body language and the tiniest hints of expressions on my face.

"She doesn't like this program," I said, just to get him to stop reading me so intently. "She doesn't like us. And she really doesn't like me."

"She doesn't dislike you as much as you think she does." Michael's voice was quiet. I found myself leaning toward him, even though I wasn't sure I wanted to hear more. "Agent Sterling isn't fond of me, because I'm not fond of rules. She's afraid to spend more than a few seconds looking at Dean, but she's not scared *of* him. She actually likes Lia, even though Lia's not any fonder of rules than I am. And Sloane reminds her of someone."

The difference between Michael's gift and mine was as obvious as it had been playing poker. He saw so much that Sterling was trying to hide. But *why* she was hiding it—that was a question for me.

"How's the studying coming along?"

I glanced up at Judd, who stood in the doorway. He was a Marine, not a den mother. The question sounded completely foreign coming out of his mouth.

"Haven't started," Michael replied flippantly at the exact same time that I said, "Almost done."

Judd arched an eyebrow at Michael, but didn't push the issue. "You mind giving us a moment?" he asked instead.

Michael cocked his head slightly to one side, taking in the expression on Judd's face. "Do I have a choice?"

Judd almost smiled. "That would be a no."

As Michael made his way out of the room, Judd crossed it and lowered himself onto the sofa next to me. He watched Michael go. Something about the way he tracked Michael's progress made me think he was forcing himself to take in the way Michael favored his injured leg.

"You know why this program is restricted to cold cases?" Judd asked me once Michael was gone.

"Because Dean was twelve when this program was started?" I suggested. "And because Director Sterling wants to minimize the chances of anyone finding out the program exists?" Those were the easy answers. Judd's silence pushed me into giving the hard one. "Because on active cases," I said softly, "people get hurt."

"On active cases, people cross lines." Judd took his time with the words. "Everything is urgent, everything is life-and-death." He rubbed his thumb across the pads of his fingers. "In the heat of battle, you do what needs to be done. You make sacrifices."

Judd was military. He didn't use the word *battle* lightly.

"You're not talking about *us* crossing the lines," I said, sorting through what I was hearing—and what I *knew*. "You're talking about the FBI."

"Could be I am," Judd allowed.

I tried to parse my way through Judd's logic. Reading interviews, going through witness statements, looking at crime scene photos—those were all things we already did. What did it matter if the files were a year old versus a day?

Theoretically, the risks were the same—minimal. But with active cases, the stakes were higher.

This UNSUB that Locke and Briggs were hunting, he was out there *now*. He might be planning his next kill *now*. It was easy enough to keep us out of the field on cold cases. But with lives on the line, if bringing us along could make a difference . . .

"It's a slippery slope." Judd rubbed the back of his hand over his jaw. "I trust Briggs. Mostly."

"You trust Agent Sterling," I said. He didn't contradict me. "What about the director?"

Judd met my eyes. "What about him?"

The director was the one who'd caved to political pressure and trotted me out as bait on the Locke case. I'd wanted to help. He was the one who'd let me.

"I heard you and Ronnie butted heads," Judd said, closing the door on further discussion. He put his palms on his knees, pushed off, and stood. "I think it would do you some good to stay out of the basement." He let that sink in. "For a few weeks."

Weeks? It took me a second to figure out what was going on here. Had Agent Sterling *tattled* on me? "You're grounding me from the basement?" I said sharply.

"You're a profiler," Judd said mildly. "You don't need to be down there. And," he added, his voice hardening slightly, "you don't need to be poking your nose into this case."

In all the time I'd been here, Judd had never told any of

us what we *needed* to do. This had Agent Sterling's finger-prints all over it.

"She's a good agent, Cassie." Judd seemed to know exactly what I was thinking. "If you let her, there's a lot she could teach you."

Locke was my teacher. "Agent Sterling doesn't have to teach me anything," I said sharply. "If she can catch who-ever killed that girl, we'll call it even."

Judd gave me a look. "She's a good agent," he repeated. "So is Briggs." He started for the door. His back to me, he kept talking, his voice so low I almost couldn't hear him.

For a long time after he left, I wondered over the words I'd barely heard. He'd said that Sterling was a good agent. That Briggs was a good agent. And then, as if he couldn't stop himself, as if he didn't even realize he was saying the words out loud, he'd said one last thing.

"There was only ever one case they couldn't solve."

YOU

At first, it felt good. Watching the life go out of her eyes. Running your thumb across the bloodstained knife. Standing over her, your heartbeat accelerating, pounding out a glorious rhythm: I did that. I did that. I did that.

But now—now, the doubts are starting to worm their way into your brain. You can feel them, wiggling through your gray matter, whispering to you in a familiar voice.

"You were sloppy," it says. "Someone could have seen you."

But they didn't. They didn't see you. You're better than that. You passed this test with flying colors. You bound her. You branded her. You cut her. You hung her.

You did it. You're done. But it doesn't feel like enough. You don't feel like enough.

Good enough.

Strong enough.

Smart enough.

Worthy.

If you'd done it right, you'd still be able to hear her screams. The press would be giving you a name. They'd be talking about you on the news, not her. She was nothing. No one. You made her special.

But no one even knows you're alive.

"I'll do it," you say. "I'll do it again."

But the voice tells you to wait. It tells you to be patient. What will be will be—in time.

CHAPTER 13

I woke up in a cold sweat in the middle of the night. I couldn't remember my nightmare, but knew that I'd had one. My heart was racing. My chest was heavy, and I couldn't shake the feeling that I was *trapped*. I threw off the covers.

My fingers found their way to the Rose Red lipstick of their own accord. On the other side of the room, Sloane turned over in her bed. I held my breath, waiting to see if she'd wake up. She didn't. As quietly as I could, I slipped out of bed and out of our room.

I needed space. I needed air. I needed to breathe.

The house was silent as I crept downstairs. I wasn't even sure where I was going until I ended up outside the kitchen door.

"I told you, I'm fine."

I came to an abrupt halt as the silence in the house gave way to the muted sound of arguing on the other side of the door.

"You're not fine, Dean. You're not supposed to be fine with this. *I'm* not fine with this."

Agent Sterling and Dean. They're fighting.

I heard the sound of a chair scraping across tile and prepared to retreat. I listened for footsteps, but none were forthcoming. It sounded like someone had just pushed back from the table—angrily.

"You left."

"Dean—"

"You left the FBI. I think we both know why."

"I left because I wasn't doing my job, Dean. I was angry. I needed to prove that I wasn't scared, and I got someone killed. Because I couldn't follow the rules. Because Tanner couldn't let even one case go."

Tanner was Briggs's first name. The fact that Agent Sterling was using it in a conversation with Dean made me wonder just how much history the two of them shared. This wasn't a conversation you had with a kid you'd met once when you arrested his father.

"What was the girl's name?" Dean's voice was lower-pitched than Agent Sterling's. I struggled to make out his words as he spoke.

"I can't tell you that, Dean."

"What was her name?"

"You're not authorized to work on active cases. Leave it alone."

"You tell me her name. I'll leave it alone."

"No, you won't." Agent Sterling's voice was getting harder to decipher. I wondered if she was speaking more softly because the alternative was starting to yell.

"I made you a promise once." Dean's voice was controlled—too controlled. "I kept it. Tell me this girl's name, and I'll promise to leave it alone."

My fingers tightened around the tube of lipstick in my hand. Briggs had let me read through Locke's file. I'd memorized the names of every one of her victims.

"Isn't it enough that I swore we would take care of this?" Agent Sterling said sharply. "We've got some solid leads. I can't tell you what they are, but I can promise you we have them. It's a copycat, Dean. Paint by numbers. That's all. Daniel Redding is in jail. He's going to be in jail for the rest of his miserable life."

"What's her name?"

"Why do you need to know?" This time, Agent Sterling's voice got loud enough that I would have heard it even if I hadn't been standing right outside the door. "You tell me that, and I'll answer your question."

"I just do."

"Not good enough, Dean."

Silence. Neither one of them spoke for at least a minute. The sound of my own breathing seemed unbearably loud. I was sure that any second, one of them would come storming out. They'd discover me standing here, listening at the door to a conversation that I *knew* was more private than anything Dean had told me.

But I couldn't move. I couldn't even remember how.

"Her name was Gloria." That was Dean, not Sterling, so I wasn't sure who the *her* in question was. "He introduced her to me. He made her say my name. He asked her if she'd like to be my mom. I was nine. I told him I didn't want a new mother. And he looked at Gloria and said, 'That's a shame.'"

"You didn't know." Sterling's voice was quiet again, but still high enough in pitch that the words carried.

"And once I did know," Dean replied, his voice on the edge of breaking, "he wouldn't tell me their names."

Another torturously long silence. The vicious beating of my own heart drowned out the sound of my breathing. I took a step backward, a tiny, silent step.

I shouldn't be here. I shouldn't be listening to this.

I turned, but even with my back to the door, I heard Agent Sterling answer Dean's question. "The girl's name was Emerson Cole."

Back in my own bed, I closed my eyes and tried not to think about what I'd overheard, as if by pushing it out of my mind, I could make up for the fact that I'd listened at the door for far too long.

I failed.

Dean and Agent Sterling hadn't just *met* each other

before. They *knew* each other. They had history. *Stop think-ing about it,* I told myself. *Don't do this.* I couldn't stop, any more than Sloane would have been able to see a mathemati-cal equation without calculating the answer.

Dean made you a promise once, Agent Sterling, and what-ever it was, he kept it. The closest I could come to granting Dean privacy was to try getting inside Agent Sterling's head instead of his. *You don't like thinking about the Daniel Redding case. You care about Dean. Michael said you're afraid to even look at him, but clearly, you don't blame Dean for what his father did.*

Another implication of their conversation finally sank in.

You know that Dean discovered what his father was doing, don't you? You know that Daniel Redding made his son watch.

The words Dean had whispered to me the day before, the secret I'd been sure he'd never told anyone—she knew it, too. Somehow, that made it harder to hold on to my resent-ment against Agent Sterling.

You think you can protect him. You think if he doesn't know what's happening, it won't affect him. That's why you didn't want to tell him Emerson's name.

If Agent Sterling knew him so well, if she cared about Dean so much, why couldn't she see that it was the *not* knowing that was going to kill him? It didn't matter if this killer was just a copycat—the fact that Dean had needed to know the girl's name told me he wouldn't be able to make that separation in his mind.

He'd blame himself for this girl, the way he blamed himself for all the others.

I told him I didn't want a new mother.

And Daniel Redding had replied, "That's a shame." In Dean's mind—and maybe in his father's—at least one of Daniel Redding's victims had died because she wouldn't make a suitable replacement mother for Dean.

Because Dean had said he didn't want her.

So much for my resolution to stick to profiling Sterling instead of Dean.

Thwap. A small, cold projectile hit me in the side of the head. For a second, I thought I'd imagined it, and then—*thwap.*

I opened my eyes, turned toward the door, and wiped the side of my face, which was damp. By the time my eyes had adjusted to the light, I'd been pelted for a third time.

"Lia," I hissed, keeping my voice to a whisper to avoid waking Sloane. "Quit throwing ice at me."

Lia popped a piece of ice into her mouth and rolled it around with her tongue. Without a word, she beckoned me into the hallway. Fairly certain she would continue throwing ice at me until I agreed, I rolled out of bed and followed her into the hall. She closed the bedroom door behind us and pulled me into the nearby bathroom. Once she'd locked that door, she flipped the light switch on, and I realized that, in addition to the cup of ice she held in her left hand, she held a sparkly mint-green shirt in her right.

My eyes went from the clothes in Lia's hands to the

clothes she was wearing: black leather pants and a silver top that was held in place by a chain around her neck and had no back whatsoever.

"What are you wearing?" I asked.

Lia answered my question with an order. "Put this on."

She thrust the shirt at me. I took a step back. "Why?"

"Because," Lia said, like the two of us hadn't fought *twice* in the past forty-eight hours, "you can't go to a Colonial University frat party dressed in your pajamas."

"A frat party," I repeated. Then the rest of her statement sunk in. Colonial University. The scene of the crime.

"This is a bad idea," I told Lia. "Judd would kill us. Not to mention the fact that Agent Sterling's already on the warpath, and all Sloane and I did was build a mock-up of the crime scene in the basement."

"Sloane built a mock-up of the crime scene," Lia corrected. "You didn't do anything other than get caught."

"You're a crazy person," I told Lia, struggling to keep my voice to a whisper. "You want us to sneak out of the house to attend a college frat party at a university where there is an ongoing FBI investigation. Forget about Judd and Agent Sterling. *Briggs* would kill us."

"Only if we get caught," Lia retorted. "And unlike certain redheads in this room, I specialize at not getting caught. Put on the dress, Cassie."

"What dress?"

Lia held up the glittery thing I'd mistaken for a shirt. "This dress."

"There is no world in which that is long enough to be a dress."

"It's a dress. In fact, as of this moment, it's *your* dress, which you are going to put on without complaining, because frat boys are more talkative when you're showing a little leg."

I inhaled, preparing to counter Lia's statement with one of my own, but she took a step forward, invading my personal space and pushing me back against the bathroom counter.

"You're the profiler," she said. "You tell me how okay Dean is going to be if the FBI botches this case. Then tell me that you are one hundred percent certain that we won't pick up on something they miss."

The FBI had profilers and interrogators. Those agents had training. They had experience. They had a million and one things that we didn't—but no one had instincts like ours. That was the whole point of the program. That was the reason Judd was afraid that if the FBI started using us on active cases, they wouldn't be able to stop.

"Who do you think college students are going to get chatty with," Lia asked me, "FBI agents or two scantily clad and passably nubile teenage girls?"

Even setting aside our abilities, Lia was right. No one would suspect we were part of the investigation. They might tell us something the FBI didn't know.

"If Sterling implied that she could, in any way, get the director to disband this program, she was lying. I can guarantee you that's outside her purview. At most, she could send one of us home, and I would bet you a lot of money that the director wouldn't let her send *you* home, because you're a nice, shiny alternative to Dean, who the director has never trusted and never liked." Lia took a step back, allowing me some breathing room. "You say you care about Dean," she told me, her voice low. "You say you want to help. This will help. I'd lie to you about a lot of things, Cassie, but helping Dean isn't one of them. I wouldn't do this for you, or for Michael, or even for Sloane. But I would waltz into hades and make nice with the devil himself for Dean, so either you put on the damn dress or you get the hell out of my way."

I put on the dress.

"Are you sure this isn't a shirt?" I asked, eyeing the hemline.

Lia manhandled my face and slathered it with base before brandishing a tube of pink lip gloss and a container of black mascara. "It's a dress," she swore.

It was times like these I really wished Lia weren't a compulsive liar.

"How are we even getting to this party?" I asked.

Lia smirked. "It just so happens I know a boy with a car."

CHAPTER 14

Michael's Porsche was a remnant of his life before the program. Watching him behind the wheel, it was easy to picture the person he'd been then, the trust-fund brat bouncing from one boarding school to another, summering in the Hamptons, jetting out to Saint Barts or Saint Lucia for a long weekend.

It was easy to picture that Michael bouncing from girl to girl.

Lia sat in the front seat beside him. She was leaning back, the leather seat caressing her cheek, her long hair whipping in the wind. She'd rolled down her window and showed no signs of wanting to roll it back up. Every once in a while, her gaze flitted over to Michael. I wished I could read the inscrutable expression on Lia's face. What was she thinking?

When she looked at Michael, what did she feel?

Michael kept his eyes locked on the road.

As hard as I tried not to profile the two of them, I kept

thinking that Lia was the one who'd asked Michael to join us on this ill-advised outing, and that he'd agreed to help her. Why?

Because opportunities for trouble were not to be missed. Because he owed her. Because as much as Michael enjoyed jabbing at Dean, he didn't like watching him bleed. The answers flooded my brain, and Michael caught my gaze in the rearview mirror. He'd told me once that when I was profiling someone, my eyes crinkled slightly at the corners.

"We'll want to make a quick detour," Lia said. Michael glanced over at her, and she gestured with the tip of one dark purple nail. "Pull off at the next exit." She glanced back at me. "Enjoying the ride?"

She was in the front seat. I was in the back. "I'm not doing this for enjoyment," I told her.

She let her gaze trail from me to Michael and then back again. "No," she agreed. "You're not doing this for enjoyment. You're doing it for Dean."

Lia lingered on Dean's name just slightly longer than the other words in that sentence. Michael's hands tightened slightly on the steering wheel. Lia wanted him to know I was doing this for *Dean*. She wanted him dwelling on that fact.

"Gas station," Lia directed, her hair whipping in the wind. He pulled in and threw the car into park. Lia smiled. "You two wait here."

It was just like her to stir things up and then leave. No matter how well he masked it, I knew Michael was sitting there asking himself what—exactly—had led me to do this for Dean. The same way I'd spent the ride wondering why Michael had said yes to Lia.

"Ta," Lia said, sounding fairly satisfied with herself. In an impressive feat of flexibility, she snaked her body out the open window without ever opening the door.

"This is a bad idea," I said as Lia sauntered toward the mini-mart.

"Almost certainly," Michael agreed. From the backseat, I couldn't see his face, but it was all too easy to imagine the unholy glint in his eyes.

"We snuck out of the house to go to a frat party," I said. "And I'm pretty sure this *isn't* a dress."

Michael turned around in his seat, took in the view, and smiled. "Green's a good color for you."

I didn't reply.

"Now it's your turn to say something about the way this shirt really brings out my eyes." Michael sounded so serious that I couldn't help cracking a smile.

"Your shirt is blue. Your eyes are hazel."

Michael leaned toward me. "You know what they say about hazel eyes."

Lia opened the passenger door and flopped back into her seat. "No, Michael. What do they say about hazel eyes?" She smirked.

"Did you get what you needed?" Michael asked her.

Lia handed a brown paper bag back to me. I opened it. "Red Gatorade and cups?"

Lia shrugged. "When in Rome, do as the Romans do. When at a frat party, drink questionable fruit punch out of a red Solo cup."

Lia was right about the punch. And the cups. It was dark enough in the dimly lit frat house that no one noticed that our drinks were a slightly different shade of red.

"What now?" I asked Lia over the deafening music.

She began to move her hips, and her upper body followed suit in a way that made it fairly clear that she'd excel at limbo. She eyed a trio of boys at the edge of the room and shoved Michael toward a blond girl with red-rimmed eyes.

"Now," she said, "we make friends."

A profiler, an emotion reader, and a lie detector went to a party. . . .

An hour later, Michael had identified the people in the room who seemed hardest hit by the murder that had rocked the campus. We'd found a few partyers who were upset for other reasons—including, but not limited to, unrequited crushes and backstabbing roommates—but there was a certain combination of sorrow, fascination, and fear that Michael had zeroed in on as marking someone a person of interest.

Unfortunately, most of our persons of interest had nothing interesting to say.

Lia had danced with at least half the boys in the room and spotted at least three dozen lies. Michael was playing sympathetic ear to the female half of the student population. I stuck to the edges, nursing my fake punch and turning a profiler's eye on the college students crammed into the frat house like jelly beans in a Guess How Many jar. It felt like Colonial's entire student body had showed up—and based on the general lack of sobriety, I was certain that none of *them* were drinking Gatorade.

"People mourn in their own ways." A boy sidled up next to me. He was just shy of six feet tall and dressed entirely in black. There was a hint of a goatee on his chin, and he was wearing plastic-rimmed glasses that I deeply suspected weren't prescription. "We're young. We're not supposed to die. Getting wasted on cheap alcohol is their misguided attempt at reclaiming the illusion of immortality."

"Their attempt," I said, trying to look like I found him intriguing—and not like I was thinking that there was a 40 percent chance he was a philosophy major and a 40 percent chance he was pre-law. "But not yours?"

"I'm more of a realist," the boy said. "People die. Young people, pretty people, people who have their whole lives in front of them. The only real immortality is doing something worth remembering."

Definitely a philosophy major. Any second, he was going to start quoting someone.

"'To live is to suffer, to survive is to find some meaning in the suffering.'"

And there it was. The challenge to getting information

out of this guy wouldn't be getting him to talk; it would be getting him to actually say something.

"Did you know her?" I asked. "Emerson Cole?"

This guy wasn't one of the students Michael had picked out, but I knew before he responded that the answer would be yes. He wasn't *mourning* Emerson, but he'd known her all the same.

"She was in my class." The boy adopted a serious expression and leaned back against the wall.

"Which class?"

"Monsters or Men," the boy replied. "Professor Fogle's class. I took it last year. Now I'm the TA. Fogle's writing a book, you know. I'm his research assistant."

I tried to catch Lia's eye on the dance floor. Professor Fogle was a person of interest in Emerson's murder. He taught a class on serial killers. And somehow, his teaching assistant had found me.

He likes being the pursuer, I thought, watching Lia dancing her way through the frat boys, listening for lies. *Not the pursued.*

"Did you know her?" the boy asked, suddenly turning the tables on me. "Emerson. Did you know her?"

"No," I said, unable to keep from thinking of the lengths Dean had gone just to learn her name. "I guess you could say she was a friend of a friend."

"You're lying." The boy reached out and tucked a stray strand of hair behind my ear. It took everything in me not to pull away. "I consider myself an excellent judge of character."

You consider yourself excellent at everything, I thought.

"You're right," I said, fairly certain those were his favorite words. "I don't even go to school here."

"You saw the story on the news," the boy said, "and you decided to come check it out."

"Something like that." I ran through everything I knew about him and settled on playing to his supposed expertise. "I heard that the professor's a person of interest because of that class he's teaching. Your class."

The boy shrugged. "There was one lecture in particular. . . ."

I took a step forward, and the boy's eyes darted down to my legs. The outfit Lia had picked for me left very little to the imagination. Behind him, I caught sight of Michael, who pointed at the boy and raised his eyebrows. I didn't nod to tell him that I had a promising lead. I didn't have to. Michael saw the answer in my face.

"I could show you the lecture in question." The boy lifted his gaze from my legs to my face. "I have all of Professor Fogle's slides on my laptop. And," he added, "I have a key to the lecture hall." The boy dangled said key in front of me. "It'll be just like sitting in on the class. Unless you'd rather stay here and drown your sorrows with the masses."

I met Michael's eyes over the boy's head.

Follow me, I thought, hoping he'd somehow manage to read my intention in the set of my features. *This is too good to pass up.*

"Take a seat. I'll get the lights." The boy's name was Geoffrey. With a G. That was how he'd introduced himself on the way to the lecture hall—like it would have been a tragedy if I'd mistakenly thought he was Jeffrey with a *J*.

I wasn't about to turn my back on a boy who'd lured me away from a frat party, so I waited for Geoffrey with a *G* to turn the lights on, my back to the wall. The lights flickered overhead and then the auditorium was flooded with light. Hundreds of old-fashioned wooden desks sat in perfect rows. At the front of the room, there was a stage. Geoffrey walked backward down the aisle.

"Getting cold feet?" he asked me. "Criminology isn't for everyone." Most people would have stopped there. Geoffrey didn't. "I'm pre-law."

"Philosophy minor?" I couldn't help asking.

He paused and gave me an odd look. "Double major."

Eyes on mine, Geoffrey climbed onto the stage and plugged his laptop into the projector.

Who brings their laptop to a frat party?

I answered my own question: *a person who was planning on bringing a girl back here for the show all along.* I took a seat, still on guard, but less wary. Geoffrey wasn't our UNSUB. He was so high on himself that I couldn't imagine him needing the validation of the kill.

Then again, I also hadn't sensed that need in Locke.

"Hope we're not late." Michael's voice echoed cheerfully through the auditorium. He'd followed me. *Good.* On the stage, Geoffrey frowned. I turned in my seat to see that Michael hadn't come alone. There was a girl with him: pretty, blond, and curvy, with hipster glasses of her own.

"Geoffrey."

"Bryce."

Clearly, Geoffrey with a *G* and Hipster Girl knew each other. Geoffrey sighed. "Veronica, this is Bryce. Bryce, this is Veronica."

Leave it to Michael to follow us *and* bring reinforcements. Reinforcements who knew Geoffrey—and, unless I was mistaken, didn't like him very much. *Michael must have plucked her from the crowd the moment she saw Geoffrey leave with me.*

"Nice to meet you," I told Bryce. She wound her arm around Michael's waist. Seeing her touch him was a thousand times worse than watching Michael with Lia.

At least Lia was *ours*.

"Geoff," Bryce said, relishing having Michael on her arm and purposefully shortening Geoffrey's name in a way designed to annoy him, "this is Tanner. We're here for the show."

I caught Michael's eye and had to duck my head to keep from bursting out laughing. I'd chosen Agent Sterling's first name as my alias, and Michael had chosen Agent Briggs's.

"You weren't invited," Geoffrey told Bryce, his voice flat.

Bryce shrugged and flopped down in a seat across the aisle from me. "I doubt you'd want Professor Fogle to know that there *was* a show," she said, in a way that left very little doubt that she'd been in my shoes, the recipient of Geoffrey's little show, before.

"Fine," Geoffrey said, capitulating. He turned to me. "Bryce is in my class," he explained. Then, for Michael's benefit, he added, "I'm the teaching assistant."

Michael smirked. "Nice."

"Yeah," Geoffrey replied tersely. "It is."

"I was talking about your goatee." Michael played casually with the tips of Bryce's hair. I shot him a look. Challenging TA Geoff could work in our favor, but not if Geoff got annoyed enough to kick Michael out.

After a tense moment, Geoffrey decided to ignore Michael *and* Bryce and got on with the show. "Welcome to Psych 315: Monsters or Men: The Psychology of Serial Murder." Geoffrey's voice carried across the auditorium, and I could practically hear the man he was channeling. Geoffrey's expression changed as he walked across the stage and flipped from slide to slide.

Body.

After body.

After body.

The images flashed across the screen in rapid succession.

"People define humanity by its achievements, by the Mother Teresas and the Einsteins and the Everyday Joes playing hero in their own ways a thousand times a day. When tragedy strikes, when someone does something so *awful* that we can't even wrap our minds around it, we pretend like that person isn't human. Like there's not a continuum from us to them, like the Everyday Joe isn't a villain in a thousand small ways every day. There's a reason we can't look away from a train wreck, a reason we watch the news when a body turns up, a reason that the world's most infamous serial killers get hundreds of thousands of letters every year."

Geoffrey was reading the words. As well as he delivered them, he wasn't the one who'd written this speech. I turned my attention to the man who had. I could tell, by listening to Geoffrey parrot his words, that Professor Fogle was a larger-than-life figure. Based on the size of this room, his class was a popular one. He was a storyteller. And he had a fascination for the subject matter—a fascination he was convinced the rest of humanity shared.

"The philosopher Friedrich Nietzsche said that anyone

who fought monsters had to fight becoming a monster himself. 'If you gaze long enough into the abyss, the abyss will gaze back into you.'" Geoffrey paused on a slide that included dozens of pictures—not of bodies, but of men. I recognized some of them—they lined our walls at home, smiling out at us from frames, a constant reminder that the kind of monster we hunted could be anyone. Your neighbor. Your father. Your friend.

Your aunt.

"Charles Manson. John Wayne Gacy. Son of Sam." Geoffrey paused for effect. "Ted Bundy. Jeffrey Dahmer. These names mean something to us. This semester, we'll touch on all of the above, but we're going to start closer to home."

The other pictures disappeared, replaced by a man with dark brown hair and eyes the exact same shade. He looked normal. Nondescript. Harmless.

"Daniel Redding," Geoffrey said. I stared at the picture, looking for a resemblance to the boy I knew. "I've studied the Redding case for the past four years," Geoff continued.

"And by *I*, he means the professor," I heard Bryce stage-whisper to Michael. Geoffrey with a *G* ignored her.

"Redding is responsible for a minimum of a dozen murders over a five-year period, beginning with his wife's desertion, days before his twenty-ninth birthday. The bodies were recovered from Redding's farm over a three-day excavation period subsequent to his arrest. Three more victims fitting his MO were identified across state lines."

A crime scene photo flashed up onto the screen. A woman, long dead, hung from a ceiling fan. I recognized the rope—black nylon. Her arms were bound behind her back. Her legs were bound together. The floor beneath her was soaked with blood. Her shirt was torn, and underneath it, I could see cuts—some long and deep, some shallow, some short. But the thing that drew my eyes was the burn on her shoulder, just under her collarbone.

The skin was an angry red: welted, blistered, and raised in the shape of an *R*.

This was what Dean's father had done to those women. This was what he'd made Dean *watch*.

"Bind them. Brand them. Cut them. Hang them." Geoffrey clicked through a series of enlarged images of the woman's body. "That was Redding's modus operandi, or MO."

Listening to Geoffrey use the technical terms made me want to smack him. He didn't know what he was talking about. These were just pictures to him. He didn't know what it was like to discover a loved one missing, or to crawl into the mind of a killer. He was a little boy playing at something he didn't understand.

"Coincidentally," Bryce cut in, "that's also the title of Professor Fogle's book."

"He's writing a book?" I asked.

"On the Daniel Redding case," Geoffrey answered. Clearly, he wasn't about to let his spotlight be usurped. "You can see why he's a person of interest in Emerson's murder. She was branded, you know."

"You said she was in this class. You knew her." My voice was flat. The fact that Geoffrey could talk so casually about the murder of a girl he knew made me reconsider my earlier analysis—maybe he would have been capable of murder.

Geoffrey met my eyes. "People mourn in different ways," he said. I might have been imagining it, but I saw the barest hint of a smile around the edges of his lips.

"She was in my small group," Bryce volunteered. "For our end-of-semester project. The professor assigned the groups. Emerson was . . . nice. Perky, even. I mean, who's perky in a class about serial killers? But Emerson was. She was nice to everyone. One of the guys in our group, you should see him— he's like a roly-poly. You say anything to him, and he just curls into a metaphorical ball. But Emerson could actually get him to talk. And Derek—the other boy in our group—he's that guy. You know, the obnoxious, if-you-don't-know-who-that-guy-is-in-your-section-then-chances-are-good-that-you-*are*-that-guy guy? That's Derek, but Emerson could actually get him to shut up, just by smiling."

Bryce couldn't match Geoffrey's detached tone. She was upset about what had happened to Emerson. This wasn't just a performance to her. She leaned into Michael.

"Emerson didn't show up for our exam." Geoffrey closed his laptop. "Professor Fogle was out sick. I printed off the tests that morning, one for every student in the class. Emerson was the only one who didn't show. I thought she was . . ." Geoff cut off. "Never mind."

"You thought she was what?" Michael asked.

Geoffrey narrowed his eyes. "What does it matter?"

It mattered, but before I could come up with a rational explanation for needing the information, Michael's phone buzzed. He pulled it out, read a text, and then stood. "Sorry, Bryce," he said. "I have to go."

Bryce shrugged. Clearly, she wasn't going to be pining away for him anytime soon. Michael turned toward the door, catching my eye as he passed. *Lia,* he mouthed.

"I should go, too," I said. "This was . . . intense."

"You're leaving?" Geoffrey sounded genuinely surprised. Apparently, he'd been under the impression that he had this one in the bag. Dead girl. Freaky lecture. Sensitive eyes. Clearly, I was supposed to be his for the taking.

"Tell you what," I told him, resisting the urge to roll my eyes. "Why don't you give me your number?"

ia's text didn't lead us back to the party. Apparently, she hadn't been quite as cautious as I was about going off with her quarry alone.

"What exactly did Lia say?" I asked.

Michael held up his phone for my inspection. There was an off-center picture of Lia with two college boys: one tall, one round, both slightly out of focus.

"'Having a fascinating chat,'" I read the accompanying text. "'Heron Hall, roof.'" I paused. "What's she doing on the roof of some random building?"

"Interrogating suspects who don't know they're being interrogated?" Michael suggested, an edge creeping into his voice.

"Any chance the boys in the picture aren't suspects?" I wanted to believe that Lia wouldn't go off alone with someone she thought might be capable of murder. "Maybe they're just friends of Emerson's."

"She sent a picture," Michael replied flatly.

In case something happens, I filled in. Lia had sent us a picture of the boys she was talking to, in case we got to the roof of Heron Hall and she was gone.

We shouldn't have left her at that party alone. I'd been so caught up in getting information out of Geoffrey that I hadn't even told Lia I was leaving.

Lia did a very good impression of someone who could take care of herself—but Lia could do a good impression of just about anything.

Dean wouldn't have left her, I thought, unable to stop myself. That was why he was the one person in this world that she'd walk through fire for, and Michael and I didn't make the cut.

I walked faster.

"She'd mock us for worrying," Michael said, as much to himself as to me. "Either that or she'd take it as a personal insult." He picked up his own pace. With each step, I imagined the ways that this could go badly.

Lia was ours. She had to be okay. *Please be okay.* Finally, we made it to Heron Hall. The towerlike building was clearly Gothic in design—and just as clearly, it was closed and locked down for the evening.

NO TRESPASSING.

Michael didn't miss a beat at the sign. "Do you want to trespass first, or should I?"

_ _ _

I heard Lia laughing before I saw her. It was a light, almost bell-like sound, musical and delighted—and almost certainly a lie.

A step in front of me, Michael opened the door onto the roof. "After you," he said. My stomach muscles unknotted themselves slowly as I stepped out and into the moonlit night. My eyes searched for Lia. Once I'd seen for myself that she was okay, I registered the fact that her flair for fashion apparently extended to her choice of rendezvous points. Not just a tower, not just a locked tower, but the roof of a locked tower. From here, we could see the entire campus stretched out below, a splattering of lights in the darkness.

From the other side of the roof, Lia spotted us. There were two people with her, both of them male. "You made it," she said, weaving on her feet toward us in a way that would have made me nervous even if we'd been on solid ground.

"Don't worry," Lia whispered, throwing her arms around me like the very happiest of drunks. "I'm on the clock. Nothing but Gatorade since we arrived. And if anyone asks, my name is Sadie."

Lia turned back toward the boys. I followed her, unable to keep from thinking that Sadie *was* Lia's real name. None of us knew why she'd changed it.

Only Lia would use the name she'd been born with as her *fake* name.

"Derek, Clark, this is . . ." Lia hiccuped, and Michael took that cue to take over the introductions.

"Tanner," he said, sticking out his hand to shake the others'. "And this is Veronica."

The boy on the left was tall and preppy, with politician hair and classically handsome features. There was a distinct chance that he was flexing his pecs. "I'm Derek," he said, slipping his hand into mine.

Definitely flexing, I thought.

Derek elbowed the boy on the right, hard enough that the boy actually stumbled. Once he regained his footing, he held out his hand. "Clark," he mumbled.

"You sound like a duck," Derek told him. "Clark, clark, clark!"

I ignored Derek and focused on Clark. His handshake was surprisingly firm, but his hands themselves were soft. In fact, *soft* was the best adjective to describe him. He was small and round and looked like he'd been made out of clay that had never quite set. His skin was blotchy, and it took him several seconds to actually meet my eye.

Suddenly, it clicked. "Derek," I said. "And Clark."

Hadn't Bryce said that one of the guys she was assigned to work with in the Monsters or Men class was named Derek? And the other reminded her of a roly-poly. . . .

How in the *world* had Lia managed this? She met my eyes slyly, and I realized that I'd underestimated her. I shouldn't have—not when the reason she was doing all of this was Dean.

"Brilliant deduction," Derek told me, with a trademark

smile that he'd probably practiced in the mirror. "Call Mensa," he said. "This girl's a genius!"

The patronizing tone in his voice told me that he didn't expect me to recognize the put-down for what it was. I suddenly knew exactly what Bryce had meant when she'd described him as "that guy." He almost certainly came from a wealthy family—I was going to guess a long line of successful lawyers, most likely with an Ivy League pedigree. He liked the sound of his own voice even more than Geoffrey did. He was the type who'd debate an issue in class just to prove that he was the better man. He probably whitened his teeth.

"Clark and Derek knew that girl," Lia said, slurring the words. "I met Derek at the party. He called Clark. I asked him to." She leaned into Derek's chest and reached a hand out to Clark's cheek. Clark flushed a brilliant red. Derek nodded at me over Lia's head, as if her presence on his chest was proof that I should want to be there, too.

I was officially *never* wearing this dress again.

"What girl?" I asked.

"The girl who got killed," Derek answered. "Emmie."

"Emerson," Clark muttered.

"What was that, Clark?" Derek said, shooting the rest of us a grin, like Clark's inability to speak up was the world's cleverest joke.

"Her name was Emerson," Clark said, flushing even brighter than he had when Lia had touched him.

"That's what I said." Derek raised one of his palms upward in a gesture I translated to mean, roughly, *What's this guy's problem—meh, what are you gonna do?*

Clark mumbled something in reply. Derek ignored him.

"She was in our class," Derek told me.

"I think I met your TA tonight." I measured their responses to that. Derek stiffened. Clark didn't appear to move at all. Beside me, I could practically feel Michael cataloging every detail of their expressions.

"That guy's a tool," Derek replied.

Quite frankly, I thought that tools who lived in tool houses probably shouldn't throw stones.

"Geoffrey seemed into death," I said. "Like, really into death. And the way he talked about Emerson, it was like he didn't even care."

Agreeing with Derek was like throwing water onto a grease fire. It just made this situation that much worse.

"TA Geoff thinks that frowning and wearing black is a substitute for genuine intelligence. I bet he told you he knew Emerson."

I nodded, willing to see where this was going.

"He didn't know her," Derek said. "He just sits up at the front of the class and grades papers. Clark and I, we knew her." He leaned back on his heels. "That stuck-up blond chick in our group, she knew her. Hey, even Fogle knew her. But TA Geoff is just blowing smoke."

"What do you mean 'Fogle knew her'?" Michael asked. "Isn't it a pretty large class?"

Derek turned his attention to Michael. Whatever he saw there, he liked. Given Michael's background, he'd probably known a dozen Dereks growing up.

"When I say that the professor knew Emmie, I mean that he *really* knew her," Derek said. "Biblically."

I looked at Lia. She nodded slightly—Derek was telling the truth. Beside her, Clark's face was growing red again.

"The dead girl was involved with the professor," Michael said. "That kind of thing could get a guy fired."

"No kidding. Person of interest?" Derek scoffed. "Try *he did it.*" Derek laughed under his breath. "He did her, and then he did *it.*"

"*Shut up,*" Clark said, the words exploding out of his mouth as his hands balled into fists at his sides. "You don't know what you're talking about." He sucked in air like he'd just run a mile. "She wasn't . . . she wasn't like that."

"Whoa there, buddy." Derek held up both palms this time. I didn't bother mentally translating the gesture. "Simmer down. I get it. Don't speak ill of the dead." Derek turned back to the rest of us and proceeded to continue blessing us with his wisdom. "I promise you, once the police find Fogle, the university will be looking for a replacement teacher for our class. Guy's guilty." Derek blanched. "I hope they don't hand the class over to TA Geoff."

Beside him, Clark sucked in another audible breath. Lia met my eyes, then Michael's. We'd gotten what we came for—and more.

CHAPTER 17

The ride home was quiet. Lia was in the back, her legs stretched out the length of the seat. Michael was driving the speed limit. I stared out the window into the black.

"That actually went better than I expected it to," Lia said finally. "If we can sneak back in without getting caught, I'm willing to call it a win."

"I thought you never got caught," I told her, pulling my eyes away from the window and turning to look at her.

Lia inspected her fingernails. "We live in a house with a trained FBI agent and a former military sniper. I'm stealthy, not *magic*. Call it an acceptable risk."

That was a very different tune than the one she'd been singing when she talked me into this.

"Are you sorry you came?" Lia gave me a pointed look. "Or, given the opportunity, would you do it all over again?"

I couldn't be sorry I'd agreed to this. We'd learned too much.

"What did you think of the TA?" I asked Michael.

"Yes," Lia said, yawning and fanning her hand over her mouth. "Do tell, Michael. What did you think of the TA who was such a promising lead that Cassie left the party to go with him, with you on her heels?"

That was the first time Lia had referenced the fact that we'd left her. She tossed the words off like she couldn't be bothered to care.

"The guy was looking at Cassie like she was some kind of specimen under a glass." Michael eyed Lia in the rearview mirror. "You really think I should have let him take her off alone?"

"I'm surprised, that's all." Lia executed an elaborate shrug. "I mean, following Cassie worked out *so well* for you last time."

The last time Michael had followed me, he'd gotten *shot*.

I deserved that. For leaving her at the party, for not even thinking twice about it, I deserved whatever verbal darts she threw out. "We shouldn't have left you there," I said.

"Puh-lease." Lia closed her eyes, like this whole conversation was boring her to tears. "I can take care of myself, Cassie. I saw you leaving. I could have joined you. I *chose* not to. And if Michael had bothered asking, I would have *told* him to go with you."

"I told *you* to stay at the party," Michael muttered.

"Excuse me?" Lia shot back. "What was that?"

"I texted you when I left. You were supposed to stay at the party!" Michael slammed the heel of his hand into the steering wheel, and I jumped. "But no, you went off with not one, but two strange—"

"Witnesses?" Lia supplied. "Trust me, I had a handle on it. I could handle the Dereks and Clarks of the world in my sleep."

I read more into those words than I would have a week ago. Lia was certain she could handle the Dereks and Clarks of the world—because, in all likelihood, she'd seen and handled much, much worse.

"Now, Michael, dearest," Lia continued, her words designed to grate, "concentrate. Cassie's TA. What were your impressions?"

Michael ground his teeth for a moment, but eventually answered. "He wasn't happy when I showed up. He was even less happy to see me with Bryce. I caught a flash of guilt when he saw her, followed by possession, condescension, and titillation."

I said a brief and silent thanks that Michael had been focused on Geoffrey's reaction to seeing him with Bryce—and not mine.

"Geoffrey considers himself above it all." I forced myself to focus on the issue at hand. "He likes holding a position of power in the class." I paused, sorting through my impressions of him. "He chose me because I look young. He expected me to lap up every word of that lecture, to be a little bit afraid of him, but also drawn to the things he could teach me."

"A leader in search of followers?" Lia said. "What does that make the professor?"

"If I had to guess," I told her, drumming my fingers contemplatively against the side of my seat, "I'd say that Professor Fogle has a magnetic personality. Geoffrey was reading his lecture slides. The professor is a performer. And if Derek was telling the truth about Emerson's relationship with Professor Fogle—"

"He was," Lia confirmed.

"—the good professor is not opposed to groupies." I turned that over in my mind. "That's part of what attracts him to this area of study. It's there in the title of his class. These men are larger than life. They're legends. They're the train wreck we can't stop watching, the forbidden, danger-ous *other*."

Michael accepted my appraisal at face value. "I'd have to see the man to tell you anything about him," he said. That was one of the key differences between Michael's ability and mine. Michael read *people*. I read personalities and behaviors—and I didn't always need a person present to do it. "But I *can* tell you that TA Geoff enjoyed talking about Redding's MO just a little too much," Michael continued. "He wanted to see an expression of horror on Cassie's face, and when he didn't get it, he turned the topic to Emerson."

"And what did his face tell you about Emerson?" Lia asked.

"No guilt," Michael reported. "Not even sadness. A tiny sliver of fear. Satisfaction. And loyalty."

"Loyalty?" I asked. "To whom?"

"I truly hate to say it," Lia said with a sigh, "but Derek might have been right. Maybe the professor is our guy. The entire time I was talking to the dynamic duo of God's Gift to the Planet and the Blushing Wonder, I only caught one interesting untruth."

"Derek?" I guessed.

"Clark." There was no question in Michael's voice. "When he was talking about Emerson."

"Point to the emotion reader," Lia drawled. Their gifts overlapped with each other's more than either's overlapped with mine. "When Clark said that Emerson 'wasn't like that,' he was lying." Lia twirled her ponytail around her index finger. "If you ask me, Clark knew that she was doing the horizontal mambo with Professor Creepy."

I turned to Michael. "What did you see?"

"In Clark?" Michael pulled off the highway. Soon, we'd be home. "I saw longing," he said. "Fear of rejection." He flicked his eyes over to mine. "Rage."

Not just anger, but rage. At Derek, for speaking badly about a girl that Clark had cared about? At us for asking the questions? At the professor? At Emerson?

"So what do we do now?" I asked. "Assuming we don't get caught the second we get home."

"We need to figure out if the FBI knows about Emerson's relationship with the professor." Lia flicked her hair back over her shoulder. "If they don't, we have to find a way of passing that information on."

"What about Dean?" I asked.

"We don't tell Dean." Lia's voice was quiet, but it cut through the air like a whip. "He needs this case solved. He doesn't need to know what we'll do to see that happen."

Dean wouldn't understand why we would go out on a limb for him, because deep down, he believed he wasn't worth saving. He would have taken a bullet for any of us, but he wouldn't want us risking anything for him.

Most people built walls to protect themselves. Dean did it to protect everyone else.

For once, Lia and I were in total agreement. "We don't tell Dean."

CHAPTER 18

"*Deviant Behavior, Criminal Minds: An Introduction to Criminal Psychology, Eighth Edition.*" Bleary-eyed and only half awake, I looked from the textbook sitting on the kitchen table to Dean, then back again. "Seriously?" I said. "Agent Sterling wants us to read an introductory textbook?"

After the night Lia, Michael, and I had had, my head was pounding, and all my body really wanted was to go back to bed.

Dean shrugged. "We've been assigned chapters one through four." He paused, his eyes drinking in my appearance. "You okay?"

No, I thought. *I'm sleep-deprived, and I can't tell you why.*

"I'm fine," I insisted. I could see Dean piecing his way through the dozens of ways that I was just a shade off this morning. "I just can't believe Agent Sterling's idea of training us is . . . *this*," I added, gesturing toward the textbook. From the moment I'd joined the program, I'd learned by doing. Real cases. Real crime scene photos. Real victims.

But this textbook? Bryce and Derek and Clark had probably all read one just like it. There were probably little worksheets to go with it.

"Maybe it is a waste of time," Dean said, plucking the thought from my mind. "But right now, I'd rather waste our time than Sterling's."

Because Agent Sterling was hunting down Emerson's killer.

I took the textbook from him and turned to chapter one. "'Criminal Psychology is the subset of psychology dedicated to explaining the personality types, motives, and cognitive structures associated with deviant behavior,'" I read, "'particularly that which causes mental or physical harm to others.'"

Dean stared down at the page. His hair fell into his face. I kept reading, falling into a steady rhythm, my voice the only sound in the room.

"'Chapter Four: Organized vs. Disorganized Offenders.'"

Dean and I had taken a lengthy break for lunch, but my voice was still getting hoarse.

"My turn," Dean said, taking the textbook from me. "If you read another chapter, you're going to be miming things by the end."

"That could get ugly," I replied. "I've never been very good at charades."

"Why do I get the feeling there's a story there?" Dean's lips twisted into a subtle smile.

I shuddered. "Let's just say that family game night is a competitive affair, and I'm also pretty dismal at Pictionary."

"From where I'm sitting, that's not exactly a character flaw." Dean leaned back in his chair. For the first time since we'd seen the body on the news, he looked almost relaxed. His arms dangled loosely by his sides. His chest rose and fell slightly with each breath. His hair still fell into his face, but there was almost no visible tension in his shoulders, his neck.

"Did someone say character flaw?" Michael sauntered into the room. "I believe that might be one of my middle names."

I glanced back down at the textbook, trying to pretend that I *hadn't* just been staring at Dean.

"Middle names, plural?" I asked.

Michael inclined his head slightly. "Michael Alexander Thomas *Character Flaw* Townsend." He shot me a lazy smile. "It has a certain ring to it, don't you think?"

"We're working," Dean told him flatly.

"Don't mind me," Michael said, waving a hand in our general direction. "I'm just making a sandwich."

Michael was never "just" anything. He might have wanted a sandwich, but he was also enjoying irritating Dean. *And,* I thought, *he doesn't want to leave the two of us in here alone.*

"So," I said, turning back to Dean and trying to pretend

this *wasn't* awkward. "Chapter four. You want to take over reading?"

Dean glanced over at Michael, who seemed amused by the entire situation. "What if we didn't read it?" Dean asked me.

"But it's our *homework*," I said, adopting a scandalized expression.

"Yeah, I know—I'm the one who talked you into reading it in the first place." Dean ran his fingertip along the edge of the book. "But I can tell you what it's going to say."

Dean had been here five years, and this textbook was Profiling 101.

"Okay," I said. "Why don't you give me the abbreviated version? Teach me."

There was a time when Dean would have refused.

"Okay," he said, staring at me from across the table. "Disorganized killers are loners. They're the ones who never quite fit in. Poor social skills, a lot of pent-up anger."

At the word *anger*, my eyes darted involuntarily toward Michael's. *Never fit in. Poor social skills.* I could tell from the look on Michael's face that I wasn't the only one thinking that sounded like a bare-bones description of Clark.

Dean paused. I forced my eyes forward and willed Dean not to think too hard about why it was that hearing a few words about disorganized killers had led to something unspoken passing between Michael and me.

"In their day-to-day lives, disorganized killers are generally seen as antisocial and inept," Dean continued after a long moment. "People don't like them, but they're not scared of them, either. If the disorganized killer has a job, it's likely to be low-paying and low on respect. Disorganized killers may behave like adolescents well into adulthood; it's statistically likely that they still live with one or more of their parents."

"So what's the difference between a disorganized killer and a loser?" Michael didn't even bother to pretend he wasn't eavesdropping.

"If you were like Cassie and me"—Dean stared Michael down—"you wouldn't have to ask."

Dead silence.

Dean had never admitted that the two of us were the same before. He'd never believed it. He'd certainly never said it to Michael.

"Is that so?" Michael's eyes narrowed, a sharp contrast to the seemingly unruffled smile on his lips. I looked down at the table. Michael didn't need to see the expression on my face—the one that said that Dean was right. I *didn't* have to ask Michael's question, because I *did* instinctively know the answer. Being antisocial and angry and inept didn't make someone a killer. Traits like those couldn't tell us whether Clark had the potential for violence, or how much. The only thing they could tell us was what *kind* of killer someone *like* Clark would be, if he ever crossed that line.

If Clark were a killer, he'd be a disorganized killer.

"Organized killers can be charming." Dean swung his

attention from Michael back to me. "They're articulate, confident, and comfortable in most social situations." His hair fell into his face, but his gaze never moved from mine. "They tend to be intelligent, but narcissistic. They may be incapable of feeling fear."

I thought of Geoffrey with a G, who'd lectured me on the meaning of modus operandi and mentioned Emerson without a whiff of grief.

"Other people aren't worthy of empathy to the organized killer, because other people are *less*. To them, being average is the same as being disposable."

I absorbed Dean's words, memorized them.

"What's the life of one more person when the world is full of so many?" Dean's voice went flat as he posed the question, and I knew he was somewhere else. "Organized killers feel no remorse."

Dean's father was an organized killer, I thought. I reached across the table and placed my hand over Dean's. He bowed his head, but kept talking. "Organized killers plan things," he said, his voice low. "Disorganized killers, they're the ones who would do things on the spur of the moment."

"They snap," I said softly, "or they give in to their impulses."

Dean leaned forward, his fingers curving around mine. "They're more likely than organized killers to attack from behind."

"Weapon choice?" I asked, my hand still intertwined with his.

"Whatever they have in reach," Dean replied. "Blunt force trauma, a nearby kitchen knife, their own hands. The entire crime scene reflects a loss of control."

"But for organized killers," I said, my eyes on him, "it's all about control."

Dean held my gaze. "Organized killers stalk their victims. They often target strangers. Every move they make is calculated, premeditated, and in service of a particular goal. They're methodical."

"Harder to catch," I supplied.

"They like that they're harder to catch," Dean returned. "Killing is only part of the pleasure. Getting away with it is the rest."

Everything Dean said made sense to me—incredible, intuitive sense, like he was reminding me of something I'd always known, rather than teaching me something new.

"You okay?" he asked me.

I nodded. "I'm fine." I glanced over at the kitchen counter, where Michael had been making his sandwich. He was gone. At some point during my back-and-forth with Dean, Michael had taken off.

I glanced down at the table. Dean slowly unfurled his hand from mine.

"Dean?" I said. My voice was soft, but cut through the room. I could still feel the exact place where his skin had touched mine. "Organized killers, they're the ones who take trophies, aren't they?"

Dean nodded. "Trophies help them relive their kills. It's

how they sate their desire to kill in between victims."

"Locke took a tube of lipstick from every woman she killed." I couldn't keep from saying those words out loud. *Narcissistic. Controlled.* It fit.

"My father was an organized killer." There was an intensity to Dean when he spoke about his father. This was the second time he'd opened up to me, tit for tat. "He said that as a child, people knew there was something wrong with him, but for as long as I could remember, he was well-liked. He planned things meticulously. He never deviated from the script. He dominated the women he targeted. He controlled them." Dean paused. "He's never once showed remorse."

I heard the front door open and shut. I thought it might be Michael, getting out of the house and away from us, but then I heard footsteps coming our way—two sets, one heavier than the other.

Sterling and Briggs were back.

They appeared in the doorway just as Dean closed the textbook on the table in front of us.

"Cassie, can we talk to Dean alone for a minute?" Agent Briggs straightened his tie. This particular gesture, from this particular man, set off alarm bells in my mind. The tie was something Briggs only wore when he was on duty. Straightening it was an affirmation of sorts. Whatever he wanted to talk to Dean about, it was *just business*.

I trusted Briggs less when business was involved.

"She can stay," Dean told Briggs. His words fell on the room like a thunderclap. For as long as I'd known Dean, he'd been pushing me away. *Alone* was the name of his game.

I caught his eye. *Are you sure?* I asked him silently.

Dean ran the heels of his hands over the fronts of his jean-clad thighs. "Stay," he told me. *Dean wants me here.* He turned back to Briggs. "What do you need?"

Agent Sterling stiffened, her lips pressed into a grim line.

"The person who killed Emerson Cole is obsessed with your father," Briggs said, ignoring the expression on his ex-wife's face. "There's a very real chance the UNSUB has written to him."

"And let me guess," Dean interjected. "Dear old dad destroys the letters once he gets them. They're all up here." Dean tapped a finger to the side of his head.

"He's agreed to assist us," Briggs said. "But only on one condition."

The tension was back in Dean's shoulders, his neck. Every muscle in his body was strung tight.

"You don't have to do anything you don't want to do," Agent Sterling cut in.

"I know what the condition is." Dean's eyes burned with an emotion I couldn't identify: not quite hatred, not quite fear. "My father won't tell *you* anything. The only person he'll talk to is me."

YOU

Daniel Redding is one of the greats. Infamous. Ingenious. Immortal. You chose him for a reason. When a man like Redding speaks, people listen. When Redding wants someone dead, they die. He is everything you want to be. Powerful. Sure of himself. And always, always in control.

"You were sloppy. Stupid. Lucky." You banish the voice and run your fingers along the edges of a photograph of Emerson Cole standing next to a tree. Proof that for a moment, you were powerful. Sure of yourself. In control.

Just. Like. Him.

Daniel Redding is not your hero. He's your god. And if you keep going down this path, you will slowly remake yourself in his image. The rest of the world will be as insignificant and powerless as ants. The police. The FBI. You'll crush them under steel-toed boots.

What will be will be—in time.

CHAPTER 19

Stone walls. *Barbed wire.* My impression of the maxi-
mum security prison that housed Dean's father was
fleeting. Dean and I were ensconced in the backseat
of an FBI-issued black SUV. Agent Briggs was driving. Agent
Sterling sat shotgun. From my position directly behind her,
I couldn't see anything but her forearm, resting on the arm-
rest. At first glance, she seemed relaxed, but the pads of her
fingertips were pressed flat and digging into the leather.

Beside me, Dean stared fixedly out the window. I laid
my hand on the seat between us, palm up. He tore his gaze
from the window and looked over, not at me, but at my
hand. He laid his hand palm-down on the seat, inches away
from mine.

I slid my hand closer to his. His dark eyes closed, his
eyelashes casting a series of tiny shadows onto his face.
After a small eternity, his hand began to move. He rotated it

slowly clockwise until the back of his hand was flat against the seat, mere centimeters from mine. I slid my hand into his. His palm was warm. After several seconds, his fingers curled upward, closing around mine.

Moral support. That was why I was there, along for the ride.

Briggs pulled into a secured lot. He parked and cut the engine. "The guards will come out to let Dean and me in." He glanced first at Sterling, then at me. "You two stay in the car. The fewer people who see another teenager here, the better."

Briggs wasn't happy I was here, but he hadn't tried to leave me behind. They needed Dean, and Dean needed something—some*one*—to tether him to the here and now.

The back door to the prison opened. Two guards stood there. They were the exact same height. One was beefy and bald, the other younger and built like a runner.

Briggs climbed out of the car and opened Dean's door. Dean set my hand lightly back into my lap. "I won't be long."

A muscle in his jaw twitched. His eyes were emotionless and hard. *He was born smiling.* The words from Redding's interview echoed in my head as Dean slammed the door.

Dean and Briggs approached the guards. The balding man shook Briggs's hand. The younger guard took a step toward Dean, looking him up and down. A moment later, Dean was against a wall being frisked.

I looked away.

"Some people will always look at Dean and see his father," Agent Sterling said from the front seat. "Daniel Redding isn't exactly a favorite among the guards here. He has a certain fondness for mind games and a penchant for picking up information about the guards' families. Briggs had to tell them that Dean was Redding's son. It would have been impossible to get this visit approved otherwise, even with permission from on high."

"Your father approved this visit?" I asked, sliding over in the seat so that I had a better angle to see her.

"It was his idea." Sterling pursed her lips. She wasn't happy about this.

"Your father wants this case closed." I worked my way through the logic of the situation. "The Locke case made the papers. The last thing the FBI needs right now is more bad press. The director needs this case to go away quickly and quietly, and he's not above using Dean to do it. But if it were up to you—"

"If it were up to me," she cut in, "Dean would never have to come within a hundred yards of his father again." She glanced out the window. Briggs, Dean, and the older guard had disappeared into the building. The younger guard— the one who'd frisked Dean—was walking toward our car. "Then again," Sterling said, unlocking her car door, "if it were up to me, once we'd arrested Redding, Dean would have gotten his chance at a normal childhood."

She opened the door and stepped out. "Can I help you?"

she asked the guard. He looked down at Agent Sterling, a slight curl to his lips.

"You can't stay in the car," he told her. "This is a secure area."

"I'm aware. And cleared to be here," Sterling said coolly, arching one eyebrow. She had the manner of someone who'd spent her life in a series of old boys' clubs. One prison guard on a power trip didn't impress her.

I could practically see the guard debating whether getting into a pissing match with a female FBI agent—particularly *this* female FBI agent—was worth it.

"Warden's on a security kick," he told her, shoving the blame off on his superior. "You'll have to move the car."

"Fine." Sterling went to climb back into the car, and the guard's eyes landed on me. He held up a hand and motioned for me to open my door. I looked to Agent Sterling. She gave a brief nod. I opened the door and stepped out.

The guard barely spared a glance for me before turning his attention back to Agent Sterling. "She friends with that Redding kid?" he asked. His voice left no question on his feelings about Dean—and Dean's father.

I was pretty sure Michael would have read it as disgust.

"If you'll excuse me," Sterling said firmly, "I'll move the car."

The guard eyed me, his earlier resolve not to get into it with Agent Sterling facing off with his dislike of Dean—and now me. He turned and said something into a handheld

143

radio. After a few moments, he turned back around, a polite smile on his face, his eyes narrowed to cold and uncompromising slits. "I put a call into the warden. I'm afraid the two of you are going to have to come with me."

"Don't say a word," Agent Sterling told me under her breath. "I'll take care of this."

The guard walked us down a hallway. Agent Sterling whipped out her phone.

"I can put you in the visitor's room," the guard offered. "Or you can wait in the offices out front."

Whoever Sterling was calling didn't answer. She turned her attention to the guard. "Mr. . . ." She trailed off, waiting for him to provide his last name.

"Webber," he said.

"Mr. Webber, there is a reason you and your colleague were asked to meet Agent Briggs at the *back* door. There is a reason that Agent Briggs is not meeting with Daniel Redding in the visitor's room. This case is sensitive and need-to-know. And *no one* needs to know that the FBI has been here to see Redding."

Prison guards held a position of power inside these walls, and this one relished his. Webber didn't like being reminded that Sterling was FBI. He didn't like her. He didn't like being talked down to.

And he really didn't like Dean. Or Redding. Or me.

This was not going to end well.

"Unless you have somewhere we can wait that is both *secured* and *private*," Agent Sterling continued, "I suggest you call your supervisor and—"

"Secured and private?" the guard said, congenial and polite enough to send chills down my spine. "Why didn't you say so?"

We ended up in an observation room. On the other side of a two-way mirror, Agent Briggs and Dean sat across from a man with dark hair and dark eyes.

Dean's eyes.

I shouldn't be here. I shouldn't be seeing this.

But thanks to a prison guard with a chip on his shoulder, I was. Dean and his father sat in silence, and I couldn't keep from wondering: how long had they been sitting there, staring at each other? What had we missed?

Beside me, Sterling's eyes were locked on Redding.

Dean's father wasn't a big man, but sitting there, a slight smile gracing even and unremarkable features, he commanded attention. His dark hair was thick and neat. There was a slight trace of stubble on his chin and cheeks.

"Tell me about the letters." Dean didn't phrase those words as a question or as a request. Whatever conversation had passed between the two of them before we'd gotten here, Dean was a man on a mission now.

Get the information he needed and get out.

"Which letters?" his father asked amiably. "The ones

that curse me to hell and back? The ones from the families, describing their journeys toward forgiveness? The ones from women proposing marriage?"

"The ones from the professor," Dean countered. "The one who's writing the book."

"Ah," Redding said. "Fogle, I believe it was? Healthy mop of hair, deep, soulful eyes, overly fond of Nietzsche?"

"So he's been to visit." Dean wasn't affected by his father's theatrics. "What did he ask you?"

"There are only two questions, Dean. You know that." Redding smiled fondly. "*Why* and *how*."

"And what kind of person was the professor?" Dean pressed. "Was he more interested in the why or the how?"

"Little of column A, little of column B." Redding leaned forward. "Why the sudden interest in my professorial colleague? Afraid he might not get your part right when he tells our story?"

"We don't have a story."

"My story is your story." An odd light came into Redding's eyes, but he managed to tamp down on it and dial the intensity in his voice back a notch. "If you want to know what the professor was writing and what he's capable of, I suggest you ask him yourself."

"I will," Dean said. "As soon as you tell me where to find him."

"For heaven's sake, Dean, I don't have the man on speed dial. We aren't *friends*. He interviewed me a few times.

Generally, he asked the questions and I answered them, not the other way around."

Dean stood to leave.

"But," Redding added coyly, "he did mention that he does most of his writing in a cabin in the mountains."

"What cabin?" Dean asked. "What mountains?"

Redding gestured with his manacled hands toward Dean's seat. After a long moment, Dean sat.

"My memory may need some refreshing," Redding said, leaning forward slightly, his eyes making a careful study of Dean's.

"What do you want?" Dean's voice was completely flat. Redding either didn't notice or didn't care.

"You," the man said, his eyes roving over Dean, drinking in every detail, like an artist surveying his finest work. "I want to know about you, Dean. What have those hands been doing the past five years? What sights have those eyes seen?"

There was something disconcerting about listening to Dean's father break his body down into parts.

Dean is just a thing to you, I thought. *He's hands and eyes, a mouth. Something to be molded. Something to own.*

"I didn't come here to talk about me." Dean's voice never wavered.

His father shrugged. "And I can't seem to remember if the professor's cabin was near Catoctin or Shenandoah."

"I don't know what you want me to say." Dean's eyes bore

into his father's. "There's nothing to talk about. Is that what you want to hear? That these hands, these eyes—they're *nothing?*"

"They're everything," Redding replied, his voice vibrating with intensity. "And there is so much more you could do."

Beside me, Agent Sterling stood. She took a step closer to the glass. Closer to Redding.

"Come now, Dean-o, there must be something worth talking about in your life." Redding was perfectly at ease, immune—maybe even unaware—of the enmity rolling off Dean. "Music. Sports. A motorcycle. A girl." Redding cocked his head to the side. "Ah," he said. "So there is a girl."

"There's no one," Dean bit out.

"Methinks you doth protest too much, son."

"I am not your son."

Redding's hands shot out. In a flash, he was on his feet. Dean must have been leaning forward, because somehow, Redding managed to get hold of his shirt. Father jerked son to his feet. "You are my son, more than you were ever your whore mother's. I'm in you, boy. In your blood, in your mind, in every breath you take." Redding's face was close to Dean's now, close enough that Dean would have felt the heat from his breath with each word. "You know it. You fear it."

One second Dean was just standing there, and the next, his hands were fisted in his father's orange jumpsuit, and Daniel Redding was being pulled bodily across the table.

"Hey!" Briggs came between the two of them. Redding let go of Dean first. He held his hands up in submission.

You never really submit, I thought. *You never give in. You get what you want—and you want Dean.*

Agent Sterling's hand clamped around my elbow. "We're going," she told me. The guard tried to stop her, but she turned the full force of her glare on him. "One more word, one more step, and I swear to God, I will have your job."

I looked back at Dean. Briggs put a hand on his chest and pushed, hard. Like a sleepwalker suddenly awakened, Dean jerked backward, dropping his hold on his father. He looked at the two-way mirror, and I would have sworn that he could see me standing there.

"Cassandra," Agent Sterling snapped. "We're going. Now."

The last thing I heard before I left was Dean's voice, empty and hard. "Tell me about the professor's cabin."

CHAPTER 20

"This was a mistake." Sterling waited until the two of us were ensconced in the car before saying those words.

"Going with the guard?" I asked.

"Bringing you here. Bringing *Dean* here. Staying in that room, watching that. All of it." When Sterling said *all of it*, I got the sense that she wasn't just talking about the way that Briggs and the director had chosen to handle this case. She meant the life Dean was living. The Naturals program. *All of it*.

"It isn't the same," I told her. "What we do as a team, and what they're having Dean do in there with his father—it's not the same." Putting Dean in a room with Daniel Redding ripped open all the old scars, every wound that man had inflicted on Dean's psyche.

That wasn't what this program was. That wasn't what we *did*.

"You should have seen Dean when we got the call that the FBI had recovered Mackenzie McBride," I said, thinking of *that* Dean. Our Dean. "He didn't just smile. He beamed. Did you know he has dimples?"

Agent Sterling didn't reply.

"Dean was never going to have a normal childhood." I wasn't sure why it felt so important to make her understand that. "There are things you don't come back from. Normal's not an option, for any of us." I thought of what Sloane had said. "If we'd had normal childhoods, we wouldn't be Naturals."

Agent Sterling finally turned to look at me. "Are we talking about Dean's father or your mother?" She let that question sink in. "I've read your file, Cassie."

"I'm Cassie now?" I asked. She wrinkled her forehead. I elaborated. "You've called me Cassandra since you showed up."

"Do you want me to keep calling you by your full name?"

"No." I paused. "But you want to keep calling me by it. You don't like nicknames. They bring you closer to people."

Sterling sucked in a breath. "You're going to have to learn to stop that," she said.

"Stop what?"

"Most people don't like being profiled. Some things are better left unsaid." She paused. "Where were you last night?"

My heart nearly jumped out of my chest. The question came out of nowhere.

I played dumb. "What do you mean?" She'd threatened the program when all Sloane had done was make use of the basement crime sets. If she knew what Lia, Michael, and I had done the night before, there was no telling what she might do.

"You think that I dislike you." Sterling was using her profiler voice, getting into my head. "You see me as the enemy, but I am not your enemy, Cassie."

"You have a problem with this program." I paused. "I don't know why you even took this job. You have a problem with what Briggs is doing here, and you have a problem with me."

I expected her to deny it. She surprised me. "My problem with you," she said, enunciating each word, "is that you don't do what you're told. All the instincts in the world are worthless if you can't work within the system. Briggs never understood that, and neither do you."

"You're talking about what happened last summer." I didn't want to be having this conversation, but there was no way out. I couldn't get out of the car. I couldn't get away from her assessing stare. "I get it. Dean got hurt. Michael got hurt. Because of me."

"Where were you last night?" Agent Sterling asked again. I didn't answer her. "Last summer, you and your friends hacked a secured drive and read through the case files for no reason, as far as I can tell, other than the fact that you were bored. Even after Briggs warned you to back off, you had no intention of doing it. Eventually, the killer made contact." She didn't give me time to recover from that brutal recitation of events. "You wanted in on the case. Your Agent Locke obliged."

"So it's my fault," I said, angry, trying not to cry, terrified that she was right. "The people Locke killed, just to send me their hair in boxes. The girl she kidnapped. The fact that she shot Michael. That's all on me."

"No." Sterling's voice was low and uncompromising. "None of that was your fault, Cassie, but for the rest of your life, you will wonder if it was. It will keep you up late at night. It will haunt you. It will never leave. I know that sometimes you wonder if I look at you and see your aunt, but that's not it. Dean's not his father. I'm not mine. If I thought you were anything like the woman who called herself Lacey Locke, we wouldn't be having this conversation."

"Then why are you having this conversation with *me*?" I asked. "You say that I don't know how to work within the system, but don't try to tell me that the others do. Lia? Michael? Even Sloane. You don't look at them the way you look at me."

"Because they're not me." Agent Sterling's words seemed to suck all the oxygen out of the car. "I didn't read your file and see your aunt, Cassie." She clamped her jaw shut. By the time she finally continued, I'd almost convinced myself that I'd misheard her. "When you break the rules, when you start telling yourself that the end justifies the means, people get hurt. Protocol saves lives." She ran a hand over the back of her neck. Midday, with no air-conditioning, the temperature in the car was approaching stifling.

"You want to know why you, in particular, concern me, Cassie? You're the one who really feels things. Michael, Lia,

Dean—they learned very early in life to shut down their emotions like *that*. They're not used to letting people in. They won't feel the need to put their own necks on the line *every single time*. Sloane cares, but she deals in facts, not emotions. But you? You won't ever be able to stop caring. For you, it will always be about the victims and their families. It will always be personal."

I wanted to tell her that she was wrong. But then I thought of Mackenzie McBride, and I knew that Agent Sterling was right. Every case I worked would be personal. I would always want justice for the victims. I would do whatever it took to save just one life, the way that I wished that someone had saved my mother's.

"I'm glad you were able to be here for Dean today, Cassie. He needs someone, especially now—but if you're serious about doing what we do, what *I* do, emotions are a luxury you cannot afford. Guilt, anger, empathy, being willing to do *anything* to save a life—that's a recipe for getting someone killed."

At some point before she'd left the FBI, she'd lost someone. Because she'd gotten emotionally involved in a case. Because in the heat of battle, she'd broken the rules.

"I need to know where you were last night." She was like a broken record. "I'm giving you a chance to make a good decision here. I suggest you take it."

Part of me wanted to tell her, but this wasn't just my secret. It was also Michael's and Lia's.

"Briggs doesn't know you snuck out. Neither does Judd."

Sterling let the implied threat hang in the air. "I'm betting you've never seen Judd really angry. I have. I don't recommend it."

When I didn't reply, Agent Sterling went silent. The temperature in the car was becoming unbearable. "You're making a bad decision here, Cassie." I said nothing, and her eyes narrowed. "Just tell me this," she said. "Is there anything I should know?"

I caught my bottom lip in my teeth and thought of Dean and the lengths he was going to, to get even the smallest bit of information out of his father.

"Emerson was involved with her professor," I said finally. I owed it to Dean to share that information. "The one who was writing a book about Dean's dad."

Agent Sterling slipped off her jacket. Clearly, the heat was getting to her, too. "Thank you," she said, turning in her seat to face me. "But listen and listen well: when I told you to stay away from this case, I meant it. The next time you take so much as a step out of Quantico without my permission, I'll have you fitted for an ankle tracker."

I barely heard the threat. I didn't reply. I couldn't form words. I couldn't even think them.

When Agent Sterling had removed her jacket, she'd dislodged her shirt slightly. It gapped in the front, giving me a view of the skin underneath. There was a scar just under her collarbone.

A brand, in the shape of the letter *R*.

Sterling looked down. Her face absolutely expression-less, she righted her shirt. The scar was covered now, but I couldn't stop staring.

Bind them. Brand them. Cut them. Hang them.

The entire time we'd been in the observation room, she hadn't taken her eyes off of Daniel Redding.

"My team was investigating the case," Sterling said calmly. "I got a little too close, and I got sloppy. Redding had me for two days before I escaped."

"That's how you know Dean." I'd wondered how they'd developed a relationship based only on the fact that she'd arrested his father. But if she'd been one of Redding's victims . . .

"I'm not a victim," Sterling said, following my line of thought so closely it was eerie. "I'm a survivor, and Dean is the reason that I survived."

156

"Was this the case you were talking about before?" I couldn't seem to find my voice. It came out cracked and hushed. "When you said that getting emotionally involved was a recipe for getting someone killed, were you talking about someone Daniel Redding murdered?"

"No, Cassie, I wasn't. And that's the last question I'm going to answer about Daniel Redding, my past, or the brand on my chest. Are we clear on that?" Sterling's voice was so even, so utterly matter-of-fact, that I couldn't do anything but nod.

The door to the prison opened, and Briggs and Dean exited. They were only accompanied by one guard, the older one. I watched as the guard handed something to Agent Briggs—a file. Beside them, Dean stood perfectly, unnaturally still. His shoulders were hunched. His head was down. His arms hung listlessly by his sides.

"Don't ask Dean about any of this." Agent Sterling issued those words as a command, desperate and fierce. "Don't even tell him you saw the brand."

"I won't. Ask him. I won't ask him anything." I struggled to form sentences and fell silent as Dean and Briggs walked toward the car. Dean opened the car door and climbed in. He shut the door, but didn't look at me. I forced myself not to reach for him. I tried to keep my eyes focused on the seat in front of me.

Briggs handed the file to Agent Sterling, slapping it down into her hand. "Visitor logs," he said. "Redding wasn't supposed to *have* visitors. The warden is out of his mind. I wouldn't even bet on the logs being complete."

Agent Sterling flipped open the file. She ran down the list of names. "Conjugal visits?" she asked.

Briggs spat out the answer. "Several."

"You think our UNSUB is on this list?" Sterling asked.

"That would make sense," Briggs replied tersely. "It would make our lives easy, so, no, Ronnie, I don't think our UNSUB is on that list, because I don't think this is going to make sense. It's not going to be easy. We're just not that lucky."

I expected Sterling to snap back at him, but instead, she reached out and touched his forearm lightly with the tips of her fingers. "Don't let him get to you," she said quietly. Briggs relaxed slightly under her touch. "If you let him in," she continued, "if you let him under your skin, he wins."

"This is stupid." Dean shook his head, his upper lip curling in disgust. "We knew what would happen if I came here. He promised he'd talk. Well, he talked, and now we have no way of knowing how much of what he said was true and how much is just him leading us around, like dogs on ropes."

It shouldn't have been me behind that glass, I thought. It should have been Lia watching the interrogation. I didn't care about the difference between active cases and cold cases. I cared about *Dean.*

Agent Sterling turned around in her seat. I expected to see the gentleness with which she'd just reproved Briggs, but instead, her eyes were glittering, hard as diamonds, as she addressed Dean. "Don't," she told him, jabbing a finger in his direction.

"Don't what?" Dean shot back. I'd never heard him so angry.

"You really want to play this game with me?" Sterling asked him, her eyebrows nearly disappearing into her hairline. "You think I don't know what it was like for you in there? You think I don't know what he said, what you're thinking? I am telling you, Dean, *don't*. Don't go there."

As Briggs drove back past the gate and off prison grounds, the three of them settled into a tense silence. I put my hand on the seat, palm up. Dean turned toward the window, his fingers curling into fists.

I looked down at my hand, open and waiting, but couldn't move it. I felt utterly out of place and useless. I'd accompanied them on this trip for Dean's sake, but I didn't need to be a profiler to know that he didn't want me here now. With a single conversation, his father had jammed a wedge between Dean and the rest of the world, cutting him off as effectively as a blade severing a ruined limb. The unspoken closeness that had been building between Dean and me was a casualty of that blow—gone, as if it had never existed at all.

I'm in you, boy. In your blood, in your mind, in every breath you take.

In the front seat, Briggs pulled out his cell phone. Seconds after he dialed the number, he was barking out orders. "Redding gave us a location on the professor's writing cabin.

Catoctin." Briggs paused. "No, I don't know whose name the deed to the cabin is under. Try the professor's parents, ex-wife, college roommates. . . . Try everyone and their damned dog, but find it."

Briggs ended the call and tossed his phone down. Sterling caught it. "If I remember correctly," she said dryly, "throwing phones was more my area than yours."

Agent Sterling was the one who had been tortured by Daniel Redding, but she was the only one of the three of them holding it together in the wake of this visit.

"Did Redding say anything about the professor being involved with Emerson Cole?" Agent Sterling's question snapped both Dean and Briggs out of it, if only for a second.

"Care to share your source on that one?" Briggs asked tightly. I could practically hear him thinking that Sterling was following leads behind his back.

"Why don't you ask Cassie?" Sterling suggested. "Apparently, she's been doing some extracurricular digging."

"Excuse me?" Briggs spat out.

Dean turned his head slowly away from the window to face me. "What kind of extracurricular digging?" he asked me, his voice low and haggard. "What did you do?"

"Nothing," I said. "It doesn't matter."

"Just you?" Dean asked. I didn't reply. He closed his eyes, his entire face taut. "Of course it's not just you. You wouldn't be lying to me about it if it were. I'm assuming Lia's involved. Sloane? Townsend?"

I didn't reply.

"This gives us motive," Agent Sterling told Briggs in the front seat. "The professor might have killed the girl to keep the truth from coming out."

"Emerson," Dean said, his voice tight. "Her name was Emerson."

"Yes," Agent Sterling said, ignoring the fury in Dean's voice. "It was. And whether you believe it or not, Dean, the information you got out of your father today, no matter how insignificant it seems, will help us find Emerson's killer. Now you just have to let us do our job." She paused. "You both do. No more digging. No more field trips."

At the phrase *field trips*, Briggs pulled the car over to the shoulder of the road and killed the engine. "You," he said, turning around and pinning me with a look. "Out of the car." With those words, Briggs got out of the car himself.

I tried not to flinch as I joined him. Briggs might have been willing to take calculated risks, like bringing Dean to see his father, but he was only okay with those risks if the calculations were *his*.

"Am I to understand that you left the house, went on some kind of *field trip*, and directly interfered with an ongoing FBI investigation?" Briggs never raised his voice, but he put so much force behind each word that he might as well have been yelling.

"Yes?"

Briggs ran his hands through his hair. "Who went with you?"

That, I couldn't tell him.

"I know you want to help," he told me through clenched teeth. "What this case is doing to Dean isn't fair. Bringing him here to talk to his father—that wasn't fair of *me*. But I didn't have a choice. Dean didn't really have a choice, but you do. You can choose to trust me. You can choose not to give Agent Sterling any more ammunition against this program. You can choose *not* to behave like an irresponsible, shortsighted teenager who can't be trusted to follow rules put in place for her own safety!"

Now, he *was* yelling.

Dean opened his car door. He didn't get out. He didn't even look at me. Briggs exhaled. I could practically see him counting to ten in his head. "I'm not going to ask where you went," he told me, each word measured and full of warning. "I'm not going to tell you that it was stupid and reckless, although I am certain that it undoubtedly was. I'm going to ask you—once and only once, Cassandra—who told you about the professor and the girl?"

I swallowed, hard. "My source's name was Derek. He was working on a group project with Emerson in Professor Fogle's class. There were two other students in the group—a girl named Bryce and a boy named Clark."

Briggs's gaze shifted briefly to Dean.

"What?" I said. I caught the significance of the look that passed between the two of them, but couldn't figure out its meaning.

Dean was the one who answered, as Briggs headed back for the car.

"My father said that if we were looking for a copycat, we were wasting our time with the professor." Dean ran a hand roughly through his hair, closing his fingers into a fist and pulling at his roots. "He said that the only truly *remarkable* letters he'd received were from a student in that class."

CHAPTER 22

y the time Briggs pulled up to the house, the silence in the car was clawing at me. Dean hadn't said a word since he'd told us about the letters.

We wanted to protect you, I thought, willing him to profile me and see that. But it was like someone had flipped a switch, and Dean had gone into lockdown mode. He wouldn't even look at me. And the worst part was that I *knew* he was sitting there thinking about the day the two of us had spent together and what a mistake it had been for him to have believed, even for a second, that he could let someone in.

"Dean—"

"Don't." He didn't sound angry. He didn't sound *anything*.

I was the first one out of the car once Briggs put it into park. I started toward the house, then slowed when I saw a heap of junk in the driveway. Calling the mound of metal a car would have been generous. It had three wheels, no paint, and a spattering of rust along the bumper. The hood—if you could call it a hood—was popped. I couldn't make out the person inspecting the engine, but I could make out his jeans. His well-worn, formfitting, oil-smudged jeans.

Michael?

When I'd first met Michael, he'd changed his clothing style every day to keep me guessing. But this Michael—wearing jeans and a ratty old T-shirt, buried elbow-deep in a junkyard car—was new.

He stood up, wiping a hand across his brow. He saw me looking at him, and for a split second, his expression hardened.

Not you, too, I thought. I couldn't deal with Michael being mad at me, too.

"I've decided to take up restoring cars," he called out, answering the question I hadn't asked and giving me some hope that I'd imagined the look on his face a moment before. "In case something happens to my Porsche."

The reference to my proposed threat did not go unnoticed.

You saw Dean and me in the kitchen, I thought, slipping into his perspective. *You got sick of watching us together. You left. . . .*

"I'm a man of many mysteries," Michael said, disrupting my thoughts. He always knew when I was profiling him and never let me get away with it for long. "And you," he added, his gaze flitting over my face, "are . . . not happy."

"All of you, inside!" Briggs snapped.

Dean headed for the house, hunched, his eyes locked

straight ahead as he brushed by us. Michael tracked Dean's movements, then glanced back at me.

I looked down and started walking. I made it halfway to the front door before Michael caught up with me. He put a hand on my shoulder.

"Hey," he said softly. I stopped, but still didn't look at him. "You okay?"

"I'm fine."

"You're not fine." The hand on my shoulder traced the edge of a tensed muscle, then turned me to face him. "What did Dean do?"

"Nothing," I said. Dean had a right to be angry. He had a right to want nothing to do with me.

Putting two fingers below my chin, Michael angled my face toward his. "He did something, if you're looking like that."

"It's not his fault," I insisted.

Michael dropped his hand to his side. "Don't take this the wrong way, Colorado, but I'm getting really tired of watching you make excuses for him."

"Enough." Briggs put one hand on Michael's shoulder and one on mine and steered the two of us into the house. "Get Lia," he said. "And Sloane. I want all of you in the living room in five minutes."

"*Or else,*" Michael intoned in a whisper.

"Move!" Agent Briggs's voice edged up on a yell. Michael and I moved.

Five minutes later, we were gathered in the living

room—Michael, Lia, Sloane, and I on the coach, Dean seated on the edge of the fireplace. Briggs loomed over us. Sterling stood back and watched.

"Tell me something: in the history of this program, have any of you ever been authorized to approach witnesses?" Briggs's voice had become deceptively pleasant.

Lia processed that question, then turned to me. "Seriously, Cassie, are you the single least stealthy person on the face of the planet, or do you just habitually *want* to get caught?"

"Lia!" Briggs said sharply. "Answer the question."

"Fine," Lia said, her voice silky. "No, we've never been authorized to approach witnesses. We've never been authorized to do anything of interest. We stay locked in the metaphorical tower while you run out and catch the bad guys. Satisfied?"

"Do I look satisfied to you?" A vein in Briggs's forehead throbbed. "Dean went to see his father today."

Nothing Briggs could have said would have had a bigger impact on Lia. Her eyes flickered over to Dean's. She sat there, frozen.

"Dean went through hell because I asked him to," Briggs continued mercilessly. "Because it was crucial for this case. I want this solved as badly as any of you, but unlike you, I'm not playing games here."

"We weren't—" I started to say.

Briggs cut off my objection. "Every second I have to spend policing you, making sure that you're not taking matters into your own hands and compromising this entire investigation, is a second that I could be spending catching this killer. Right now, I should be following up a lead on the professor's writing cabin, but instead I'm here, because you seem to need a reminder about what this program is and what it isn't."

Lia finally managed to look away from Dean. She turned to Briggs, her eyes flashing, her fingers curled into fists. "You're reading us the riot act for trying to put our abilities to use, but letting that SOB play with Dean's head in exchange for whatever table scraps of information you can get your hands on, *that's* okay?"

"Enough." Dean didn't raise his voice. He didn't have to. Lia turned to him. For five or six seconds, they just sat there, staring at each other.

"No, Dean. It's not enough." Her voice was soft, until she turned back to Briggs. "You need to let me watch the tape of your interview with Redding. Don't even try to tell me you didn't tape it. You tape every conversation you have with the man. The question isn't if he's lying—it's what he's lying about, and we both know that I'm your best chance at answering that question."

"You're not helping," Briggs told Lia. He held her gaze, and I realized that he wasn't just denying her request. He was telling her that we really weren't helping the situation, that everything we'd done up until this point had *hurt* Dean.

Maybe he was right, but I couldn't help thinking that

Lia was right, too. What if she *could* see something in the interview that the rest of us had missed?

Briggs's phone rang. He answered it, turning his back on the rest of us. Agent Sterling stepped forward.

Dean preempted whatever she was going to say. "I'll stay out of it." His tone was expressionless, but there was something bitter in his eyes. "That's what I excel at, isn't it? Staying out of things until it's too late."

I thought of the *R* burned into Agent Sterling's chest.

Briggs pocketed his phone and turned back to Sterling. "We've got a possible address for the professor's cabin."

"Go on, then." Judd spoke up from behind us. I wondered how long he'd been there. "You two, get out of here," he said to Briggs and Sterling. "I may be old, but I'm still capable of making sure none of these miscreants leave the house."

We miscreants didn't leave the house. We convened in the basement.

"I want to know exactly where Cassie got the information she gave Briggs," Dean said. The fact that he was talking about me and not to me cut deeper than it should have.

"Well, I want to know why you thought that being in the same room with your father was anything but the worst idea ever," Lia retorted.

"He knew something," Dean told her.

"Or he wanted you to think he knew something. You shouldn't have gone. And if you had to go, you should have taken me with you." Lia turned her back on Dean, but not

169

before I realized that she wasn't just angry. She was hurt. Dean had gone to see his father for the first time in five years. I'd gone with him. She hadn't.

"Lia," Dean said softly.

"No," she snapped without turning back around. "I watch your back. You watch mine. He's hard to read, but he's not impossible, Dean. I could have listened in. I could have helped."

"You can't help," Dean told her. He turned the topic back to his original question. "You know how Cassie got the information, don't you, Lia?"

"Of course I know," Lia said. "It was my idea! And it was our risk to take, Dean."

"Risk?" Dean repeated, his voice silky and low. "Lia, what did you do?"

"They snuck out," Sloane piped up from beside me. All of us turned to look at her. She'd been uncharacteristically quiet since Briggs had called all of us downstairs. "According to my calculations, Cassie was gone for two hours, forty-three minutes, and seventeen seconds. And she was only wearing two-fifths of a dress."

"Sloane!" I said.

"What?" she shot back. "If you wanted me to keep my mouth shut, you should have taken me with you."

We hurt her feelings, I realized suddenly. It hadn't even occurred to me to ask her.

"Next time," Lia told her.

"There's not going to be a next time!" Dean exploded. He took a deep breath, calming himself. "Tell me you didn't go to Colonial."

"We didn't go to Colonial," Lia replied without missing a beat.

Dean stared at her for a few seconds, then turned to me. Clearly, I was easier prey. "You went to a college campus *knowing* that a murder had just been committed there, wearing two-fifths of a dress and looking for people who might be connected to the killer?"

"If it's any consolation," Michael told Dean, "I went along for the ride."

Dean went very still. For a second, I thought he might actually hit Michael. "Why in the world would that be a consolation?"

"Because," Michael replied, a glint in his eyes, "if I hadn't been there, Cassie would have gone off *alone* with a college senior who has an unhealthy fascination with your dad's case."

"Michael!" I said.

"Cassie!" Dean turned a thunderous look on me.

I threw Lia under the bus. "At least I didn't actually go off by myself with *two* strange guys in Fogle's class."

Dean turned back to Lia.

"I have no idea what she's talking about." Lia's innocent act was as good as they came. Dean threw his hands up in the air.

"Do you all have a death wish?" he asked.

"No!" I couldn't hold the objection back. "We all wanted to help *you.*"

Those were the very last words I should have said. The whole point of not telling Dean had been to keep him from feeling responsible for our actions. From the moment he'd come back from the interview with his father, he'd been pulling away, and I'd just given him the final shove.

He left. When Lia tried to follow him, he said something to her, his voice so low that I couldn't make out the words. She blanched, the blood draining completely from her face, and stood there, frozen in place as Dean stalked off. After several seconds of shocked silence, Lia fled, too.

Michael looked at Sloane and then at me. He strolled toward the door. "I think that went well."

CHAPTER 23

Sloane and I were the only ones left in the basement.

"I thought you weren't supposed to be down here," she said abruptly. Her terseness surprised me, until I remembered the look on her face when she'd mentioned us sneaking out without her.

"I'm not," I said.

Sloane didn't respond. She walked over to a bathroom set and stood just outside the shower. She stared at it, like I wasn't even there.

"Are we okay?" I asked her.

Dean was furious. Michael had taken off for parts unknown. When the dust settled, Lia would probably blame this whole mess on me. I needed Sloane cheerful and spouting statistics. I needed not to be alone.

"You're okay, and I'm okay. It would seem to follow logically that we're okay." Sloane's gaze settled on the shower drain. It took me a moment to realize she was counting—counting the holes in the drain, counting the tiles on the shower floor.

"We didn't mean to leave you out," I told her.

"I'm used to it."

With the way Sloane's brain worked, she'd probably spent her whole life before the program on the outside looking in. I was her roommate, and I was a profiler—I should have known better.

"Dean is my friend, too." Sloane's voice was small, but fierce. She looked up from the floor, but still didn't turn to face me. "I'm not good at mingling, or at parties. I say the wrong thing. I do the wrong thing. I know that—but even numbers are better than odd, and if I'd been there, Lia wouldn't have had to go off alone." Sloane paused and bit her lip. "She didn't even ask." She swallowed hard. "Before you came, Lia might have asked me." Sloane finally turned to look at me. "There's only a seventy-nine-point-six percent chance, but she might have."

"Next time," I told Sloane, "*I* will ask you."

Sloane considered my words carefully, then accepted them with a nod. "Are we going to hug now?" she asked. The question was absolutely clinical. I slipped an arm around her shoulder and squeezed.

"Statistically," Sloane told me, sounding more like her usual self, "the bathroom is the deadliest room in the house."

I found Michael working on his car. Or, more specifically, I found him holding some kind of power sander and staring at his car with a diabolical expression.

"Judd let you play with the power tools?" I asked.

Michael turned the sander on and off experimentally, then he smiled. "Judd is a man of discerning tastes and good sense."

"Meaning that Judd doesn't know that you're playing with the power tools," I concluded.

"I'm going to have to plead the Fifth on that one," Michael told me.

There was a beat of silence, and then I asked the question I really wanted an answer to. "Are we okay?"

"Why wouldn't we be?" Michael turned the power sander on and attempted to attack the rust on the car's front bumper, drowning out all conversation.

I'd thought that I could keep things from changing, but they were changing anyway. With Michael and me. With Dean and me.

"Michael," I said, my voice soft enough that he couldn't hear it over the sound of metal on metal.

Michael turned the sander off. Then he turned to me. I felt naked, the way I always did when I knew my face was giving me away. Why couldn't he just be a normal boy, one who couldn't take one look at me and know exactly which emotions were churning around in my gut?

"We're fine, Cassie. It's just that sometimes, when you're in the business of being devastatingly handsome and admirably patient, you need an outlet. Or two. Or seven."

He was taking his frustrations with me out on this car.

"Nothing happened between Dean and me," I said.

"I know that," he replied.

"Nothing is going to happen between Dean and me," I said.

"I know that, too." Michael leaned back against the car. "Better than you do. You look at Redding and see all the ways the two of you are the same. I look at him, and I see someone who's so angry and so terrified of that anger that there's not room for anything else. Or any*one* else."

I realized, suddenly: "That's your problem with Dean."

"That he's incapable of romancing a female?" Michael smirked. "As far as I'm concerned, that's his best quality."

"No," I said, turning the thought over in my mind. "That he's angry and holding it in." In Dean's shoes, I would be angry, too. I understood why he wouldn't let himself express it, why he'd fight tooth and nail against throwing a punch. He couldn't risk flipping that switch and not being able to turn it off.

But I'd never thought about the effect that being around a person like Dean would have on someone like Michael.

Michael gave me a look. "You're profiling me."

I shrugged. "You read my emotions all the time."

He paused for a moment. "What do you see?"

That was as close to permission to poke around inside his head as I was going to get. "You grew up in a house where everything seemed perfect—you had every advantage that money could buy. But it wasn't perfect." Michael had told me that much, but I pushed forward, tiptoeing into more dangerous waters. "You learned to read emotions because your father was hard to read, and you needed to be able to tell when he was angry."

No response.

"Even if there was a smile on his face, even if he was laughing, if he was angry, you needed to see it." I swallowed the ball of emotion rising in my throat. "You needed to avoid it."

To avoid getting hit.

"Dean said pretty much the same thing to me once." Michael crossed his arms, his eyes on mine. "Only he wasn't nearly as nice about it."

When I'd met Michael, he'd had an ingrained distrust of profilers—and a strong personal dislike of Dean. It had never occurred to me that Dean might have done something *to* Michael to justify those feelings.

"What did he say to you?" I asked, my throat going suddenly dry.

"Does it matter?" Michael glanced over at the house. "He's got dibs on the screwed-up childhood, right? He's the one with the get-out-of-jail-free card." Michael smiled, but there was an edge to it. "No pun intended."

"Tell me," I said.

Michael took a casual stroll around the car, examining it from all angles. When he spoke, it wasn't to answer my question. "Anger," he said offhandedly. "This might come as a surprise, Cassie, but I don't always react well to it." An edge crept into his voice. "In fact, I tend to have a very particular reaction."

I thought about Michael making veiled comments about *The Bad Seed* in Dean's hearing. Michael letting Lia use him to get a rise out of Dean.

"You're the guy who waves the red flag in front of the bull."

"If you can't keep them from hitting you," Michael said, "you *make* them hit you. At least that way, you're ready. At least that way, it's not a surprise."

It was easy to see now, what it must have been like when Michael was drafted to join the program. He wasn't happy about coming here, but at least he'd escaped living with a ticking time bomb. And then he'd arrived to find Dean, who had every reason in the world to be angry and was fighting that rage every step of the way.

"One night, Lia and I stayed out until sunrise." Michael never hid the fact that he had a history with Lia. I was so focused on the picture he was painting for me that I barely noticed. "Believe me when I say *that* had nothing to do with Dean. But when we got back that morning, he was waiting for us, practically vibrating, holding it in check, but just barely."

I could see it: Michael being Michael, and Lia being Lia, both of them self-destructive with a taste for chaos and a desire to cause the FBI a little trouble. And I could see Dean, worrying about Lia out all night with an unknown entity that neither one of them had a reason to trust.

"So you said something to push Dean that much closer to the edge." I wasn't sure I wanted to know *what* Michael had said.

"I took a metaphorical swing," Michael told me. "Redding hit back."

"But not with his fists," I clarified. Dean's gift was like mine. We knew exactly what to say to hurt someone the most. We knew what people's weak spots were. And Michael's was his father. The idea that Dean might have used that to get at Michael made my stomach twist sharply.

"I punched him," Michael added in the kind of casual tone most people reserved for chatting about the weather. He took a step toward me, giving me that patented Michael smile. "I get it, you know."

"Get what?"

"You. Redding. I get it. I get that he's going through something, and I get that you need to be there. That's who you are, Cassie. You care about people. You need to help. Believe me when I say that I am trying to step back and let you do whatever it is you need to do. But it's not easy." Michael tore his eyes from mine and picked the power sander back up. "I haven't had a lot of practice at being a decent person. It's not something at which I particularly excel."

Before I could reply, Michael turned the sander on, drowning out the sounds of the night. I stood there for a couple of minutes watching him. Agent Sterling's car eventually pulled into the driveway. It was getting dark enough that I couldn't make out much of her posture or the look on her face, but as she cut across the lawn, Michael tilted his head to the side. He turned the sander back off.

"What?" I said.

"She's not happy," he told me. "Brisk pace, no bounce to her step, hands glued to her sides. I'm guessing the exploration of the professor's writing cabin did not go particularly well."

My stomach dropped. I could suddenly hear the sound of my own breathing, my own heartbeat.

Now it was Michael's turn to ask: "What?"

I'd been so focused on Dean when I'd been on the other side of that observation glass that I hadn't spent much time thinking about his father. I hadn't let myself really dissect him or the things he'd said. But now, all I could think was that Redding had—at great cost to Dean—finally given the FBI a tip about where the professor might be hiding.

As an organized killer, Daniel Redding was a man who thrived on mind games. On misdirection. On power. If Redding had thought, even for a moment, that the professor was the killer, he wouldn't have told Briggs where to find him. The only way Redding would have really told Briggs where to find the professor was if Redding suspected, based on the letters he'd received, that finding the professor would remind Briggs—and Sterling and everyone else at the FBI— that they weren't nearly as smart as they thought they were.

The only truly remarkable letters were from students.

When I didn't respond, Michael called after Agent Sterling. "Professor's cabin a bust?"

She didn't answer him. She went into the house and shut

the door behind her. And that, as much as anything else, told me that I was right.

"It wasn't a bust," I told Michael. "I think they found the professor." I swallowed. "We should have seen this coming."

"Seen what coming?"

"I think they found the professor," I said again, "but our UNSUB found him first."

YOU

The professor was a problem. You're a problem solver. It was quick and clean—a single bullet to the back of his skull. And if there was no artistry to it, no method, at least you were showing initiative. At least you were ready, willing, and able to do what needed to be done.

It makes you feel powerful, and that makes you wonder, just for an instant, if this isn't the better way. Guns and neat little bullet holes and the glory of being the one to pull the trigger. You could knock the next girl out, tie her up, take her to the middle of nowhere. You could let her loose deep in the forest. You could track her, catch her in your sights.

You could pull the trigger.

Just thinking about it sets your heart to pounding. Take them. Free them. Track them. Kill them.

No. You force yourself to stop thinking about it, to stop imagining the sound of bare feet running through the brush— running away from you. There is a plan. An order. A bigger picture.

You will abide by it. For now.

terling didn't say a thing about the professor. Dean didn't say a word to any of us. Living in the house with the two of them—and a vulnerable, seething Lia—was like trying to tap dance through a minefield. I felt like any second, everything would explode.

And then Director Sterling showed up.

The last time the FBI director had put in an appearance at our house, a senator's daughter had just been kidnapped.

This did not bode well.

The director, Sterling, and Briggs locked themselves in Briggs's office. From the kitchen, I couldn't make out what they were saying, but every few minutes, voices were raised.

First Sterling's.

Then the director's.

Briggs's.

Finally, there was silence. And then they came for us.

— — —

The past twenty-four hours hadn't been kind to either Sterling or Briggs. Briggs looked like he'd slept in his clothes. Beside him, Agent Sterling's jaw was clenched. Her shirt was buttoned all the way up. So was her suit jacket. Since she was the kind of person who used clothes as armor, the subtle changes told me that she'd gotten dressed today expecting a fight.

"Three hundred and seven," the director said grimly, looking at each of us in turn. "That's how many students are enrolled in Fogle's serial killer class. One hundred and twenty-seven females, a hundred and eighty males." Director Sterling paused. The first time I'd met him, he'd reminded me of a grandfather. Today, there was nothing grandfatherly about him. "That's a lot of suspects, and I'm a man who believes in utilizing all of his resources."

Director Sterling was whatever kind of man he had to be to stay on top. When confronted with a problem, he analyzed all possible solutions: costs versus benefits, risks balanced out against rewards. In this case, the risks and likelihood of compromising the investigation and exposing the Naturals program compared to the potential benefits of utilizing all of his "resources" to catch this killer.

I thought of Judd and his talk of slippery slopes.

"We were told to stay away from this case on pain of death." Lia smiled like a predator toying with its prey. She didn't like that we'd gotten caught, she didn't like that she'd been told to back off, and she hated that Dean wouldn't even look at her. "Am I to take it that certain parties have been overruled?"

Lia let her gaze roam to Briggs when she said *certain parties*, but my eyes were on Agent Sterling. There was a reason she had dressed for battle this morning. Whatever the director was about to ask us to do, his daughter had argued against it.

"The risks are minimal to nonexistent," the director said firmly. "And given recent events, it's my understanding that giving you something useful to do might actually keep you *out* of trouble."

I took that to mean that the director knew about our little trip to Colonial.

"The five of you won't be interviewing witnesses." Briggs stood with his hands loose by his sides, eyeing us one by one. "You will not be going to crime scenes." Briggs's gaze flicked over to Lia. "You won't be analyzing any of our interviews with Daniel Redding."

I wasn't sure what that left.

"Your involvement on this case begins and ends with social media." Briggs turned to Sterling and waited. For a moment, I thought she'd turn on her heels and march out the door, but she didn't.

"Our preliminary profile says the UNSUB is male." Sterling's voice was perfectly even and perfectly calm in a way that told me that she was on the verge of snapping. The closer she was to losing it, the more viciously she reeled it in. "Redding suggested we might be dealing with a college student. I would have put the UNSUB's age between twenty-three and twenty-eight. Above-average intelligence, but not necessarily educated. But what do I know?" An edge crept into her voice.

"Thank you, Agent Sterling," the director cut in. He turned to the rest of us. "With the university's cooperation, we've obtained copies of the class schedules and transcripts for every student in that class. What that doesn't tell us is who they are, what they're capable of. That's where you come in."

"Social media," Sloane interjected, picking up on what Briggs had said earlier. "Upwards of three hundred million photos are uploaded to leading social media sites every day. Among smartphone owners in our UNSUB's demographic, somewhere between sixty and eighty percent of time spent using that device will be spent on social networks, rather than direct communication."

"Exactly," Director Sterling told her. "We don't have the manpower to search through every post, and even if we did, your eyes might catch something that Briggs's team wouldn't. We're not asking you to do anything that adolescents all over the country don't do every day." Director Sterling wasn't looking at us when he said those words. He was looking at his daughter. "You're teenagers. This internet stuff is practically your native language."

"And you're okay with this?" Michael asked Agent Sterling, arching one eyebrow. To me, there was no noticeable change in her expression, but Michael must have seen something. "Not okay with it," Michael interpreted, "but also not as convinced that it's a bad idea as you'd like to be." He gave her his most beatific smile. "We're growing on you."

"Enough, Michael." Briggs turned the focus away from Agent Sterling and back to the case. "If the UNSUB is enrolled in Fogle's class, the profile predicts that he would be an older student—he may not have the credits to be a junior or senior, but he would be in that age range. He probably comes from a working-class family and may live at home and commute to campus."

Agent Sterling threaded her fingers together in front of her. Her profile had put the younger end of the age range at twenty-three. Briggs had just expanded that downward by at least a year or two.

"Veronica?" the director prompted.

"We're looking for someone who gets pleasure out of dominating others, but who may not be fully confident in his ability to do so," Agent Sterling said after a sizable silence. "His father was present, but volatile, and likely left the family around the time our UNSUB entered puberty. His mother may have dated a string of men, but she did not remarry until the UNSUB was at least eighteen. This UNSUB is comfortable around firearms. He will not have a girlfriend or spouse. It's likely that he drives a dark-colored truck or SUV, and if he has a dog, expect it to be a larger breed, such as a German shepherd."

I was used to making profiles. Doing the reverse—trying

to figure out the specific pieces of evidence that had led Sterling to those conclusions—was harder. A dark-colored SUV and a large-breed dog suggested a need for power and domination. I wasn't sure where firearms came in—unless the professor had been shot?—but there must have been something about Emerson's murder that suggested both a need for control and a lack of confidence on the killer's part. The presentation of the body and the methodical way Emerson had been killed were both characteristic of an organized killer. So where was Sterling getting the lack of confidence?

The fact that he's copying another killer's MO? Victim selection? Did the UNSUB's initial attack come from behind? Did he drug her?

I tried to figure out how Sterling had arrived at her conclusions, but operating with a tiny subset of the relevant case details was like trying to swim with a cinder block tied to each knee and a squirrel stuffed in your pocket. I'd seen Emerson's body on the news, but that wasn't enough.

"How was the professor killed?" I asked.

The director, Sterling, and Briggs all turned to stare at me. So did Dean. I realized belatedly that no one had ever *said* that the professor was dead. That was information that we weren't supposed to know. It was a guess.

Based on their reactions, I knew I'd guessed right.

"You don't need to know the details," Briggs replied curtly. "Consider this nothing more than another training exercise. Find whatever internet profiles you can for each of the students on the class list. Check out their status updates or likes or whatever it is college kids are doing online these days, and let us know if you run into anything suspicious."

Lia narrowed her eyes at Briggs. "You don't think we'll find anything." She punctuated her words by drumming her fingers, one by one, against the arm of the sofa. "Interesting."

"You don't think the UNSUB is a student." Dean picked up where Lia left off. "But you can't rule out the possibility, because that's what my father does: he doles out tiny kernels of truth and dresses them up like lies." Dean looked at Sterling, then at Briggs. "He wants you questioning your instincts about everything."

"I'm not questioning anything," Briggs said, a muscle tensing in his jaw. "If there's something to his comment about the students in that class, there will be red flags. If there are red flags, the five of you will find them."

"And if there aren't," Dean said, filling in the blanks, "you won't have wasted your time."

Every hour we spent wading through social media sites was an hour Briggs's team was free to hunt down other leads. *That's why you agreed to this,* I thought, focusing in on Briggs. *If Redding lied, you haven't lost anything. If he's telling the truth, we'll see it. Either way, he's not the one calling the shots. You are.*

I thought about what Dean had said about Briggs's competitive streak and what Judd had said about crossing lines. *You were all for keeping us out of this,* I thought, *and then you found the professor's body.*

"Dean, if you'd rather sit this one out, that would be fine." The director straightened the front of his suit as he gave Dean a tight, close-lipped smile.

"You mean that you would rather I sat this one out." Dean stayed hunched over on the fireplace, but he lifted his eyes to meet the director's. "Because I'm 'too close to it,' but really, because you don't trust me." Dean waited a bit, but the director didn't contradict him. "Not on this case," Dean continued. "Not with my father." He stood. "Not with your daughter."

CHAPTER 25

You killed Emerson Cole. You killed the professor. You liked it.

As I waded through online profiles, those words were never far from my mind. Spread out around me, Michael, Lia, and Sloane were focused on their respective laptops. Dean's absence was palpable.

I tried to focus on the profile Agent Sterling had given us. *Early twenties,* I reminded myself. *Commutes from home. No father in the picture. May have acquired a stepfather sometime in the past few years. Comfortable around firearms.*

Those weren't exactly the kinds of things that a person advertised on social media sites. I could pick up the gist of an individual's personality from their favorites—favorite books, favorite movies, favorite quotes—but the most reliable information came from the pictures and status updates. How often did they update? Did they converse with friends?

Were they in a relationship? Sloane had developed some kind of method for screening pictures for dark-colored trucks and SUVs, but I was more interested in the stories the pictures told.

Snapshots uploaded by other people gave me a candid look at a person. How self-conscious were they? Were they at the center of group pictures, or at the edge? Did they make the same facial expression in every picture, rigidly controlling what they showed to the world? Did they stare down the camera or look away? What kind of clothes did they wear? Where were the pictures taken?

Bit by bit, I could build a model of someone's life from the ground up—which would have been more useful if I'd actually been the one to profile the UNSUB, rather than just being given a list of boxes to check off.

Okay, I told myself after my eyes had gone blurry from scrolling through too many profiles, very few of which set off my spidey senses. *Sterling and Briggs gave you a few key things to look for. So do what you always do. Take a handful of details and get to the big picture.*

Sterling thought the UNSUB was young, but not adolescent. Why? He'd chosen a college sophomore as his first victim. Someone who desperately longed to dominate other people would start with easy prey—a laughing, smiling young girl who wasn't physically imposing in the least. He was probably at least a couple of years older than she was, and since a quick glance at Emerson's profile told me that she was twenty, that explained the lower end of Sterling's estimated age range. How had she determined that the UNSUB wasn't an older man, like the professor?

You imitate another man's kills. You admire him. You want to be like him. I let that thought sit for a moment. *But you also risked getting caught to display your kill in a very public location—something Daniel Redding wouldn't have done. You brought black rope with you to hang her, but the news report said you strangled her with the antenna from her own car.*

To put it in terms of the textbook Dean and I had read, this was an organized kill, but there was something disorganized about it, too. The attack had obviously been planned, but there was also something impulsive about it.

Did you plan to leave her on the president's lawn? Or was that something you thought of once your adrenaline started pumping?

Displaying the victim in public suggested a need for recognition. But recognition from whom? From the public? From the press?

From Daniel Redding? That was a possibility I couldn't shake, and somehow, other pieces of Sterling's profile began to make sense. An impulsive copycat who idolized Redding would be younger than the man was himself, probably by a decade or more.

You've felt powerless, and you admire his power. You've felt invisible, and you want to be seen.

SUVs and trucks were large. They sat up higher on the

road. German shepherds were also large. They were intelligent, strong—and often police dogs.

You don't just want power. You want authority, I thought. *You want it because you've never had it. Because the people in your life who do have it make you feel weak. You didn't feel weak when you killed Emerson.*

I thought about the professor and wished again that I knew how he'd died. *If you were in Fogle's class, you admired the professor—at first. But later, you resented him for being all talk and no show. For not paying enough attention to you. For paying too much to Emerson.*

Organized killers frequently chose victims they did not know to reduce the chances that the crime could be traced back to them. But my gut was telling me that it wasn't a coincidence that Emerson had been in a relationship with the professor and now they were both dead. These victims weren't chosen randomly. They weren't chosen by a stranger.

"Hey, Sloane?"

Sloane didn't look up from her computer. She held up the index finger on her right hand and continued typing rapidly with her left. After a few more seconds, she stopped typing and looked up.

"Can you compare the other students' schedules to Emerson's and see how much overlap there is?" I asked. "I'm thinking that if our UNSUB was fixated on Emerson, this might not be the only class they shared."

"Sure." Sloane didn't move to reach for any of the files.

She just sat there, her hands now folded into her lap, a bright smile on her face.

"Could you do it now?" I asked.

She held up the index finger on her right hand again. "I am doing it now." Sloane had an incredible memory. The same skill set that allowed her to rebuild the crime scene apparently meant she didn't need to go back over the data to analyze it.

"Emerson was an English major," she rattled off. "She was taking Professor Fogle's class as an elective. All of her other classes counted toward her major, except for Geology, which I assume fulfills some kind of natural science requirement. Most of the other students in Fogle's class were psychology, pre-law, or sociology majors, and as a result, they shared very few classes with Emerson, with the exception of two students."

If my instincts were right, if Emerson hadn't been a random target, then I was very interested to know who those two students were.

Sloane thumbed expertly through the stack of files on the counter and handed me two of them. "Bryce Anderson and Gary Clarkson."

Michael looked up from whatever he was doing at the sound of Bryce's name. "Bryce didn't mention that she and Emerson had any other classes together."

I went back to my computer and searched for Gary Clarkson's profile. Unlike most of his peers, the profile itself was set to private, so all I could see was the profile picture.

"Gary Clarkson," I said, turning my computer around so the others could see. "He goes by Clark."

Clark had known Emerson. He'd known she was sleeping with the professor. He was angry. And we were staring at a picture of him wearing an orange hunting vest, holding a gun.

CHAPTER 26

Y *ou were in most of Emerson's classes.* I slipped into Clark's mind without even thinking about it. *You liked watching her. She was nice to you. You thought she was perfect. And if you found out she wasn't . . .*

"You got something?" Michael asked me from his spot across the room.

I caught my bottom lip in my teeth. "Maybe."

I could see Clark targeting Emerson, but if he'd been the one to attack her, I would have expected it to be messier. I'd thought it myself the day before: if Clark was a killer, he'd be a disorganized killer. Emerson wasn't murdered on an impulse. The UNSUB never lost emotional control.

And yet . . .

A phone rang, breaking me from my thoughts. It took me a second to realize that the ringtone was mine. I reached for my phone, but Lia beat me there. She snatched it and held it just out of reach.

197

"Give it here, Lia."

Selectively deaf, she turned the phone around so I could see the caller's name. TA GEOFF flashed across the screen. *What the* . . . He'd given me his number. I'd plugged it into my phone, but I'd never given him mine.

"The two of you have been texting," Lia informed me pertly. "You've really grown quite close."

I made a mental note to change the password on my phone.

"Shall we see what he has to say?" Lia didn't wait for a response before she answered the call.

"Geoffrey. I was *just* talking about you." She smiled at whatever he said in response, then put the phone on speaker and laid it on the coffee table between us, daring me to hang up.

I didn't.

"Did you hear about the professor?" Geoffrey asked, his voice grave. "It's all over the news."

So the story about the professor's death had broken.

"This must be so hard for you," Lia said, putting her feet up on the coffee table. Her tone oozing sympathy, she gave an exaggerated roll of her eyes.

"You have no idea," Geoffrey said in response. "The professor didn't deserve this."

And Emerson did? I bit back the question.

"First that girl, now the professor," Lia said, sounding every inch the tragedy groupie, ready to hang on Geoffrey's every word. "Who do you think it is?"

"We're dealing with what I like to call an *organized killer,*" Geoffrey intoned. "Highly intelligent and hard to catch."

I didn't know what was more off-putting: the way Geoffrey was acting like he'd invented the phrase "organized killer"—while demonstrating only the smallest fraction of understanding of what that really meant—or the fact that "highly intelligent" was probably a descriptor he'd use to describe himself.

"I'll probably have to take over the class now that Fogle is gone," Geoffrey added. "I don't know what will happen to his book, *Bind Them, Brand Them, Cut Them, Hang Them: The Daniel Redding Story.*"

Geoffrey couldn't resist dropping the book's title. Listening to him talk, I thought back to the way Dean had looked, saying those same words: eyes unseeing, face pale.

"Do you think it could be someone in the class?" Lia asked. "*Your* class?"

She was so good at changing the direction of the conversation that Geoffrey didn't even realize she'd done it.

"If there were a student in this class with the potential for that kind of thing," Geoffrey said, his tone saturated with smugness, "I think I would know it."

My first reaction to those words was that *of course* he thought he'd recognize a killer. But my second reaction sat heavier in my stomach. He'd used the word *potential.*

Potential as in *capability,* or potential as in *talent?*

"What about the kid who's setting the curve in the class?" Lia gave Geoffrey another verbal nudge.

"No way," Geoffrey scoffed. "Gary something. He wouldn't hurt a fly."

Gary Clarkson. As in Clark. I wouldn't have pegged him as the curve-setting type, and that disturbed me. Maybe he was more of a planner, more type A, more *organized* than I'd realized.

Lia snatched the phone up and abruptly hung up. The sudden movement jerked me out of my thoughts and I tracked her gaze. Dean was standing in the hallway behind me.

He didn't comment on what he'd overheard. He didn't threaten to tell Briggs we'd broken the rules. Again. He just turned and walked, his footsteps heavy, toward the stairs.

I snatched my phone back. Lia didn't stop me. It rang. I expected it to be Geoffrey calling back, but it wasn't.

"There's someone I need you to look up," Briggs said, forgoing the customary greeting.

"Same to you," I told him. "Gary Clarkson. He's comfortable with guns, shared a high percentage of Emerson's classes, and was setting the curve in Fogle's class." I hesitated just a second, then plowed on. "You should also check out the professor's TA."

The FBI hadn't given us a file for Geoffrey, but that was an oversight on their part. He wasn't a student in the class, but he *was* a student at the university—and it would be just like Dean's father to get off on telling the FBI something misleading, but true.

"I'll look into it," Briggs promised, "but right now, I need you to see what you can find out about a Conrad Mayler. He's a senior who took Fogle's class two years ago."

"Why am I looking him up?"

There was silence on the other end. For a moment, I thought Briggs wouldn't answer the question, but after a second's hesitation, he did. "He's the one who posted the video of the crime scene."

Briggs had a way of punctuating the end of sentences that shut the door completely on further conversation.

"Okay," I said. "Conrad Mayler. Got it."

Twenty minutes later, I'd discovered everything there was to online-know about Conrad Mayler. He was a journalism major. He claimed to listen only to indie bands. His favorite movies were documentaries. He had a blog where he wrote snarky recaps of a variety of reality shows. According to his profile, he'd attended a private high school and worked part-time at the student radio station.

His relationship status was "It's complicated." The girl implicated in said relationship was Bryce Anderson.

Your name just keeps coming up. I pictured the blond girl in my mind. I'd made the error once before of erroneously assuming an UNSUB was male. No matter what my gut was telling me this time, I couldn't risk making the same mistake twice.

Scrolling through Conrad's status updates and profiles, it wasn't hard to see that he fancied himself a journalist. He'd probably claim that he'd taken the video of Emerson's body and posted it anonymously online because the public had a right to know. I was half-surprised he hadn't actually posted it to his profile.

Seemingly in answer to my thoughts, the page in front of me updated itself. Conrad had posted a new video. Preparing myself for the worst, I clicked play, but instead of a corpse, I saw rows of wooden seats, filled with students. The time stamp on the video read 7:34 A.M.

"Professor George Fogle once said that he scheduled his class for 7:30 in the morning as a way of separating the students who were taking his class on a lark from those who were serious about the study of criminology." The camera panned the room, and I recognized the auditorium.

I'd been there before.

"Three days ago, three hundred and seven serious students took the first of three Monsters or Men exams. The three hundred and eighth student, Emerson Cole, was found dead that morning."

"There's no white noise," Sloane commented, sidling up behind me. "Whoever taped the narration has decent equipment. The video, on the other hand, was taken by some kind of smartphone. At least 1080p resolution, maybe higher."

The video cut from the auditorium scene to familiar footage—the clip of Emerson's body. The narration continued, but I tuned it out.

"I'd ask if this kid was serious," Michael said, coming to join us, "but I can tell that he is. He thinks this is cutting-edge journalism. On his profile page."

"He didn't kill Emerson," I said tiredly. Conrad didn't fit the profile. Our killer didn't have a snarky blog. He didn't have a girlfriend like Bryce—even if it *was* complicated. And the person who'd killed Emerson, who'd displayed her like a dog dropping a dead bird at the feet of his master, would never have started his "video coverage" of the event with footage of the class.

For the UNSUB, the rest of the class would have been beside the point.

"Play it again," Sloane ordered. "From the beginning."

I did. Sloane shoved me gently out of the way and took over, using keyboard shortcuts to pause the video, play it, pause it. Her eyes flitted back and forth over the screen. "The voice-over was right," she said finally. "There are three hundred and seven students in that classroom taking that test. Including your suspect," she told me, pointing to an unmistakable face—round, with dull eyes—in the third row. Clark. He was sitting two seats away from Bryce, a row behind Derek.

"Who's filming the test?" I asked. "And why?"

"I don't know." Sloane's tongue darted out in between her lips in a look of intense concentration. "The news report said that Emerson's body was discovered early that morning," she said finally. "The question is how early?"

I followed her line of thought. According to the time stamp, this footage was taken at 7:34 A.M.

"Time of death." I said the obvious out loud. "We need the time of death."

Sloane grabbed my phone and dialed a number from memory. When no one answered, she called again. And again. And again.

"What?" Irritation made Briggs's voice loud enough that I could hear it from a distance.

"It's considered impolite to talk above seventy-five decibels," Sloane sniffed. "I believe it's called shouting."

I couldn't hear Briggs's reply.

"Is the autopsy in on Emerson Cole?" Sloane held the phone to her ear with her shoulder and used her free hands to pull her hair out of its ponytail and refasten it. "We need time of death. Cause of death would also be helpful."

I was fairly certain Briggs wouldn't want to part with that information. There was quite a bit of distance between profiling college students on social media and being read in to the nitty-gritty of a classified autopsy.

"You're at seventy-eight decibels," Sloane said, unfazed by Briggs's objections. "And we still need time of death." She paused again. "Because," Sloane said, drawing out the word as if she were talking to a very small, very slow child, "we're sitting here looking at a video that was taken at 7:34 that morning. If I'm remembering the campus maps correctly—and you know I am—Davies Auditorium is a twenty-five-minute walk and a ten-minute drive from the president's house. Which means that if the death of Emerson Cole (a) required the UNSUB's presence and (b) took place after 7:25 A.M. and before the end of that test, then every single student in that class has an alibi."

Sloane was quiet for longer this time. Then she hung up the phone.

"What did he say?" Michael asked her.

Sloane closed her laptop and pushed it away. "He said that the body was found at 8:15 that morning. Time of death was estimated at 7:55."

CHAPTER 27

The time stamp on the video was verified. It was official: Emerson Cole had been strangled to death while the students in Professor Fogle's class were in Davies Auditorium, taking their midterm.

The FBI tracked the video back to our good friend TA Geoff, who explained that it was Professor Fogle's policy to have a video record of tests to discourage ringers from taking it on another student's behalf. The full-length video also included close-ups of each student as they turned in their tests. Each and every one of our 307 potential suspects—308 if you counted Geoffrey—was present and accounted for.

As far as alibis went, this one was ironclad.

"I told Briggs he should have let me watch the interview with Daniel Redding." Lia slammed the door to the freezer and then took her frustration out on the silverware drawer. She banged it open, sending the contents rattling. "We've been chasing a nonexistent lead because nobody will let me tell them when that soulless, Machiavellian piece of . . ."

Lia had several colorful ways of describing Dean's father. I didn't disagree with any of them. I slid in front of her and withdrew two spoons from the silverware drawer. I held one out to her. After a long moment, she took it. Then she eyed the spoon in my hand suspiciously.

"You're sharing the ice cream," I told her. She twirled the spoon back and forth in her fingers, and I wondered if she was planning my demise.

"Dean's not talking to me, either," I told her. "And I'm just as frustrated as you are. Everything we've done—everything we tried to do—it was for nothing. The UNSUB isn't in that class. It doesn't matter that Geoffrey has minimal empathy and a fascination with the dark side, or that Clark had a thing for Emerson and a lot of pent-up rage. None of it matters, because neither of them killed Emerson."

The one thing the FBI had allowed us to do was a wild-goose chase, courtesy of Dean's psychotic father. And I couldn't help feeling so *stupid* for thinking that we could just waltz onto a college campus or look at some internet profiles and find a killer. Dean was still furious with us, and we had nothing to show for it.

"Lia—"

"All right, already," Lia said, cutting me off. "Enough with the bonding, Cassie. I'll share the ice cream, but we're eating it somewhere else. I'm not in the mood to play well with others, and the next person who asks me to share something dies a slow, painful death."

"Fair enough." I cast a glance around the kitchen. "You have someplace in mind?"

At first, I thought Lia was leading me to her bedroom, but once she shut the door behind us, I realized that wasn't her endgame. She shoved open her window and, with one last wicked glance over her shoulder, climbed out onto the roof.

Great, I thought. I stuck my head out the window just in time to see her disappear around a corner. I hesitated for a split second, then climbed carefully out the window myself. The roof's slope was gentle outside of Lia's room, but I kept a hand on the side of the house anyway. I edged my way toward the corner I'd seen Lia take. When I'd made the turn, I let out a heavy breath.

The roof flattened out. Lia was sitting with her back up against the siding, her mile-long legs stretched out nearly to the edge of the gutter. Watching my step, I made my way toward her and slid into a sitting position myself. Wordlessly, Lia tilted the carton of rocky road toward me.

I dug my spoon into the ice cream and gouged out a hefty spoonful.

Lia delicately arched one brow. "Someone's courting an ice cream headache."

I nibbled a bite off the end of my spoon. "We should have brought bowls."

"There're a lot of things we should have done." Lia sat perfectly still, her eyes fixed on the horizon. The sun was just now setting, but I got the distinct feeling that if I hadn't been with her, she would have stayed out here all night, two stories off the ground, her feet brushing up against the edge. She was a person who hated being boxed in. She hated being trapped. She always had an exit strategy.

She just hadn't needed one in a very long time.

"Dean will get over it." I said that instead of the other things I was thinking—about exit strategies and Lia's child-hood and the way that she had, in all likelihood, learned to lie. "He can't stay mad at us forever," I continued. "We were just trying to help."

"Don't you get it?" Lia finally turned her head toward mine, her dark eyes gleaming with tears she would never let herself shed. "Dean doesn't *get* mad. He doesn't let himself. So if we went to talk to him right now, he wouldn't be angry with us. He wouldn't be *anything*. That's what he does. He shuts down, and he shuts people out, and that's fine. I get it. Of all people, I do." Lia closed her eyes and clamped her lips together. She took several ragged breaths and then opened them again. "But he doesn't shut *me* out."

Dean knew Lia better than any of us, and that meant that he knew exactly what shutting her out would do. He knew that he was the one person she trusted, that their relationship was the one thing that kept her from feeling trapped all the time. Michael's defense mechanism growing up had been to recognize anger, and if he couldn't defuse it, to provoke it. Lia's had been to bury herself away under so many layers of deception that whatever anyone else did to her, they couldn't really hurt her, because they couldn't touch the *real* girl.

Dean was the exception.

"When I came here, it was just Dean and Judd and me." Lia abandoned her spoon in the carton and leaned back on the heels of her hands. I wasn't sure why she was telling me this, but for once, I knew in my gut that everything she was telling me was true. "I was ready to hate him. I'm good at hating people, but Dean never pressed. He never asked me a single question that I didn't want to answer. One night after I'd been here a couple of months, I went to sneak out. Running away is something I'm good at."

I filed that away under the growing list of things I knew about Lia's past.

"Dean caught me. He said that if I was going, he was going with me. I called his bluff, but it turned out, he wasn't bluffing. I ran away. He followed. We were gone for three days. I'd lived on the streets before, but he hadn't. He stayed up nights so I could sleep. Sometimes I'd wake up and I'd see him keeping watch. He never looked at me the way most guys look at me. He was watching out for me, not watching me." She paused. "He never asked for a thing in return."

"He wouldn't."

Lia's smile was brittle. "No," she agreed. "He wouldn't. The last day before we came back, he told me about his dad, about how he'd come to be here, about Briggs. Dean is the only person I've ever known who's never lied to me."

And now he wasn't talking to her at all.

"Agent Sterling was one of his father's victims," I said softly. Lia's eyes flew to mine. From the sharp intake of breath that followed, I knew that she'd recognized my words as the truth and didn't know how to handle it.

Telling Lia didn't feel like betraying Dean. She was his family. She'd opened up to me in a way that Lia didn't open up to people, and that told me how badly she needed to know that he wasn't shutting her out just because she'd screwed up. Dean's life was a minefield right now.

"Sterling has a brand, right here." I held my fingertips to my chest. "She got away somehow. I think Dean helped her escape."

Lia digested that information, her face unreadable. "And now, she's back," she said finally, her eyes fixed on a place in the distance. "And all Dean can think is that he didn't help her enough."

I nodded. "Then Emerson Cole turns up dead, and Dean ends up in an interrogation room with his father." I leaned back, allowing my head to clunk lightly against the side of the house. "Going into that room, listening to what Daniel Redding had to say, that's what made Dean shut down. It was like someone had drained his soul from his body. Then Agent Sterling lets him know that we went digging on our own—"

"Which *you* let slip," Lia interjected.

"Sterling already knew that I'd snuck out," I told her. "And besides, I didn't tell her what *we* did. I didn't even tell her you were there. I just told her what we learned."

"None of which even matters," Lia cut in, "because every student in that class—not to mention the TA—has an iron-clad alibi. And instead of using us, the way they should, the FBI, in all their glorious wisdom, leaves us locked up here, where we can't do anything to solve the case or to help Dean." Lia wound a thick strand of jet-black hair around her finger. "And here's our favorite person now."

I followed Lia's gaze. A dark car had pulled into the driveway. Agent Sterling got out.

"Where do you suppose she's been?" Lia asked me.

Sterling had stopped by the house earlier, just long enough to pick up the students' files, then she'd left. I'd assumed she'd gone back to meet Briggs, but he wasn't with her now.

The passenger side of Sterling's car opened, and the director climbed out. The two of them had the look of people who had just endured a very tense, very silent car ride.

"Think he's back to see us?" I asked, lowering my voice, even though they were far enough away that I wasn't sure I needed to.

Lia clapped a hand over my mouth and pulled me back so that we were partially obscured from view. Her eyes narrowed. I nodded, to show that I understood, and a moment later, I discovered why Lia was so fond of the roof.

The acoustics were excellent.

"You're welcome to borrow the car to see yourself home," Agent Sterling said. She was using her interrogator's voice, implacable and even-keeled.

"I asked you to drive me here," the director returned. His

voice was baritone, just as unruffled as hers. "I'd like to talk to the boy."

"You don't need to talk to Dean."

"I think you're forgetting which one of us is the director here, Agent."

"And I think you're forgetting that after the Locke debacle, I wasn't the only one asking questions." She paused, waiting for those words to hit their target. "I have contacts at National Intelligence. People in Washington are talking. What do you think would happen if it got out that the FBI was consulting with Redding's teenage son on this case?"

"This is the one case for which exposure isn't a concern." The director's tone never changed. "The FBI would be talking to the boy on this case whether he was working for us or not. If the director of National Intelligence asks—and he won't—it would be easy enough to explain. Redding's son was there the first time around. He knows the ins and outs of Redding's psyche better than anyone—including you."

"I agreed to come here and evaluate this program because you said that reporting the Naturals program to Washington would be a mistake." A tiny hint of emotion crept into Agent Sterling's voice, though whether it was frustration or something else, I couldn't tell. "You told me that I needed to see it myself to understand exactly what I would be shutting down."

I'd wondered why the director would send his daughter here, knowing she thought this program was a mistake, and now I knew.

"You listened to me then," the director countered calmly. "You could have filed that report, and you didn't."

"Like you left me any choice!"

"I did nothing but tell you the truth." The director looked down at his watch, as if to mark exactly how much time he was wasting on this conversation. "This program is the only thing keeping *that boy* from the edge. You think he'd fare better in foster care? Or maybe you'd like me to send Lia Zhang back onto the streets? She'd get caught again eventually, and this time, I guarantee you she'd end up getting tried as an adult."

I felt Lia stiffen beside me.

"You wanted me to come here," Sterling said, gritting out the words. "I came here. But when I did, you promised that you would listen to my recommendations."

"If you were being reasonable, I *would* listen. But keeping Dean Redding away from this case isn't reasonable." The director gave her a moment to reply to that, and when she didn't, he continued. "You can stand there and tell me how *wrong* this program is, but inside, you want to shut down this killer just as badly as I do. It's everything you can do not to use the Naturals to do it, and sooner or later, you'll forget all about your principles. You'll be the one telling *me* we need to cross that line."

I expected Sterling to tell him he was wrong. She didn't. "Of course I want to use them!" she shot back. "But this isn't about me. Or you. Or the Bureau. This is about the five teenagers who live in that house. Five actual people whose only protection is rules that you put in place and then break, again and again. You're the one who let Cassie Hobbes work on the Locke case. You're the one who insisted we bring Dean to talk to Redding. You're making rules and breaking them, sending mixed messages—"

"That's not what this is about," the director broke in. Unlike his daughter's voice, his remained completely impassive. "You're not upset about whatever messages you think I'm sending. Five years later, you're still upset that I sided with your husband on this program instead of with you."

"Ex-husband."

"You left him. You left the FBI."

"Go ahead and say it, Dad. I left *you*."

"Do you know what kind of position that put me in, Veronica? How am I supposed to command the loyalty of the entire Bureau when my own daughter couldn't be bothered to stick around? After the incident with the Hawkins girl on the Nightshade case, morale was low. We needed to present a united front."

Agent Sterling turned her back on her father, and when she turned back around, the words shot out of her like bullets from a gun. "Her name was Scarlett, and it wasn't an *incident*. A psychopath snuck into *our* labs and murdered one of *our* people. Tanner and I both had something to prove—" She cut herself off, breathing in raggedly. "I left the Bureau because I didn't belong there."

"But you came back," the director said. "Not for me. You came back for the boy. What Redding did to you, what happened to Scarlett on the Nightshade case—it's all tied up in your mind. You couldn't save her, so you've decided to save him."

Sterling took a step toward her father. "Someone has to. He's seventeen years old."

"And he was helping dear old daddy out when he was twelve!"

It was all I could do not to fly off the roof and go at the director myself. Beside me, all the tension melted out of Lia's body. She looked relaxed. Friendly, even. For Lia, that meant she was almost certainly out for blood.

Some people will always look at Dean and see his father, I thought dully. The director didn't just hold Dean responsible for the sins of his father—he considered Dean an accomplice.

"I am done talking about this with you, Veronica." The director's temper frayed. "We need to know if any of Redding's visitors is a likely suspect on this case. Do I need to tell you who some of Colonial University's alumni are? The pressure to put this one to bed is coming from on high, Agent." His voice softened slightly. "I know you don't want to see the bodies stacking up."

"Of course I want to catch this guy before anyone else gets hurt." Agent Sterling had cautioned me against making cases personal, but this one had snuck through the chinks in her armor. "That's why I went to see Redding myself."

The director froze. "I intercepted you before you executed that ill-thought-out plan."

Agent Sterling smiled at him, baring her teeth. "Did you?"

"Veronica—"

"Right now, I think I prefer *Agent*. You wanted someone to get underneath Daniel Redding's skin. You don't need Dean for that. I'm the one who got away, Director. You know what that means to a man like Redding."

"I know that I don't want you anywhere near him." For the first time, the director actually sounded like a father.

"Let me talk to Dean." Sterling wasn't above pressing her advantage, however slight it might have been. "Let me be the one who shows Dean the visitor logs. If he knows anything that might prove relevant, he'll tell me. Dean trusts me."

After a good ten or fifteen seconds of silence, the director nodded curtly. "Fine. But if you and Briggs can't get me results, I'll bring in someone who can."

ia and I did not say a word until both Agent Sterling and the director were out of sight.

"And I thought my family had issues." Lia got up and stretched, arching her back and then twisting from one side to the other. "She was telling the truth when she said that she had our best interests at heart. Not the whole truth, but it was true. Heartwarming, isn't it?"

I was too busy sorting through the implications of what we'd heard to reply. After last summer, Sterling had threatened to shut down the program. The director had kept her from going over his head by pointing out exactly what I'd told Sterling: that normal wasn't an option for any of us anymore. At least I had somewhere to go back to. Dean didn't. Lia didn't. Michael's father was abusive. There was a very high likelihood that Sloane's family were the ones who'd hammered home the idea that she said and did the wrong thing 86.5 percent of the time.

My mother was dead, my father barely involved in my life. And I was the lucky one.

"The director calls Dean *the boy.*" I paused to consider the significance of that. "He doesn't want to see Dean as a person. *The boy* is an extension of his father. *The boy* is a means to an end."

This from the man who referred to his own daughter as *Agent.*

She's the one who followed in your footsteps. Of all your children, she's the most like you. She was your legacy, and then she was gone.

"The director really does believe that Dean helped his father." Lia let me chew on that for a few seconds before continuing. "What exactly he thinks Dean helped Redding do is up in the air, but that wasn't conjecture I heard in his voice. For him, Dean's culpability is fact."

"Dean was twelve when his father was arrested!" The objection burst out of me. Realizing that I was preaching to the choir, I reined in the indignation a bit. "I know that Dean knew," I said softly. "I know he thinks that he should have found a way to put a stop to it, that if he'd done things differently, he could have saved those women, but according to Professor Fogle's lecture, Redding had been killing for five years before he was caught. Dean would have been seven."

Dean had told me once that he hadn't known about his father *at first.* But later . . .

He made me watch. Dean's words stuck in my head, like food wedged between my teeth.

I forced my attention back to the present, to Lia. "Was Sterling—our Sterling—telling the truth when she said she'd ask Dean about the visitor logs?" I asked.

"Yeah," Lia replied. "She was."

"Maybe she's starting to realize that she can't protect Dean from this," I said. "All she can do is run interference and make sure he's not going through it alone."

My words hung in the air. I'd thought all along that Sterling and Briggs weren't doing Dean any favors by keeping him in the dark, but from his perspective, Lia, Michael, and I had done the exact same thing. *When I was the one at the center of a case,* I thought slowly, *if I'd discovered that the others were investigating behind my back, I wouldn't have felt protected.*

I would have felt betrayed.

"Whatever you say, Cassandra Hobbes." Lia pivoted and began making her way back to her bedroom window. She walked on the tips of her toes, like the roof was a tightrope and she was seconds away from performing a death-defying move.

"You forgot the ice cream," I called after her.

She glanced back over her shoulder. "And you forgot the most interesting thing we learned from this little excursion."

I'd been so focused on the sequence of events that had led Agent Sterling here and the director's comments on Dean that I hadn't let myself process the rest of their conversation.

"The Nightshade case?" I grabbed the ice cream and went to stand, but Lia's response froze me to the spot.

"The Nightshade case—whatever that is—*and* the person who paid the price for however that case went down."

"Scarlett," I said, thinking back to my realization outside the prison that Agent Sterling had lost someone and that she blamed herself.

Lia turned the corner. I couldn't see her anymore, but I had no trouble hearing her. "Not just Scarlett," she countered. "Scarlett *Hawkins*."

CHAPTER 29

The person Agent Sterling had lost because she cared too much, because she was willing to do whatever it took to save lives, shared Judd's last name.

His daughter, I guessed. Judd was about the same age as the director, and the way he treated Agent Sterling wasn't just familiar—it was fatherly. Now Judd's feelings about the director made total sense. Judd had lost a child, and Director Sterling's primary concern had been *morale.*

I pieced together what I knew. Scarlett Hawkins and Agent Sterling were friends. They both worked at the FBI. Scarlett was killed. Briggs started going to Dean for help on cases. Agent Sterling left the FBI . . . and her husband.

When the director had discovered what Briggs was doing, he'd made it official. Dean had moved into this house. With Judd.

I was so caught up in thought that I almost didn't see

the figure creeping across the front lawn. The sun had fully set, so it took me a moment to recognize the way the person moved, hands stuffed into his pockets, shoulders rounded and hunched. The hoodie the figure was wearing almost masked his face. His hair—in desperate need of a trim—finished the job.

Dean. Sneaking out of the house. I was halfway back to Lia's window before I'd even registered the fact that I was moving. I forced myself not to look down and finished the journey. Thankful that Lia had left the window open, I climbed back into her room and raced down the stairs.

For once, I didn't run into anyone. By the time I made out it the front door, Dean was already halfway down the block. I ran to catch up to him.

"Dean!"

He ignored me and kept walking.

"I'm sorry," I called after him. My words hung in the night air, insufficient, but dear. "Lia and I should have told you we were going to that party. We thought we might pick up on something the FBI missed. We just wanted this case over."

"For me." Dean didn't turn around, but he stopped walking. "You wanted this case over for me."

"Is that so bad?" I asked, coming to a standstill behind him. "People are allowed to care about you, and don't tell me that when people care about you, they get hurt. That's not you talking. That's something you were told. It's something your father wants you to believe, because he doesn't want you to be close to anyone else. He's always wanted you all to himself, and every time you push us away, you're giving him *exactly* what he wants."

Dean still didn't turn around, so I took three steps, until I was standing in front of him. The tip of his hood hung in his face. I pushed the hood back. He didn't move. I put a hand on each side of his face and tilted it up.

The same way that Michael had tilted my face up to his.

What are you doing, Cassie?

I couldn't pull back from Dean, not now. No matter what it might mean. Dean needed this—physical contact. He needed to know that I wasn't afraid of him, that he wasn't alone.

I brushed the hair off his cheekbones, and dark eyes met mine.

"Anyone ever tell you that you see too much?" he asked me.

I managed a small smile. "I've been told that I should keep some of it to myself."

"You can't." Dean's lips curved almost imperceptibly upward. "You didn't plan on saying any of those things. I'm not sure you even knew them until they came out of your mouth."

He was right. Now that I'd said it, I could see that it was true—Dean's father didn't want to share him. *I made him,* he'd said in that interview with Briggs. He wanted Dean to blame himself for each and every woman Redding had killed, because if Dean blamed himself, if he thought he didn't deserve to be loved, he'd keep the rest of the world at arm's length. He'd be his father's son—and nothing else.

"Where are you going?" I asked Dean. My voice came out as a whisper. I dropped my hands from his face, but they only made it as far as his neck.

This is a mistake.

This is right.

Those thoughts came on the heels of each other, playing in stereo. Any second, Dean was going to pull back from my touch.

But he didn't.

And I didn't.

"I can't just sit here and wait for the next body to show up. The director thinks that he can just put me in a drawer and pull me out when I'm *useful*. Agent Sterling tried to cover for her father, but I know what he's thinking."

He's thinking that you owe him this, I thought, feeling Dean's pulse jump in his throat under my touch. *He's thinking that he's doing the world a favor by making you his tool.*

"Where are you going?" I repeated the question.

"Agent Sterling showed me a list." Dean put his hands on my wrists and pulled my hands away from his neck. He didn't let go, just stood there on the sidewalk, his fingers working their way from my wrists to my fingers, until our hands were interwoven. "She wanted to know if I recognized any of my father's visitors, if anything jumped out to me."

"And did anything jump out to you?"

Dean nodded curtly, but didn't release my hands. "One of the visitors was a woman from my hometown."

I waited him to elaborate.

"Daniel killed people in that town, Cassie. My fourth-grade teacher. Travelers just passing through. The people in that town, our friends, our neighbors—they couldn't even stand to *look* at me after the truth came out. Why would anyone there go to visit him?"

Those weren't rhetorical questions. They were questions Dean was set on answering himself. "You're going home," I said. I knew it was true, long before Dean confirmed it for me.

"Broken Springs hasn't been home for a very long time." Dean took a step backward and dropped my hands. He pulled his hood back up. "I know the type of women who visit men like my father in jail. They're fascinated. Obsessed."

"Obsessed enough to re-create his crimes?"

"Obsessed enough that they won't cooperate with the FBI," Dean said. "Obsessed enough that they'd *love* to talk to me."

I didn't tell Dean that everyone from Briggs to Judd would kill him for doing this. I did, however, take issue with his timing. "How late is it going to be when you get there? And for that matter, *how* are you going to get there?"

Dean didn't answer.

"Wait," I told him. "Wait until morning. Sterling will be out with Briggs. I can go with you, or Lia can. There's a killer out there. You shouldn't be going anywhere alone."

"No," Dean said, his face twisting like he'd tasted something sour. "That's Lia's job."

I'd apologized for digging into this case without him. She hadn't. I knew Lia well enough to know that she wouldn't. Dean knew that, too.

"Go easy," I told him. "Whatever you said to her, she's taking it hard."

"She's supposed to take it hard." There was a stubborn set to Dean's jaw. "I'm the only one she listens to. I'm the one who cares if she goes off with two strange men in the middle of a murder investigation. You think that anything anyone else says is going to keep her from doing it again?"

"You made your point," I told him. "But you're not just the only person she listens to. You're the only person she trusts. She can't lose that. Neither can you."

"Fine," Dean said. "I'll wait until morning to head for Broken Springs, and I'll talk to Lia before I go."

Once Lia was involved, I doubted she'd sit back and let him go off on his own. If he wouldn't take her or me, he could at least take Michael. That might be a recipe for a road trip that ended in a fistfight, but at least Dean would have backup.

Michael doesn't hate Dean. He hates that Dean is angry and holding it in. He hates that Dean knows what his childhood was like. He hates the idea of Dean with me.

I turned and started walking back toward the house, my mind a mess of thoughts about Michael and Dean and me.

I'd made it six feet when Dean fell in beside me. I didn't want to think about the heat of his body next to mine. I didn't want to want to reach for his hand.

So I forced myself to stick to safer ground. "Have you ever heard of Judd having a daughter named Scarlett?"

The next morning, I woke up to find that Michael was outside working on his car again. I stood at my bedroom window, watching him going at the bumper with the power sander like rust removal was an Olympic sport. *He's going to destroy that car,* I thought. Restoration was not Michael's strong suit.

"You're up."

I turned from the window to face Sloane, who was sitting up in her own bed. "I'm up."

"What are you looking at?"

I grasped for a way to avoid answering the question, but came up empty. "Michael," I said.

Sloane studied me for a moment, the way an archaeologist might look at paintings on the wall of a cave. Given the way her brain worked, she probably would have had better luck reading hieroglyphics.

"You and Michael," Sloane said slowly.

"There's nothing going on with Michael and me." My reply was immediate.

Sloane tilted her head to one side. "You and Dean?"

"There's nothing going on with Dean and me."

Sloane stared at me for another three seconds, and then: "I give up." Clearly, she'd expended her capacity for girl talk. Thank God. She disappeared into the closet, and I was halfway out the door before I remembered my promise.

"I may be going somewhere today," I told her. "With Dean."

Sloane popped out of the closet, half-dressed. "But you said—"

"Not like that," I cut in hastily. "For the case. I'm not sure what the plan is, but I'm getting ready to find out." I paused. "I promised I'd deal you in next time. This is me dealing you in."

Sloane pulled on a shirt. She was quiet for several seconds. When she spoke, she beamed. "Consider me dealt."

We found Dean in the kitchen with Lia, who was sitting on the kitchen counter, wearing white pajamas and red high heels. Her hair was loose and uncombed. The two of them were talking softly enough that I couldn't make out the words.

Lia caught sight of me over Dean's shoulder, and with an unholy glint in her eye, she hopped off the counter. Her heels didn't so much as wobble when she landed.

"Lover boy here says you stopped him from doing something stupid last night." Lia smirked. "Personally, I don't want to know how you *persuaded* him to hold his horses. Horses were held. Let's save my tender ears the details, shall we?"

"Lia," Dean barked.

Sloane raised her hand. "I have questions about these tender details."

"Later," Lia told Sloane. She reached over and patted Dean's cheek. He narrowed his eyes, and she folded her hands primly in front of her body. "I'll behave," she promised. "Scout's honor."

Dean muttered something under his breath.

"Blush. Grimace. Smirk." Michael strolled into the room, labeling each of us as he passed. "And Sloane is perplexed. I miss all the fun."

I could practically feel him trying not to read anything into Dean's grimace and my blush. Michael was *trying* to give me space. Unfortunately, he couldn't turn off his ability, any more than I could turn off mine.

"Townsend." Dean cleared his throat.

Michael turned his full attention to the other boy. "You need something," he said, studying the set of Dean's jaw, the thin line of his lips. "You really hate asking." Michael smiled. "It's like a Band-Aid—just pull it off."

"He needs a ride," Lia said so Dean wouldn't have to. "And you're going to give it to him."

"Am I?" Michael did a passable job of sounding surprised.

"I'd appreciate it." Dean shot Lia a look, which I read to mean *Stay out of it*.

"And where, pray tell, are we going?" Michael asked.

"To talk to someone." Dean clearly didn't feel like sharing more than that. I expected Michael to draw this out, to actually make Dean ask, but Michael just stared at him for several seconds and then nodded.

"No comments on my driving," Michael said lightly. "And you owe me."

"Deal."

"Excellent." Lia looked altogether too pleased with herself. "So Michael will go with Dean and Cassie, and Sloane and I will provide the distraction."

"I like this plan," Sloane declared brightly. "I can be very distracting."

Michael and Dean weren't so enthused. "Cassie's not going." The two of them spoke in unison.

"Well, this is awkward," Lia commented, looking from one boy to the other. "Are you two going to start braiding each other's hair next?"

Someday, I was fairly certain that Lia would write a book entitled *Making an Awkward Situation Worse*.

"Cassie's a big girl," Lia continued. "She can make decisions for herself. If she wants to go, she can go."

I wasn't sure why she was so gung ho on my accompanying them, or why she was volunteering to stay home herself.

"Dean and I are both profilers," I pointed out. "Doesn't

that make me kind of redundant?" The only thing I would bring to this venture was objectivity. Lia's ability made her the more obvious choice.

"No offense"—Lia began her next sentence in a way that more or less guaranteed the next words out of her mouth would be insulting—"but you simply cannot lie, Cassie. Agent Sterling got the truth about our last little *adventure* out of you so quickly, it's embarrassing. Really. If you stay here, you'll get us all caught. Besides," she added, a smirk settling over her features, "Tweedledee and Tweedledum over here will be less likely to get themselves killed—or to kill each other—if you're along for the ride."

I thought of Lia and Michael dancing together just to get a rise out of Dean, and Michael's inability to keep from poking bears with sticks. Michael, Lia, and Dean locked in a car together would be a disaster.

"Dibs on being Tweedledee," Michael said blithely.

"Fine," I told Lia. "I'll go with them."

For a moment, I thought Dean would protest, but he didn't. "I'm ready when you two are," he said gruffly.

Michael smiled, first at Dean, then at me. "I was born ready."

We passed the ride to Broken Springs, Virginia, in tense and uncomfortable silence.

"Okay, I'm calling it," Michael announced when the quiet got to be too much. "I'm turning on the radio. There will be singing. I would not be opposed to car-dancing. But the next person whose facial expression approaches 'brood' is getting punched in the nose. Unless it's Cassie. If it's Cassie, I punch Dean in the nose."

A strangled sound came from Dean's direction. It took me a second to realize that the garbled sound was laughter. The threat was so very Michael—completely irreverent, even though I had no doubt he'd follow through with it.

"Fine," I said, "no brooding, but no radio, either. We should talk."

Both of the occupants of the front seat seemed somewhat alarmed by that suggestion.

"About the case," I clarified. "We should talk about the case. What do we know about this woman we're going to see?"

"Trina Simms," Dean said. "According to the visitor logs Agent Sterling showed me, she's visited my father with increasing frequency over the past three years." He gritted his teeth. "There's reason to believe that it may be romantic, at least on her part."

I didn't ask Dean to elaborate on what that reason was. Neither did Michael.

"I doubt she knew him before he was incarcerated," Dean continued, saying each word like it didn't matter—because if he let it, it would matter too much. "She's in her forties. In all likelihood, she's either convinced herself that he's innocent or that the women he killed deserved to die."

The real question wasn't how Trina Simms had justified her interest in a man most people considered a monster. The real question was whether or not she was a killer herself. If so, had she considered the murders a romantic gesture? Had she thought Dean's dad would be proud of her? That it would bring them closer together?

I knew instinctively Daniel Redding didn't care about this woman. He didn't care about people, period. He was callous. Unemotional. The closest he could come to love was whatever it was he felt for Dean, and that was more narcissistic than anything else. Dean was worth caring about only because Dean was *his*.

"What's our game plan?" Michael asked. "Do we just knock on the front door?"

Dean shrugged. "You got a better idea?"

"This is your rodeo," Michael told him. "I'm just the driver."

"It would be better if I went in alone," Dean said.

I opened my mouth to tell him that he wasn't going anywhere alone, but Michael beat me to it.

"No can do, cowboy. They call it the buddy system for a reason. Besides, Cassie would try to go after you, and then I would go after her, so on and so forth. . . ." Michael trailed off ominously.

"Fine," Dean capitulated. "We go in as a group. I'll tell her you're my friends."

"A clever ruse," Michael commented. It hit me then that Michael hadn't agreed to drive Dean here for me, or for Lia. Despite everything he'd told me about their history, he'd done it for Dean.

"I'll do the talking," Dean said. "If we're lucky, she'll be so fixated on me that she won't be able to pay attention to either of you. If you can get a read on her, great. We get in. We get out. With luck, we'll be home before anyone realizes we've left."

On the surface, the plan sounded simple, but *lucky* wasn't an adjective I would have applied to a single person in this car. That thought lingered in my mind as Michael drove past a sign: WELCOME TO BROKEN SPRINGS, POPULATION 4,140.

rina Simms lived in a one-story house the color of
an avocado. The lawn was overgrown, but the flower
beds had clearly been weeded. There was a pastel
welcome mat on the front porch. Dean rang the doorbell.
Nothing happened.

"Bell's broken." A boy with a buzz cut came around the
side of the house. He was blond-haired and fair-skinned and
walked like he had someplace to be. At first glance, I'd put
his age at close to ours, but as he came closer, I realized that
he was at least a few years older. His accent was like Dean's,
magnified. He offered us a polite smile, more a reflex in this
part of the country than a courtesy. "You selling something?"

His eyes skimmed over Dean and Michael and landed
on me.

"No," Dean replied, drawing the man's attention back to
him.

"You lost?" the man asked.

"We're looking for Trina Simms." Michael's eyes were locked on the man. I took a small step sideways, so I could get a better look at Michael's face. He would be the first to know if the polite smile was hiding something else.

"Who are you?" the blond guy asked.

"We're the people looking for Trina Simms," Dean said. There was nothing aggressive about the way he said it, no hint of a fight in his voice, but the smile evaporated from the stranger's face.

"What do you want with my mother?"

So Trina Simms had a son—a son who was significantly taller and bigger than either Michael or Dean.

"Christopher!" A nasal shriek broke through the air.

"You should go," Trina's son said. His voice was low, gravelly and soothing, even when the words he was saying weren't. "My mother doesn't like company."

I glanced down at the pastel welcome mat. The front door flew open, and I nearly lost my balance hopping out of the way.

"Christopher, where is my—" The woman who'd come out of the door came to a standstill. She surveyed us for a moment with squinted eyes. Then she beamed. "Visitors!" she said. "What are you selling?"

"We're not selling anything," Dean said. "We're here to talk to you, ma'am—assuming you are Trina Simms?"

Dean's accent was more pronounced than I'd ever heard it. The woman smiled at him, and I remembered what

Daniel Redding had said about Dean being the kind of child people loved on sight.

"I'm Trina," the woman said. "For goodness' sakes, Christopher, stop slouching. Can't you see we have company?"

Christopher made no move to stand straighter. From my perspective, he wasn't slouching at all. I turned my attention back to his mother. Trina Simms had hair that had probably been up in rollers all morning. She wasn't wearing any makeup except for red lipstick.

"I suppose it's too much to hope you're friends of Christopher's?" she said to us. "He has all of these friends, but he never brings them by."

"No, ma'am," Dean replied. "We just met."

If by "met" Dean meant "silently assessed each other."

"You're a pretty one." It took me a moment to realize that Trina was talking to me. "Look at all of that hair."

My hair was slightly longer and slightly thicker than average—nothing worth commenting on.

"And those shoes," Trina continued, "they're precious!"

I was wearing canvas tennis shoes.

"I always wanted a girl," Trina confessed.

"Are we inviting them in or aren't we, Mother?" Christopher's voice had a slight edge.

"Oh," Trina said, stiffening suddenly. "I'm not sure we should."

If your son hadn't said anything, you would have invited us in yourself, I thought. There was something about the dynamic between the two of them that made me uncomfortable.

"Did you ask them why they're here?" Trina's hands went to her hips. "Three strangers show up on your mother's porch, and you don't even—"

"He asked, but I hadn't gotten to introduce myself yet," Dean cut in. "My name is Dean."

A spark of interest flickered in Trina's eyes. "Dean?" she repeated. She took a step forward, elbowing me to the side. "Dean what?"

Dean didn't move, didn't blink, didn't react in any way to her scrutiny. "Redding," he said. He glanced over at Christopher, then back at Trina. "I believe you know my father."

CHAPTER 32

The inside of the Simms house contrasted sharply with the overgrown front lawn. The floors were immaculately clean. Porcelain figures sat on every available surface. Dozens of framed pictures hung on the hallway walls: Christopher in school picture after school picture, the same solemn stare on his face in each. There was only one picture of a man. I took a closer look and froze. The man was smiling warmly. There were a few wrinkles near the edges of his eyes. I recognized him.

Daniel Redding. What kind of woman had a fondness for doilies and hung a serial killer's picture on her wall?

"You have his eyes." Trina ushered us into the living room. She sat opposite Dean. Her gaze never left his face, like she was trying to memorize it. Like she was starving, and he was food. "The rest of you . . . Well, Daniel always said you had a lot of your mother in her." Trina paused, her lips pursed. "I can't say I knew her. She didn't grow up here, you know. Daniel went to college—always so smart. He came back with her. And then there was you, of course."

"Did you know my father growing up?" Dean asked. His voice was perfectly polite. He seemed perfectly at ease.

This was hurting him.

"No," Trina said. Another purse of the lips was followed by an explanation. "He was quite a few grades younger than me, you know—not that a lady ever tells her age."

"What are you doing here?" Christopher threw that question at Dean from the entryway to the room, his arms crossed over his chest. His face was cast in shadows, but his voice left no doubt to his feelings about this turn of events. He didn't want Dean in his house. He didn't want Dean's father's picture on his walls.

Not that I blamed him.

"Dean is welcome here," Trina said sharply. "If things go well with the appeal, this could be his home."

"Appeal?" Dean said.

"Your father's appeal," Trina said patiently. "The evidence they planted."

"*They* being the FBI?" Michael asked. Trina waved a hand at him like she was waving away a fly.

"None of those searches were legal," Trina said. "None of them."

"My father killed those women." Dean paused. "But you know that, don't you?"

"Your father is a brilliant man," Trina said. "Every brilliant man needs outlets. He can't be expected to live as other men can. You know that."

The familiarity with which Trina spoke sickened me. She thought she knew Dean. She thought he knew her.

But did she kill Emerson Cole? Did she kill the professor? That was why we had come here. That was what we needed to know.

"It must be hard for a man like Daniel," I said. Dean's hand found mine. He squeezed in warning, but I already had Trina's attention. "To be caged, like an animal, like he's *less* when really—"

"He's *more*," Trina finished.

"That's enough," Christopher said, crossing the room. "You need to go." He reached for my elbow and wrenched me off the couch. I stumbled, trying to catch a look at Christopher's eyes, to know what he was thinking, whether he'd *meant* to grab me so hard—

One second Dean was next to me, and the next he had Christopher pinned to the wall, his forearm pressed against Trina's son's throat. The contrast in their skin tones was striking—Dean's tan and Christopher's pale.

"Christopher!" Trina said. "This young lady is our *guest*." Her chest heaved with agitation. *No, not agitation,* I realized. Seeing the look in Dean's eye, the way he'd moved, she was *excited*.

Michael walked over to Dean and hauled him off his prey. Dean fought Michael's hold for a second, then went still. Michael let him go and patted the front of Christopher's shirt, like he was dusting off the lapels of a suit jacket, even though Christopher was dressed in a worn and battered tee.

"Touch her again," Michael told Christopher conversationally, "and Dean will be the one trying to pull me off of you."

Michael told me once that when he lost it, he *really* lost it. I could hear it beneath his pleasant tone—if Christopher laid another hand on me, Dean might not be able to pull Michael off.

Christopher's hands knotted themselves into fists. "You shouldn't have come here. This is sick. You're all sick." The fists stayed by his sides, and a moment later, he stomped out of the living room and out of the house. The front door slammed.

"I'm afraid Christopher doesn't quite understand my relationship with your father," Trina confided to Dean. "He was only nine when his own father left, and well . . ." Trina sighed. "A single mother does what she can."

Dean came back to sit beside me. Michael stayed standing, and I realized he was watching Trina from an angle that decreased the chances that she would notice his attention.

"How long have you and Daniel been together?" I asked. *You aren't together,* I thought. *He's using you.* For what, I wasn't sure.

"We've been seeing each other for about three years," Trina replied. She seemed pleased to be asked—which was, of course, why I'd chosen that question. If she believed that we were on board with the relationship, it would feed into the happy little picture she'd painted in her mind. Dean was *visiting*. This wasn't an interrogation. It was a conversation.

"Do you think this new case will affect his chances of an appeal?" I asked.

Trina frowned. "What new case?" she asked.

I didn't reply. Trina looked from me to Dean.

"What's she talking about, Dean?" she asked. "You know what a crucial time this is in your father's legal situation."

His legal situation is that he's a convicted serial killer, I thought. Based on my interactions with Briggs and Sterling— and Dean himself—I was almost certain this appeal was as fictional as Trina's misguided belief that if the older Redding was released, Daniel and Dean would move in here.

"That's why I'm here," Dean said, casting me a sideways glance as he followed my lead. "That girl who was killed at Colonial? And then the professor who was writing the book?"

"The FBI tried to talk to me about *that*." Trina sniffed. "They know I'm your father's support. They think they can turn me against him."

"But they can't," I said soothingly. "Because what you have is real." I swallowed back the guilt I felt, playing on this woman's delusions. I forced myself to remember that she knew Daniel Redding for what he was: a killer. She just didn't care.

"This case has nothing to do with Daniel. *Nothing.* The FBI would love to pin something else on him. Left on a public lawn?" Trina scoffed. "Daniel would never do something so rash, so sloppy. And to think that someone else is out there—" She shook her head. "Claiming credit, trading on his reputation. It's a crime, is what it is."

Murder is *a crime*, I thought, but I didn't say it out loud. We'd gotten what we needed here. Trina Simms wasn't concerned with continuing Daniel Redding's work—to her, the copycat was a plagiarist, a counterfeiter. She was female, a neat-freak, and controlling. Our UNSUB was none of the above.

Our UNSUB was a male, in his twenties, subjugated by others.

"We should go," Dean said.

Trina clucked and protested, but we made our way to the door. "If you don't mind me asking," I said, as we were leaving, "what kind of car does Christopher drive?"

"He drives a truck." If Trina thought it was an odd question, she didn't show it.

"What color is the truck?" I asked.

"It's hard to say," Trina said, her voice taking on the tone she'd used repeatedly with Christopher. "He never washes it. But last I checked, it was black."

I shivered as I thought of the profile Agent Sterling had given us and felt the ghost of Christopher's grip on my arm.

"Thank you for having us," I managed to say.

Trina reached a hand out and touched my face. "Such a sweet girl," she told Dean. "Your father would approve."

CHAPTER 33

"**H**ere." Michael tossed his keys to Dean. Dean caught them. "You drive," Michael said, sauntering over to the passenger side of the car. "You look like you could use it."

Dean's grip tightened on the keys, and I wondered what game Michael was playing. He never let anyone else drive his car—and Dean was the *last* person he'd make an exception for. Dean was probably thinking the same thing, but he accepted the offer with a nod.

Michael climbed into the backseat with me. "So," he said as Dean pulled away from the house, "Christopher Simms: understandably upset that his mom has a thing for serial killers, or budding psycho himself?"

"He grabbed Cassie." Dean let that statement hang in the air for a moment. "He could have gone for me. He could have gone for you. But he went for Cassie."

"And when you threatened him," I added, "he left."

You shouldn't have come here. I went back over Christopher's words. *This is sick. You're all sick.*

"What's the holdup?" Michael asked. For a second, I thought he was talking to me, but then I realized the comment was aimed at Dean. The car wasn't moving. We were sitting at a stop sign.

"Nothing," Dean replied, but his eyes were locked on the road, and suddenly, I realized Michael hadn't just let Dean drive on a whim. This was the town Dean had grown up in. This was his past, a place he never would have chosen to go if it weren't for this case.

"What's down that road?" I asked Dean.

Michael caught my eye and shook his head slightly. Then he leaned back in his seat. "So, Dean, are we headed back to the house, or are we taking a detour?"

After a long moment, Dean turned down the road. I could see his knuckles tightening over the steering wheel. I glanced at Michael. He shrugged, as if he hadn't planned this. As if he hadn't seen something on Dean's face on the way into town that had made him want to let Dean drive on the way out.

We ended up parked on the pavement next to a dirt road that snaked back into the woods. Dean turned the car off and got out. My gaze caught on a mailbox. Somewhere, buried in those woods, at the end of that road, there was a house.

Dean's old house.

"You wanted him to come here," I whispered furiously to

Michael, watching Dean from inside the car. "You gave him the keys—"

"I gave him a choice," Michael corrected. "I've seen Dean angry. I've seen him disgusted and drowning in guilt, scared of himself and what he's capable of, scared of *you*." Michael let that sink in for a moment. "But until today, I've never once seen him raw." Michael paused. "It's not the bad memories that tear a person apart like that, Cassie. It's the good ones."

We fell into a momentary silence. Outside, Dean started walking down the dirt road. I watched him go, then I turned back to Michael. "Did you give him the keys because he needed to come here, or because once upon a time, he threw *your* past in your face?"

Coming here might help Dean—but it would, without question, hurt, too.

"You're the profiler," Michael replied. "You tell me."

"Both," I said. *Pseudo-rivals. Pseudo-siblings. Pseudo-something else.* Michael and Dean had a complicated relationship, one that had nothing to do with me. Michael had arranged this to help Dean *and* to hurt him.

"Do you want to go after him?" Michael's question took me by surprise.

"You're the emotion reader," I retorted. "You tell me."

"That's the problem, Colorado," Michael replied, leaning toward me. "You want me to tell you what you feel. I want you to *know*."

Slowly, my hand crept toward the door handle. Michael leaned across the seat toward me. "You were always going to go after him," he told me, his lips so close to mine that I thought at any minute he might close the gap. "The thing you need to figure out is *why*."

I could still feel Michael's breath on my face when he leaned across me and pushed open the car door.

"Go on," he said. "I'll be waiting."

But this time, I heard an underlying edge in his voice— something that told me Michael wouldn't be waiting for long.

I caught up to Dean outside a picket fence. It might have been white once, but now it was dirt-stained and weather-worn. The siding on the house behind it was the same color. A bright yellow tricycle lay on its side in the yard, a stark contrast to everything around it. I followed Dean's gaze to a patch of bare grass just outside the fence.

"They tore down the toolshed," Dean commented, like he was talking about the weather and not the building where his father had tortured and murdered all those women.

I stared at the tricycle on the lawn, wondering about the people who had bought this place. They had to know its history. They had to know what had once been buried in this yard.

Dean started walking again, halfway around the side of the house. He knelt next to the fence, his fingers searching for something.

"There," he said. I knelt beside him. I moved his hand so I could see. Initials. His and someone else's.

MR.

"Marie," Dean said. "My mother's name was Marie."

The front door to the house opened. A toddler came bar-reling toward the tricycle. The little boy's mother stayed on the front porch, but when she saw us, her eyes narrowed to slits.

Teenagers. Strangers. On her property.

"We should go," Dean said quietly.

We were halfway back down the dirt road before he spoke again.

"We used to play Go Fish." He stared straight ahead as he spoke, walking at the same steady pace. "Old Maid, Uno, War—anything with cards."

We. As in Dean and his mother.

"What happened to her?" That was a question I'd never asked. Daniel Redding had told Briggs that his wife had left—but I hadn't processed the fact that she hadn't just left Daniel Redding. She'd left Dean, too.

"She got bored." Dean walked like a soldier, eyes straight ahead, pace never faltering. "Bored with him. Bored with me. He'd brought her back to this small town, cut off all contact with her family." He swallowed once. "One day I came home and she was gone."

"Did you ever think—"

"That he killed her?" Dean stopped and turned to face me. "I used to. When the FBI dug up the bodies, I kept wait-ing for them to tell me that she hadn't just left. That she was still there, in the ground." He started walking again, slower this time, like his body was weighed down with cement.

"And then my social worker found her. Alive."

"But . . ." That one word escaped my mouth before I managed to clamp down on the question on the tip of my tongue. I refused to say what I was thinking—that if Dean's mother was alive and they knew where she was, how had Dean ended up in foster care? Why was it that the director claimed that if it weren't for this program, he wouldn't have anywhere else to go?

"She was dating someone." Dean scuffed a foot into the dirt. "I was Daniel Redding's son."

He stopped there—nine words to explain something I couldn't even fathom.

You were her son, too, I thought. How could a person look at their own child and just say "No, thanks"? *Go Fish and Old Maid and carving their initials into the fence.* I knew then that Marie Redding was the reason Dean had come back here.

It's not the bad memories that tear a person apart. It's the good ones.

"What was she like?" The question felt like sandpaper in my mouth, but if this was what he'd come here for, I could listen. I would make myself listen.

Dean didn't answer my question until we'd made our way back to the car. Michael was sitting in the driver's seat. Dean walked around to the passenger side. He put his hand on the door, then looked up at me.

"What was she like?" he repeated softly. He shook his head. "Nothing like Trina Simms."

CHAPTER 34

When we got back, Judd was sitting on the front porch, waiting for us. *Not good.* I spent about five seconds wondering if we could claim to have spent the day in town. Judd held up his hand and stopped the words before I could form them.

"I always believed, you give kids enough space, they make their own mistakes. They learn." Judd said nothing for several seconds. "Then one time, my daughter was about ten. She and her best friend got it into their minds that they were going to go on a *scientific expedition*."

"You have a daughter?" Michael said.

Judd continued on as if he'd never spoken. "Scarlett was always getting ideas like that one. She'd get it in her brain that she was going to do something, and there was no talking her out of it. And her little friend—well, if Scarlett was in it for the *science*, her friend was the expedition type. The scale-down-the-side-of-a-cliff-for-a-*sample* type. They damn near got themselves killed." Judd fell into silence again. "Sometimes, some kids, they need a little help with the learning."

Judd never raised his voice. He didn't even look angry. But suddenly, I was very sure that I did not want Judd's "help."

"It was my fault." Dean's voice was a perfect complement for Judd's, and I realized that some of his mannerisms were the older man's as well. "Michael and Cassie only went with me so I wouldn't go alone."

"Is that right?" Judd asked, giving the three of us one of those stares that only someone who'd been a parent could manage, the one that—when your own parent made it—reminded you that they'd changed your diapers and could recognize your BS, even now.

"I needed to do this." Dean didn't say any more than that. Judd crossed his arms over his chest.

"Maybe you did," he allowed. "But I'd think of a better excuse in the next five seconds, son, because you're going to need it."

I heard the sound of heels on tile. An instant later, Agent Sterling appeared in the doorway behind Judd. "Inside," she barked. "Right now."

We went inside. So much for not getting caught. Sterling herded us into Briggs's office. She gestured to the couch. "Sit."

I sat. Dean sat. Michael rolled his eyes, but took a seat on the arm of the couch.

"It was Dean's fault," Michael announced solemnly. "He needed to do this."

"Michael!" I said.

"Do you know where Briggs is right now?" Agent Sterling's question wasn't what I expected. My mind started searching for reasons that Briggs's location might be relevant to this discussion, to what we'd done. Was he out looking for us? Meeting with the director to do damage control?

"Briggs," Agent Sterling said tautly, "is at the Warren County police station, meeting with a man who thinks he has information about the Emerson Cole murder. You see, a serial killer's son paid his mother a visit this afternoon, and Mr. Simms believes the boy might be violent." She paused. "The gentleman has a bruise on his neck to back up the claim."

Christopher Simms had reported Dean to the police? I hadn't seen that one coming.

"Luckily," Agent Sterling continued, making the word sound more like an indictment than an expression of luck, "Briggs had asked the locals to route anything relevant to this case through him, so he's the one who took the statement. He's still there, taking the statement. As it turns out, Christopher Simms has quite a lot to say—about Dean, about the rest of you, about his mother's relationship with Daniel Redding. He's just a *fount* of information."

"He drives a black truck." I stared at my hands, but couldn't keep from speaking up. "He has a connection to

Daniel Redding. His mother berates him constantly. He lost his temper while I was there and grabbed me, so you've got impulsivity, but his movements and mannerisms are also controlled."

"You slammed Christopher into the wall when he grabbed Cassie?" Agent Sterling asked Dean. Of everything I'd said, it figured that she'd latch on to that.

Dean shrugged unapologetically. Agent Sterling took that as a yes.

Sterling turned to Michael. I expected her to ask him something, but instead she just held out her hand. "Keys."

"Spatula," Michael replied. She narrowed her eyes at him. "We aren't just saying random nouns?" he asked archly.

"Give me your keys. Now."

Michael dug his keys out of his pocket and tossed them blithely to her. She turned back to Dean.

"I told my father that I trusted you," she said. "I told him I could handle this."

Her words dug their way under Dean's skin. He pushed back. "I never asked you to handle me."

Sterling actually flinched. "Dean . . ." She looked like she was about to apologize, but she stopped herself. The expression on her face hardened. "From this point on, you're not alone," she told Dean sharply. She gestured to Michael. "You two are bunking together. If you're not with Michael, you're with someone else. Now that you've flung yourself onto the local PD's radar, if and when our UNSUB strikes again, you might need an alibi."

Agent Sterling couldn't have devised a better punishment for Dean. He was a solitary person by nature, and after the day's events, he'd want to be alone.

"You're dismissed." Agent Sterling's voice was crisp. All three of us were on our feet in an instant. "Not you, Cassie." Sterling fixed me in place with her stare. "You two," she told the boys, "out!"

Michael and Dean glanced at each other, then at me.

"I won't ask you again."

Agent Sterling waited until the door shut behind the boys before she spoke. "What were you and Dean doing out at the old Redding house?"

I opened my mouth, then closed it again. Was there *nothing* she didn't know?

"Christopher Simms wasn't the only one who contacted the police," Sterling informed me. "The local police hear 'teenage prowlers' out on Redding's old property, mere minutes after someone files a complaint about Dean, and one guess where their minds go."

Even I had to admit this didn't look good.

"He needed to go back," I said, my voice soft but unwavering. "Just to see it."

Sterling's jaw clenched, and I wondered if she was thinking of the time she'd spent on that property, bound hand and foot in a toolshed that no longer existed.

"Dean needing to go back there, it wasn't about his father." I paused to let that sink in. "This visit, it had nothing to do with Daniel Redding."

Sterling turned that over in her mind. "His mother?" she asked.

I didn't answer. I didn't have to. After another tense moment of silence, a question burst out of my mouth. "Has anyone talked to her?" I just kept thinking that my mother had had many faults, but she never would have *left* me. And Dean's mother hadn't just left—she'd had a chance to get him back, and she'd said no. "If our UNSUB is obsessed with Redding, Dean's mother could be a target," I continued. There were reasons to talk to Marie that had nothing to do with wanting to shake some sense into her—or at the very least, make her face what she'd done to Dean.

"I talked to her," Sterling said shortly. "And she's not a target."

"But how could you—"

"Dean's mother lives in Melbourne," Sterling said. "As in Australia—halfway across the world and well out of the reach of this killer. She didn't have any information relevant to the case and has asked that we leave her alone."

Like she left Dean?

"Did she even ask about him?" I asked.

Sterling pursed her lips. "No."

Given what I knew about Agent Sterling and her relationship with Dean, I was betting that she'd gone into that call the same way I would have: hating Marie for what she'd done, but halfway convinced that if she just said the right thing or asked the right question, she could undo it. Agent Sterling hadn't ever wanted to believe that the Naturals

258

program was Dean's best option, but now I could practically hear her thinking, *If it weren't for this program, he'd have nowhere else to go.*

"You should add Christopher Simms to your suspect list," I said. When she didn't immediately shut me down, I continued, "He's not a small person, but he doesn't have the kind of presence you'd expect from someone his size. He moves slowly, talks slowly, not because he's unintelligent or uncoordinated, but because he's deliberate. He's inhibited. Not shy, not awkward, just holding something in."

"Cassie—" She was going to tell me to stop, but I didn't give her the chance.

"Christopher was outside when we approached the house. If I had to guess, I'd say he does all the outdoor chores. The lawn was overgrown—maybe it's his way of striking out at his mother, even as he does her bidding in everything else. He's pulling at the bit, but he's old enough that if he really wanted to, he could move out." The words were pouring out of my mouth, faster and faster. "His mother mentioned that he has plenty of friends, and I saw nothing to make me think that he was antisocial or particularly inept. So why doesn't he move out?" I answered my own question. "Maybe he thinks she needs him. Maybe he wants her approval. Maybe she guilts him into it. I don't know. But I do know that when he snapped, it happened in an instant, and he didn't go for Michael or Dean. He went for me."

I finally stopped for a breath. For a few seconds, Sterling just stood there.

"You said that the UNSUB was comfortable with firearms, but less sure of himself when it came to unarmed confrontations. I was the easy target in that room, and I was the one he went for."

Maybe Christopher had reached for me because I was the one talking. Maybe he'd been actively trying *not* to start a fight and thought that I was the only one of the three of us who wouldn't respond with a punch.

Or maybe he was the kind of guy who liked asserting himself against women.

"Were there any firearms in the house?" Sterling asked. I got the sense that the question had slipped out. She hadn't meant to ask it.

"I didn't see any guns."

Agent Sterling's phone buzzed, and she held up her hand, effectively putting me on hold.

"Sterling." She answered the phone with her name. Whatever the person on the other end of the phone had to say, it wasn't good news. She was like a spring that had been coiled tight, every muscle tense. "You're kidding me. When?" Sterling was silent for long enough to make me think that "when" wasn't the only question being answered. "I can be on the road in five."

She ended the call abruptly.

"Bad news?" I asked.

"Dead body."

Those words were probably meant as a conversation ender, but I had to ask. "Our UNSUB?"

Sterling tightened her hand around her phone.

"Is this the point where you tell me to stay out of it?" I asked.

Sterling closed her eyes and took a deep breath before opening them again. "The victim is Trina Simms, and neighbors heard screaming and called 911 *while* her son Christopher was at the police station with Briggs." Sterling ran a hand through her hair. "So, yes, this is where I tell you to stay out of it."

Whether she'd wanted to or not, she'd listened to what I had to say about Christopher. Hearing from Briggs had been like a splash of cold water in her face.

I was wrong, I thought. The bits and pieces I'd picked up from my visit to Broken Springs—none of that mattered now. Trina was dead, and Christopher had been with Briggs when it happened.

He's just a guy. A guy with a dark truck and a mother who is a real piece of work. Who was a piece of work.

I pictured Trina, who thought my shoes were precious and that Daniel Redding would be released from prison on an appeal.

"Does Dean's dad have any open appeals?" I asked.

Agent Sterling didn't bat an eye at the change of subject. "None." She walked over to Briggs's desk and pulled something out of one of the drawers. She shut the drawer and walked back to me. "Put your foot on the couch," she ordered.

That was when I remembered. *The next time you take so*

much as a step out of Quantico without my permission, I'll have you fitted for an ankle tracker.

"You can't be serious," I said.

"Do I look like I'm joking?" Sterling asked. She looked like Judd had when we'd arrived back at the house. "I made you a promise," she told me, "and I always keep my promises." I didn't move, and she knelt down and clipped the tracker in place. "If you leave the yard, I'll know it. If you try to remove the tracker, I'll know it. If you violate the perimeter set into this anklet, a silent alarm will go off, sending a text directly to my phone and directly to Briggs's. The GPS in this anklet will allow us to pinpoint your location, and I will drag you back here kicking and screaming."

She stood back up. My mouth was dry. I couldn't force out an objection.

"You have good instincts," Sterling told me. "You have a good eye. Someday, you could be a very good agent."

The tracker was lighter than it looked, but the added weight, however slight, made my entire body feel heavy. Knowing I couldn't leave, knowing that I couldn't do anything—I hated it. I felt useless and weak and very, very young.

Sterling stood up. "But that day, Cassandra, is not today."

YOU

You can picture Trina Simms's last moments perfectly in your mind. In fact, now that the deed is done, you can't stop picturing it, over and over again.

Hands bound together. Plastic biting into fleshy wrists. Knife. Blood.

Your brain re-creates the moment in bright, Technicolor detail. Her skin isn't unblemished. It isn't smooth. The brand sinks in, in, in. . . .

Burning flesh smells the same whether or not it's supple, whether or not it's young. Just thinking about the brand sinking in, you can smell it. With each breath, you picture—

Rope around her neck. Dull, lifeless eyes.

Trina Simms was always shrill, deluded, demanding. She's not so demanding now.

CHAPTER 35

very lead we'd managed to turn up in this case had ended with a brick wall. We'd discovered that Emerson was having an affair with her professor, and then he'd turned up just as dead as she was. We'd sifted through the students' internet profiles only to find that every single one of them had an alibi. Michael, Dean, and I had gone to talk to Trina Simms. We'd been able to rule her out as a suspect, but hadn't realized that the killer had her in his sights.

If my instincts are so good, I wondered, *then why didn't I see this coming? Why was I so focused on Christopher Simms?*

I was supposed to be a Natural. I was supposed to be good at this. *Yeah, right.* So good that I hadn't realized Locke was a killer. So good that for all I knew, while I'd been profiling Christopher and talking myself into suspicions, the UNSUB might have been lurking nearby, just waiting for us to leave.

Nothing we'd done on this case had turned out the way

it was supposed to, and now I'd been put on an electronic leash. Like a criminal.

"As far as accessories go, it leaves something to be desired." Lia's response to the tracker secured around my ankle was predictably blasé. "Although that exact shade of black plastic does bring out the color of your eyes."

"Shut up."

"Cranky, cranky." Lia waggled a finger at me. I smacked her hand away. "You have to admit that it's deliciously ironic," she said, stowing her waggling finger safely away.

I didn't *have* to admit anything.

"Of all of us," Lia continued, "you're the least likely to be arrested. In fact, you might be the only one of us who *hasn't* been arrested. And yet . . ." She gestured toward my ankle.

"Yuk it up," I told her. "You might be next. Agent Sterling probably orders these things in bulk."

"Bit of a double standard, don't you think? The boys sneak out and get sentenced to each other's company. You sneak out, and—"

"Enough," I told Lia. "Sitting around and talking about it isn't going to change anything. Besides, this isn't our biggest problem."

Somebody still had to tell Dean what had happened to Trina Simms.

"We went to see her, and now she's dead." Dean summarized the entire situation in a single sentence.

"Temporal proximity doesn't imply causation," Sloane said,

patting him on the shoulder—the Sloane version of a comforting *there, there.*

"That's the question, isn't it?" Michael cut in. The five of us were gathered in the room the boys were now—apparently—sharing. Michael leaned back against the doorjamb and crossed one ankle over the other. "Was Trina already in the killer's sights, or did our visit somehow set the UNSUB off?"

Dean considered the question. "Emerson's murder was fairly well-planned." Flipping into profiler mode kept him from getting dragged back under to the dark place, but even when Dean was trying to distance himself from what had happened, he never stopped referring to Emerson by name. "The presentation of her corpse was precise. Based on our interactions with Sterling and Briggs over the last few days, I'm guessing they don't have much in the way of physical evidence. We're looking at someone with a high level of attention to detail—all of which suggests that our killer would be methodical in selecting his victims."

I closed my eyes and willed the tangled mass of thoughts in my mind to sort themselves out. "If the UNSUB is doing this because he identifies with Daniel Redding," I said, working through the logic as I spoke, "it makes sense that he would seek out someone who actually knows Redding for victim number two."

"Victim number three," Sloane reminded me. "You forgot the professor."

She was right. I'd left out the professor, because even

though Briggs and Sterling hadn't said a single thing about how he'd died, my gut didn't believe that the UNSUB had tortured the professor the way he'd tortured the females. Daniel Redding's original victims had all been female. Binding the women, branding them—that was about ownership. An UNSUB who identified with the method and brutality of this particular MO wouldn't relish the death of an older male the same way. The women were the main event; Fogle was just in the way.

Some things you do because you want to, I thought, *and some things you do because you* need *to.*

Dean didn't say anything about my omission of the professor from the victim list. He had tunnel vision of his own. "Emerson was twenty years old, blond, friendly, and well-liked by her classmates. Trina was in her late forties, brunette, neurotic, and based on her reaction to having visitors, socially isolated, except for two people: my father and her son."

Most killers had a type. What did Trina Simms and Emerson Cole have in common?

"Emerson's young. She's pretty." Dean's voice took on an odd hum. "She's sleeping with a man who fancies himself an expert on Daniel Redding. Maybe that's why I chose her."

When I profiled an UNSUB, I used the word *you.* When Dean profiled killers, he said *I.*

"Or maybe," Dean said, his lids heavy, his eyes nearly closed, "I chose a girl who wouldn't sleep with me, and then one who *was* sleeping with the man I'm emulating."

Dean's voice was eerily reflective. I could feel him sinking deeper and deeper into the possibilities. "If Redding weren't in prison, he would have killed Trina Simms himself. He would have sliced her up and strung her up and laughed every time she screamed."

Dean opened his eyes. For a few seconds, I wasn't sure if he was seeing us—any of us. I had no idea what he was thinking, but I knew somehow that something had changed—the air in the room, the look on his face.

"Dean?" I said.

He reached for the phone.

"Who are you calling?" Lia asked.

Dean barely looked up. "Briggs."

By the time Briggs answered the phone, Dean was pacing. "It's me," he said. Briggs started to say something back, but Dean cut him off. "I know you're at a crime scene. That's why I'm calling. I need you to look for something. I don't know what, not exactly." Dean sat down. It was the only way he could stop pacing. "Yell at me later, Briggs. Right now, I need to know if there's anything other than doilies and porcelain figures on the end tables or the coffee table at the Simms house." Dean rested his forearm on his knees and pressed his head into his arm. *"Just look and tell me what you see."*

Silence fell over the room for a minute, maybe more. Lia sent me a questioning look, but I shook my head. I was just as clueless about what was going on as she was. One second, he was profiling our UNSUB, and the next, he was on the phone, barking out orders.

"Nothing?" Dean said. He exhaled and sat up. "No baseball cards or Matchbox cars or fishing lures." Dean seemed to be trying to convince himself, more than anything else. "No books. No games." Dean nodded in response to some query the rest of us couldn't hear, then seemed to realize that Briggs wouldn't be able to see the nod. "No. I'm fine. I just had a thought. It's nothing. I'm sure it's nothing." I could see Dean trying to stop there, trying not to say anything else. He failed. "Can you look in her pockets?"

Another long silence. But this time, I saw the exact moment when Briggs replied. Dean's body went rigid. No more nervous energy. No more questions.

"Well, that's not good," Michael murmured beside me.

"We have a problem." Dean's voice was stiff, his posture the same. "I don't think our UNSUB is a copycat." He paused, then forced out a clarification. "I think my father has a partner."

CHAPTER 36

riggs and Sterling arrived back at the house late that night. None of us were asleep. We'd gathered in the kitchen, first to eat and then to wait. Around midnight, Judd had come in to chase us all to bed, but he'd ended up putting on a pot of coffee instead. By the time Agents Briggs and Sterling pushed open the door to the kitchen to see us crowded around the table, Sloane was just starting to wind down. The rest of us were silent—and had been for most of the night.

"Contents of Trina Simms's pockets." Briggs threw a clear plastic bag lightly down onto the table in front of us. Inside the bag was a single playing card—the king of spades.

"I wanted to be wrong." That was all Dean said at first. He slid the evidence bag to the edge of the table, but didn't pick it up. "I should have been wrong."

"What put the idea in your head?" Agent Sterling sounded hoarse. I wondered if she and Briggs had spent the evening yelling orders at people, or if finding out that the man who had kidnapped and tortured her now had a partner on the outside had taken a toll.

"I was profiling our UNSUB." Dean wasn't hoarse. He spoke in slow, even tones, his fingers playing with the edge of the card through the plastic. "I thought our guy might have targeted Trina Simms because if my father weren't in prison, he would have killed her himself. It made sense, the UNSUB's believing that killing Trina was a step toward becoming my father. But then"—Dean pulled his hand back from the card—"I thought about the fact that we'd gone to see her, Cassie and Michael and me."

I wasn't sure why that made a difference, why our visit had taken Dean from thinking that this was a copycat to thinking his father was involved, but he spelled it out for us, in brutal, uncompromising terms.

"I met her. I didn't like her. She died."

Like Gloria, the woman that Daniel Redding had introduced to his young son. *I told him I didn't want a new mother. And he looked at Gloria and said, "That's a shame."*

"I wanted that to be a coincidence," Dean continued. His hands folded themselves into fists in his lap, his fingernails digging into the palms of his hands. "But then I thought about the fact that when I was in the interrogation room with my father, he knew where to look for the professor." Dean shrugged. "That made sense. The professor had interviewed him multiple times. He was writing a book. Of course he might have mentioned his writing cabin." Dean turned to address the next words to Agent Briggs. "We should have known."

Lia picked up Dean's train of thought. "He told you the truth about the professor's location, but not the whole truth. That's what he does. He deals in technicalities and half-truths and seemingly white lies."

Dean didn't turn to look at Lia, but underneath the table, I saw his hand find its way briefly to hers. She grabbed hold of his and squeezed, hard enough that I wasn't sure she'd ever let go.

"I always knew that he was messing with our minds," Dean said. "I knew that he was manipulating us, but I should have at least considered the possibility that he was pulling our UNSUB's strings as well. People are just puppets to him, players on his stage."

"You told Briggs to look in the victim's pocket." I tried to get Dean to focus on specifics. Talking about concrete details was the only thing I could think of to help him keep the big picture at bay. "How did you know there would be something there?"

"I didn't." Dean lifted his eyes to mine. "But I did know that if my father was involved, if Trina died because I went to see her, he'd want me to know."

He'd want to send a message. That Dean was *his*. That Dean had always been *his*. He wasn't his mother's. He didn't belong to the FBI. He didn't even belong to himself. That was the message that Daniel Redding had sent his son, all with one little card.

"It's not just for you, Dean." Agent Sterling had been remarkably quiet this whole time. "It's for us, too—Briggs and me. He wants us to know that we're playing his game." Her lips pulled back, halfway between a grimace and a hard-edged smile. "He wants us to know that he's winning."

She pressed her lips together, then bared her teeth. "We should have seen it." The words that Agent Sterling had been holding back this entire conversation burst out of her mouth. "*I* should have seen it. The first murder showed all the hallmarks of an organized killer—the planning, the lack of physical evidence, the supplies the UNSUB brought to the scene. But there were things that didn't fit. The use of the car antenna to strangle the girl. The fact that the UNSUB attacked from behind. Dumping the body in a public location. That's impulsiveness, deviation from a set plan, and signs of self-confidence issues." Sterling blew out a long breath, willing her temper to dispel. "Organized. Disorganized. When a crime scene has the hallmarks of both, you're either dealing with an inexperienced UNSUB who's refining his technique—or you're dealing with two UNSUBs."

Dean let out a breath of his own. "A dominant, who makes the plans, and a subordinate, who helps carry it out."

Agent Sterling had put the UNSUB's age between twenty-three and twenty-eight, but she'd worked those numbers out based on the assumption that the UNSUB was acting alone. Factoring Redding into the equation changed things. It was still a safe bet that our UNSUB idolized Redding, that he longed for power and authority and control. The lack of a father figure in the UNSUB's adolescent years was still probably right on target. But if that was the role Redding was playing for the UNSUB, what was Dean's father looking to get out of it?

The same thing Locke wanted from me.

Suddenly, I was back at the safe house. Dean was lying unconscious on the floor. Michael had been shot. And Locke wanted—desperately, madly—for me to take the knife. She'd wanted me to be like her. She'd wanted me to be *hers*. At least she'd seen me as a person. To Daniel Redding, Dean was a thing. A marvelous creation, purely his, body and soul.

Maybe Redding was looking to re-create that with our UNSUB. Or maybe this whole case had just been a way to remind his wayward son who was in charge, to force Dean to come and see him, face-to-face.

"We should adjust the lower end of the age range for our UNSUB." I sounded calm, the way I always did when this part of my brain took over, converting even the most horrifying and personal situations into a puzzle to be solved. "To seventeen."

I didn't explain my reasoning, but I saw the second that the meaning behind those words registered to Dean. *He* was seventeen.

Briggs stared at me for a few seconds. "What are you thinking?"

He could have told me that this wasn't *our* UNSUB. He hadn't. I waited for Agent Sterling to object. She didn't.

This was the heat of the battle. We weren't dealing with a copycat. We were dealing with the man who had held Agent Sterling captive, tortured her. Redding was playing mind games with her from behind bars.

He was playing with Dean.

I didn't dwell on it, or think about how Agent Sterling would feel about all this a day from now, or a week, or a month. I turned back to Agent Briggs and answered his question.

"Our UNSUB and Redding aren't partners," I said. "Men like Daniel Redding don't have *partners*. They don't think they have *equals*." I searched for the right word. "The person we're looking for isn't a partner," I said finally. "It's an apprentice."

CHAPTER 37

The next morning, Agent Briggs brought Lia a DVD. "Recordings of every meeting we've had with Redding since this case started," he told her. "They're all yours."

Lia snatched the DVDs before Briggs could rethink the offer. Beside him, Sterling cleared her throat. "You don't have to do this," she said. "The director has approved your involvement on this case, but you're allowed to say no."

"You don't want us to." Michael took in the way she was standing, the look on her face. "You hate that you're even asking, but you hope to God we say yes."

"I'm in." Lia cut Michael off before he could read the agent any further. "So is Cassie, and so is Sloane."

Sloane and I didn't contradict her.

"I don't have anything better to do," Michael offered. His tone was casual, but his eyes were glittering with the same emotion I'd seen in him when he'd pulled Dean off of Christopher Simms. No one played games with the few people in this world he cared about.

"Lia, Michael, and Cassie, you'll be in the media room, going over these interviews with a fine-tooth comb." Briggs issued orders curtly and efficiently. "Redding thinks he has the advantage here. That changes *today*."

Agent Sterling focused her attention on Dean. "If you're up for it," she said, her voice quieter than it had been when she'd spoken to the rest of us, "Briggs is going to see your father."

Dean didn't say anything. He just pulled on a lightweight coat over his battered white T-shirt and turned toward the door.

Sterling turned to Briggs. "I guess that means he's up for it."

Asking Dean to do this had hurt her, but doing nothing, doing anything less than *everything she could* to put an end to this would have hurt her more. Agent Sterling wasn't wearing makeup. Her shirt wasn't tucked in. There was an energy to her, a raw determination that told me that I was looking at the Veronica Sterling that Dean had known.

The one who reminded Agent Sterling of me.

"You okay here?" Briggs asked her.

"You know me." Sterling smiled—all lips, no teeth. "I always land on my feet."

Briggs watched her for a beat, then followed Dean to the door.

"What about me?" Sloane called after him.

Agent Sterling was the one who answered. "How are you with geography?"

Sloane disappeared to the basement with a handful of maps to work up a geographical profile of Redding's partner. The rest of us sequestered ourselves away in the media room. Michael and I sat at opposite ends of the couch. Lia popped the DVD Briggs had given her into the player and plopped down between us, one leg pulled to her chest and the other stretched out. Agent Sterling took up a spot in the doorway, watching us watch the DVD as it began to play.

Daniel Redding was seated on one side of a long table. His hands were cuffed together and chained to the table, but from his posture, you'd have thought he was at a job interview. A door to his left opened and Agent Briggs came in, carrying a thin file. He sat down opposite Redding.

"Agent Briggs." There was something musical about the monster's voice, but it was his eyes that drew your attention: dark, soulful eyes, with the faintest hint of wrinkles at the corners. "To what do I owe this most inestimable pleasure?"

"We need to talk." Briggs was all business. He didn't rush the words. He didn't drag them out. "I understand that you've been getting an unusual amount of mail as of late."

Redding smiled. The expression looked self-effacing, almost boyish. "I'm an unusual man."

"The prison screens and catalogs your mail, but they don't keep copies of the letters."

"Rather sloppy of them," Redding opined. His hands were

folded on the table. He leaned forward, just a fraction of an inch. "One can never be too careful about one's . . . *records*."

Something in the way he said *records* made me think that he was really talking about something else—something targeted to get under Agent Briggs's skin.

Did Redding keep records of the women he'd killed?

Briggs didn't rise to the bait. "Have you received any letters you would classify as fan mail?" he asked, his voice taking on a slight mocking tone, like Daniel Redding was a member of some long-forgotten boy band and not a restless predator locked in a cage.

"Why, Agent Briggs, I do believe you need something." Redding feigned surprise, but the hum of pleasure in his voice was real. "Now, why would a man like you be interested in the letters received by a man like me? Why would you want to know that women write to tell me that they *love me*, that every day, my legacy lives on, that the lonely and the heartsick and the deliciously, darkly lost sheep of this world pour their souls into ink on the page, begging me, beckoning me toward them, so desperate are they for a shepherd."

Redding's voice was silky, his delivery of those words impossible to ignore.

"Why I'm asking these questions doesn't matter. What matters is that I can make your life significantly less pleasant if you don't answer them. How would you feel about a transfer? I hear there are some federal facilities that are *lovely* this time of year."

"Now, now, Agent Briggs. There's no need to resort to

threats. I think we both know that given even the slightest opportunity, you'd throw me in the deepest, darkest hole you could find. The fact that you haven't already means that you can't." Redding leaned forward, his eyes on Briggs's. "I wonder—do you ever get tired of the things you can't do? Can't catch every killer." Redding's voice took on a pouting tone, but his expression reminded me of a hawk, sharp-eyed and merciless, focused on one thing and one thing alone. "Can't keep a wife. Can't keep from coming back here. Can't get me out of your mind."

"I'm not here to play games with you, Redding. If you can't give me something, I have no reason to stay." Briggs leaned forward. "Maybe you'd prefer I left," he said, his voice as low and silky as Redding's.

"Go ahead," Redding replied. "Leave. I think we both know that you're not my type. Now the delectable Agent Sterling, on the other hand . . ."

A muscle in Briggs's neck visibly tensed, but he didn't snap. Instead, he pulled a photograph out of the file folder and laid it on the table. He pushed the photo forward, keeping it just out of Redding's reach.

"Well," Redding said, mesmerized, "this is an interesting turn of events."

He reached for the photograph and Briggs pulled it back. He placed it back in the folder and stood up. It took me a moment to realize what had just happened. This interview had been taped shortly after the first victim had turned up dead. I was willing to bet a lot of money that Briggs had just showed Redding a photograph of Emerson's body.

I could see in the killer's eyes that he wouldn't be able to tamp down the desire to see it again.

"They say that imitation is the sincerest form of flattery." Redding's gaze was no longer on Briggs's face. It was on the folder. "Where was she found?"

Briggs took his time answering the question, but ultimately doled out the answer—just enough to whet Redding's appetite for more. "Colonial University. The president's front lawn."

Redding snorted. "Showy," he said. "Sloppy."

His eyes were still on the folder. He wanted to see the picture. He wanted to study it.

"Tell me what I want to know," Briggs said evenly, "and I'll tell you what you want to know."

Briggs was counting on Redding's narcissism. He assumed the man would want to know everything he could about this imitator. What Briggs didn't know—and what we knew now—was that Redding wasn't criticizing the work of an imitator. He wasn't looking to see his infamy reflected in this girl's body.

He was a teacher, evaluating the performance of a prize pupil.

"I'm not interested in anything you have to say." Redding managed to pull his gaze from the folder. He leaned back in his metal chair, as far as he could with his wrists chained to the table. "But it's possible that I have some information that could be relevant to you."

"Prove it." Briggs threw down the challenge—to no avail.

"I want to talk to my son," the killer said flatly. "You've kept him from me for five years. What reason could I possibly have to help you?"

"Basic human decency?" Briggs suggested dryly. "If there were anything human or decent in you, maybe your son would want to see you."

"'Doubt thou the stars are fire,'" Redding responded in a singsong tone. "'Doubt that the sun doth move. Doubt truth to be a liar. . . .'"

Briggs finished the quote for him. "'But never doubt I love.' Shakespeare." He stood, gathering his things and slamming the door on the conversation. "You're not capable of loving anyone but yourself."

"And you're not capable of letting this go." Redding smiled again, equal parts serene and smug. "You want me to talk? I'll talk. I'll tell you who's been writing to me, and who's been a very, very bad boy. I'll lay out everything you want to know—but the only person I'm talking to is Dean."

The screen went black. Redding and Briggs were gone, replaced a moment later by an eerily similar scene, except that this time, Dean was the one sitting opposite his father, and Briggs sat adjacent to Dean.

"Dean." Redding relished the word. "You've brought me a gift, Agent Briggs," he said, never taking his eyes off his son. "Someday, I will return the favor."

Dean stared at a spot just over his father's shoulder. "You wanted me here. I'm here. Now talk."

Redding obliged. "You look like your mother," he said, drinking in Dean's features like a dying man in the desert. "Except for the eyes—those are mine."

The way Redding said the word *mine* made my stomach roll.

"I didn't come here to talk about my mother."

"If she were here, she'd tell you to get your hair cut. Sit up straight. Smile every once in a while."

Dean's hair fell into his face, his eyes narrowed to slits beneath it. "There's not much to smile about."

"Don't tell me you've lost the taste for life already, Dean. The boy I knew had so much *potential*."

A muscle in Dean's jaw twitched. He and Redding sat staring at each other. After a full minute of silence ticked by, Dean's eyes narrowed, and he said, "Tell me about the letters."

This was where Agent Sterling and I had come in the first time around. It was harder to watch the second time: Dean trying to get his father to part with some scrap of information, Daniel Redding sparring with him verbally, bringing the topic back to Dean again and again.

"I want to know about you, Dean. What have those hands been doing the past five years? What sights have those eyes seen?"

You knew Briggs would come to see you as soon as the first body turned up. You knew that Dean would come if you refused to talk to anyone else. You planned this, step by step.

"I don't know what you want me to say." On the screen,

Dean's voice was getting louder, more intense. "There's nothing to talk about. Is that what you want to hear? That these hands, these eyes—they're *nothing*?"

"They're everything." This time, I could see a manic intensity in Redding's eyes. He looked at Dean, and the only thing he saw was himself—a god, not subject to man's laws, above things like empathy and guilt. I thought about the card that Briggs had found in Trina's pocket—the king of spades.

Redding wanted immortality. He wanted power. But more than anything, he wanted an heir.

Why now? I thought. *Why is he doing all of this now?* He'd sat in that prison for five years. Had it taken that long to find someone to do his bidding on the outside, or had something happened to push him into doing this?

On the screen, Dean's father had just asked if there was a girl. Dean denied it. Redding called him "son," and Dean said the five words that triggered the man to lash out.

"I am not your son."

Even knowing it was coming, the sudden rush of violence took me off guard. Redding's fists were buried in the front of Dean's shirt. He jerked him close and told him that he was and would always be his father's son.

"You know it. You fear it."

This time, I saw the instant Dean snapped, the moment when the anger that Michael had told me was always present beneath the surface bubbled up and overflowed. Dean's face was like stone, but there was something wild in his eyes as he grabbed his father, pulling him halfway across the table, as far as the other man's chains would allow.

This time, as Briggs broke up the fight, I saw Redding smile. He'd gotten what he wanted. A hint of violence. A taste of Dean's *potential*.

My eyes were riveted on the screen. This was the last thing I'd seen the first time around. Briggs waited a moment or two, to make sure Dean was finished, before he backed off—but I noticed that this time, he didn't sit, positioning himself just behind Dean.

"Where is the professor's cabin?" Briggs asked.

Dean's father smiled. "Catoctin," he said. "I don't know anything more specific than that."

Dean asked two or three more questions, but his father didn't have anything else useful to say.

"We're done here," Briggs said. Dean stood. His father remained sitting, perfectly relaxed. Briggs put a hand on Dean's shoulder and began steering him out of the room.

"Have you ever told Briggs precisely what you did to his wife, Dean?" Daniel Redding didn't raise his voice, but the question seemed to suck all the oxygen out of the room. "Or does he still think it was me who drew the knife slowly down her shoulders and thighs, me who sank the brand into her flesh?"

Briggs's grip on Dean tightened. If he'd been steering him toward the door before, he was shoving him now—anything to get Dean out of there. But Dean's feet were suddenly glued to the floor.

Go, I told Dean silently. *Just go.*

But he didn't.

Redding relished the moment. "Tell your agent friend there what you did, Dean. Tell him how you came out to the barn where I had Veronica Sterling bound hand and foot. Tell him how I went to cut her—how you took the knife from my hand, not to save her, but to do it yourself. Tell him how you made her bleed. Tell him how she screamed when you burned an *R* into her flesh. Tell him how you asked me for her." Redding closed his eyes and tilted his head toward the ceiling, like a man offering thanks to his gods. "Tell him she was your first."

First victim. For Redding, that was the only *first* that mattered, no matter how much innuendo he might jam into the word.

Briggs slammed the door open. "Guard!"

A guard—the one who'd given Agent Sterling and myself a front-row seat to the first half of this show—appeared, disgust barely contained on his face. He went to restrain Redding. "Even if you find the professor in his cabin," Dean's father called after him, his voice echoing, surrounded by metal walls, "you won't find what you're looking for. The most interesting letters I've received, those that show rather remarkable *attention to detail*—those letters didn't come from the professor. They came from one of his students."

286

The room fell into silence. Lia paused the DVD. I stood up and walked toward the door, my back to Michael and Lia. In the doorway, Agent Sterling calmly met my eyes. She didn't comment on the contents of the interviews.

Did Dean really brand you? I asked her silently. *Did Dean—our Dean—torture you?*

She had no answers for me.

"I only caught Redding in one lie."

I turned back toward Lia, hoping that she'd tell me what I wanted to hear—that Redding had lied about Dean.

"When he told Briggs that he wasn't interested in anything he had to say—that wasn't true. He wanted to know everything about Emerson Cole's murder. He was hungry for the details, which means that he didn't have them already. Whoever his protégé is, our UNSUB didn't exactly record the nitty-gritty and send them to his good old sensei."

"That's it?" I asked Lia. "Everything else he said was true?"

Lia looked down at the ground. "Everything."

"That means that he did get some remarkable letters from a student in Fogle's class," I said. "To a man like Redding, 'attention to detail' probably means some pretty explicit descriptions of violence."

"And yet," Michael chimed in, "every student in that class has an alibi."

"Misdirection." Lia said the word lightly, but I heard the bite buried in her tone. "You can deceive people without lying. Liars are like magicians: while you're watching the beautiful assistant, they're slipping the rabbit out of a sleeve."

Watching these interviews—particularly the one with Dean—had been almost physically painful. I refused to believe that we'd learned nothing about this case.

"So assume everything about the letters and the professor was the beautiful assistant," I said. "What's left? What did we learn?" *Other than the fact that Redding claims that Dean tortured Agent Sterling himself.*

"Daniel Redding's emotions are flat." Michael dangled his legs over the edge of the couch, and I knew that—like me—he was avoiding the elephant in the room. "He doesn't feel fear, ever. He can feel pleasure, but not happiness. No regret. No remorse. Most of the time, his expression is dominated by more cerebral emotions: self-satisfaction, curiosity, amusement, a desire to twist the knife. He's calculated, restrained, and the only thing that gets real emotion out of him is Dean."

My every impression of Dean's father had been confirmed. Redding was possessive. He'd snapped every time Dean had denied their relationship. He'd done everything he could to make Dean think that they were the same—to separate him from everyone else, starting with Agent Briggs.

"Did Briggs know?" I asked. "About . . . what Redding said at the end? About Dean?"

I couldn't put more than that into words.

"He knew." Agent Sterling spoke for the first time since we'd started watching the videos. Without elaborating, she walked over to Lia, grabbed the remote, and pressed play. A third interview started a moment later.

A guard—one I'd never seen before—escorted Sterling into the room. Instead of taking a seat across from Redding, she remained standing.

"Veronica Sterling." Dean's father said those words like the beginning of some kind of incantation. "I have to say, I'm surprised your dearest husband—excuse me, *ex*-husband—allowed you in such close quarters with the devil incarnate."

Sterling shrugged. "You're just a man. A pathetic little man living in a cage."

"Briggs doesn't know you're here, does he?" Redding asked. "What about your father? No, he doesn't know, either, does he? So tell me, Ms. Sterling, why are you here?"

"You know why I'm here."

"That pesky little case of yours?" Redding said. "I'm afraid I've told your Agent Briggs and my Dean everything I know."

"Liar." Sterling said the word on the screen at the exact same time that Lia muttered the word beside me.

Redding responded. "I'm hurt—and here I thought we had a very special relationship."

"Because I'm the one that got away?" Sterling asked. A muscle in Redding's cheek twitched.

"Direct hit," Michael murmured.

Redding recovered quickly. "Have the scars faded? The knife wounds were shallow enough—it was the boy's first time taking the lead, you know. But the brand—the brand won't fade, will it? You'll have my initial stamped into your flesh for the rest of your life. Can you still smell your scorching skin? Can you feel it?"

"No," Agent Sterling said, taking a seat. To my surprise, she reached up and lowered her shirt, exposing the scar. Redding's lips parted.

"Correction," Michael commented, "there are two things that bring out real emotion in Daniel Redding."

I wasn't the expert Michael was with emotions, but I could see it, too—the way the convicted killer was singing hallelujah with his eyes.

Agent Sterling let her own lips part and traced the letter on her chest. For the first time, she was firmly in control of this interview. He should have seen the steel in her expression, but he didn't.

"This isn't your initial," she said, dropping her voice to just above a whisper. "This is *Dean's* initial. We knew you were listening. We knew you'd be back to check his work, and that the only way you'd believe that he didn't have ulterior motives was if there was proof." Her finger made another loop of the *R*. "I told him to do it. I begged him to, I made him *promise* to, and he did—no matter how sick it made him, no matter how much it has haunted him ever since, *he did it*. And it worked."

"No."

"You believed the act. You trusted him, because you wanted to believe that he was *your* son, that there was nothing of his mother in him. More fool, you." Sterling righted her shirt. "I didn't *escape*, Daniel. Dean let me go. He covered for me."

"You're lying." Redding could barely get the words out around clenched teeth.

"He warned me away from you. I wasn't listening. I didn't understand, and when I came by without backup, when you jumped me—he was watching. He had a plan, and he executed that plan at all costs." She smiled. "You should be proud. He's just as brilliant as you are, smart enough, even, to pull one over on dear old dad."

Redding leaped for Agent Sterling, but she leaned back, and the chain caught him.

"Like a dog on a leash," she said.

"I will kill you." Redding's voice was dull, but the words did not ring hollow—not at all. "You have no idea what I'm capable of. None at all."

Sterling didn't reply. She walked back out of the room, and the screen went black.

"You asked Dean to *brand you*?" Lia was the first one to find her voice.

"We needed Redding to believe that Dean was going to kill me and that he didn't need to be supervised." Sterling met Lia's gaze. "Sometimes you do what you have to in order to survive."

Lia knew that—the same way Dean knew it, the same way Michael knew it. I thought of Sloane counting holes in a shower drain and working obsessively through the night and me telling Locke that I'd killed my own mother—stalling so that Michael could kill her.

You do what you need to do to survive.

"Whatever," Lia said. "I'm going to see how Sloane is doing." She didn't want to talk about survival, and I filed that away for future reference. Needing to get away, I followed Lia to the basement. We found Sloane sitting in the middle of a fake foyer, maps and geographical surveys spread out all around her.

"Found anything?" I asked.

Sloane lifted her head from the maps, but her eyes didn't quite focus on us. She was still stuck in her head, calculating something, her thoughts loud enough that the rest of the world just faded away.

Lia nudged her with the tip of her toe. Sloane snapped out of it and met Lia's eyes. "Geographical profiling is surprisingly unsatisfying," she said, sounding mildly disgruntled.

She rearranged the papers in front of her and gestured for us to take a closer look. I knelt down.

"Most killers target victims within a set radius of their home." Sloane gestured to three sets of circles on the map, each with a different center. "Emerson Cole. Professor Fogle. Trina Simms. Fogle's cabin is a three-hour drive from Colonial, which is just as far from Broken Springs." Together, the three dots on the map resembled a piece of pie. "Even if you set the radius at a two- to three-hour drive, the overlap is still tiny."

"Isn't that a good thing?" I ventured. "The smaller the overlap, the fewer places we have to look."

"But that's just it," Sloane said. "There's really only one thing that jumps out about that small slice of the map."

Lia saw it before I did. "The prison where they're keeping Dean's dad."

"It makes sense," I said. "Redding calls the shots. Redding is the focal point."

"But we already *knew* that!" Sloane was almost shouting. She bit her bottom lip, and I realized how helpless she felt down here: alone, unable to make a difference, no matter how many times she did the math.

"Come on," I said, hooking an arm through hers and making her stand up. "Let's go fill Agent Sterling in."

Sloane looked like she might argue, but Lia preempted it.

"It's always the little things," she told Sloane gently. "A tenth of a second, a single piece of information—you never know what will make a difference."

A second after we made it to the first floor, the front door slammed. For a moment, Lia, Sloane, and I froze, then we made a beeline for the entryway. Sterling and Michael met us on the way there. We all came to a standstill at once.

Dean was taking off his coat. Briggs had his arms folded over his chest, waiting. Clearly, he'd expected the rush.

"Anything?" he asked Lia.

"Nothing other than the obvious: he's been dancing a long, slow waltz around the truth."

"You?" Sterling asked Briggs.

"Do you want the good news first or the bad news?"

"Surprise me," Sterling said dryly.

"We have DNA." Briggs allowed himself a brief smile— the FBI agent's version of dancing a jig. "Trina Simms got our UNSUB with her fingernails."

Was it normal for an UNSUB to leave no evidence behind at the first two crime scenes and let his victim scratch him at the third? After all, practice made perfect—and Daniel Redding struck me as the type who valued perfection, planning, and attention to detail.

"DNA doesn't do us much good without a suspect to match it to," Dean said under his breath.

Michael arched an eyebrow. "I'm guessing that means you two didn't get anything out of ye olde mastermind?"

That was the first time in my memory that Michael hadn't referred to Daniel Redding either as Dean's father or by name. It was a subtle kindness coming from a boy who frequently called Dean by the last name he shared with the monster, just to get under his skin.

"My father," Dean said, negating Michael's efforts, "refused to see us. We forced a meeting, and he wouldn't talk."

"That's not true." Lia shot Dean an apologetic look, but preemptively waved off any protests. "He did say something."

"Nothing that bears repeating." Dean met Lia's eyes, daring her to call him a liar again.

"Nothing you want to repeat," she corrected quietly.

Briggs cleared his throat. "Redding said that he didn't feel like talking today. He said he might feel like talking tomorrow. We've got him in complete isolation—no visitors, no phone calls, no mail, no contact with other prisoners. But we have no idea what instructions he's already communicated to his partner."

He might feel like talking tomorrow. Briggs's words echoed in my mind, and I whipped my head to look at Dean. "You think that someone else is going to die tomorrow."

That was just Redding's style, to refuse to talk until he had something else to gloat about. The refusal to see Dean, though—that would have surprised me if I hadn't just seen Agent Sterling clueing Daniel Redding in to the fact that his son had betrayed him. Dean's father would want to punish him for that, almost as much as he wanted to punish Agent Sterling for having the gall not just to live, but to steal from him the one thing that mattered most.

His son.

"What else?" I asked. I knew that Dean and Briggs were leaving something out. Redding wouldn't have let Dean walk out of that room without doing something to reestablish his power—to hurt Dean, to make him suffer for betraying his father.

Briggs exhaled loudly. Then he turned to me. "There was one other thing."

"*No.*" Dean's objection was immediate and absolute.

"Dean—"

"I said no."

"That's not your decision to make," Briggs told Dean. "The hardest part of this job isn't being willing to put yourself on the line—your safety, your sanity, your reputation. The hardest part is letting people you care about do the same."

Dean turned toward the kitchen. I thought he would walk away, but he didn't. He stood there, his back to the rest of us, as Agent Briggs told us about Redding's parting shot.

"He said that if we wanted to talk to him sooner, rather than later, that Dean wouldn't come alone next time."

"He wasn't alone," I replied, wondering if Redding had been angling for another visit from Sterling.

"If you're going to tell them, you may as well tell them exactly what he said." Dean turned back around. He tried to look at Michael, at Sterling, at Briggs—anywhere but at me. He failed. "He said, *Next time, bring the girl.*"

YOU

A mistake.

That's what this is. Not the fact that Trina Simms is dead—that was part of the plan. But leaving evidence behind?

Sloppy. Stupid. Unworthy.

It won't happen again. You'll make sure of that. There won't be any more mistakes.

Hidden in the shadows, you slide your finger along the flat side of the knife. You cut the perfect length of rope. The brand is heavy in your hand. You swing it once, through the air, like a baseball bat. You imagine the satisfying thunk of metal hitting skull—

No.

That's not how it's done. That's not what you're going to do in five . . . four . . . three . . . two . . .

"What are you doing here?"

You take a swing with the brand. Down your quarry goes, and you don't regret it.

Bind them. Brand them. Cut them. Hang them.

No one said you couldn't knock them out first.

You toss the brand to the ground and take out the zip ties. Emerson Cole was an assignment, but this—this is going to be fun.

CHAPTER 39

"**H**ow does Redding even know there *is* a girl?" Director Sterling paced the length of the kitchen, past Briggs, past his daughter, past all of us until he came to a stop in front of Dean.

"He asked," Dean answered flatly. "I told him there was no one."

From the kitchen table, Judd kept watch over Director Sterling as the director's weighty gaze settled on Dean.

"So either Redding didn't believe you, he knows something, or he's playing the odds." The director considered those possibilities. "I don't like the idea of bringing any of the others into an interrogation. If the wrong people got wind of it . . ." He trailed off.

You already brought Dean into an interrogation, I thought, *but if anyone found out you'd used Dean to get information out of his father, you could explain.*

"Can't say I'm too fond of the idea of putting any of you in a room with a serial killer, either," Judd commented, nursing his coffee. "Not that anyone asked."

"*However*," the director continued, ignoring Judd, "I could put another call into the warden. If we can install our own people as security and clear the cell block of prisoners and guards, I'm willing to entertain the idea of sending one of the girls in."

"Me," I said, speaking for the first time since Briggs had told us about Redding's request. "It has to be me."

I was the one who'd gone with Dean to Broken Springs. If the UNSUB had managed to communicate that to Redding, I was the one he wanted.

"I could do it." Lia didn't bother prefacing those words with anything else. "Daniel said he'd talk if you brought the girl. He never said which one."

"Lia." Dean said her name quietly. She turned around in her seat to face him. "If I don't want Cassie in a room with him, what makes you think I would be any happier putting you on the chopping block?"

"I can take care of myself." Lia sounded remarkably like Dean—the words were simple and soft, with none of her normal flare.

"And I can't?" I asked, insulted.

"Maybe I should go," Sloane said thoughtfully.

"No," everyone in the room—including the director—said at once.

"I know jujitsu," Sloane cajoled. "And besides, from what I've gathered, this particular witness specializes in mind games and subtle suggestion, and that won't work on me. I get numbers and facts and the literal meanings of words. Subtle gets lost in translation."

No one could argue with Sloane's logic.

"I can probably offend him without even trying to!" Sloane was sounding altogether too enthusiastic now. "If things get too intense, I'll tell him some statistics about domesticated ferrets."

"That's . . . errr . . . a very generous offer, Sloane, but I'd prefer you stay behind the scenes." The director's voice came out somewhat strangled. "There's a two-way mirror. Once we've secured the area, there's no reason the rest of you can't observe."

"I can think of a few." Judd set his coffee down.

"With all due respect, Judd," the director replied tightly, "this is FBI business." And Judd wasn't FBI. After a tense moment of silence, our caretaker stood and walked out of the room.

"Cassie, Dean, and Briggs will go in," the director declared in the resulting silence.

"Why?" Dean took a step toward the director. "Why send anyone in? We haven't gotten a thing out of him, and we're not going to. He's going to play with us, and someone else is going to die. We're wasting time. We're doing exactly what he wants."

"He's on edge." Agent Sterling responded before the director could. "He's a narcissist. If we give him enough rope, he'll hang himself, Dean."

"I guess that's why he was so easy to catch the first time," Dean retorted.

"I went to see him. I riled him up, and that's going to work to our advantage." Agent Sterling took a step toward Dean. "He doesn't just want to win this game. He wants to win in a way that haunts us—and that means that if he thinks he's got the upper hand, he *will* tell us something. There *will* be clues, because he will want me up at night five years from now, wondering why I didn't see it."

"You won't have to see it," Michael interjected. He looked at Lia. "If we're on the other side of that glass, *we* will."

"What happened to keeping us out of this case?" Dean appealed to Agent Sterling, his voice hard. "Wasn't that what you wanted—for us to be *normal* and *safe*?"

That was a low blow.

"If I could give you *normal*, I would." Agent Sterling's voice was sharp. "But I can't, Dean. I can't erase the things that have happened to you. I can't make you—any of you—*want* normal. I tried to keep you out of it. I've tried treating you all like kids, and *it doesn't work*. So, yes, I'm an enormous hypocrite, but if the five of you can help us stop that man from taking even one more life, I'm not going to fight you on it." She looked at her father. "I'm *done* fighting you on it."

The interrogation room was smaller than it had looked on-screen and more claustrophobic than it had felt from the other side of the mirror. Dean, Briggs, and I arrived first. One of the agents on Briggs's team, who I recognized as

Agent Vance, went to get Dean's father from the prison officials. Once the director had pointed out that Redding's involvement in this case had happened under the warden's nose, the warden had been accommodating—a nice contrast to what Agent Sterling and I had dealt with on our *last* visit.

I took a seat at the table and waited for Dean and Briggs to sit down beside me.

They stayed standing, hovering over my shoulder like a pair of Secret Service agents flanking the president. The door to the room opened with a creak, and it took everything in me not to turn and track Daniel Redding's progress from the door to the table. Agent Vance fixed the chains, tested them, and then stepped back.

"So," Redding said, eyes only for me. "You're the girl."

There was a musical quality to his voice that hadn't come across in the recordings.

"You're quiet," Redding commented. "And pretty." He flashed me a subtle smile.

"Not that pretty," I said.

He tilted his head to the side. "You know, I think you believe that." He paused. "Modesty is such a refreshing trait for someone in your generation. In my experience, most young people *over*estimate their traits and abilities. They get too confident too quickly."

The DNA under Trina Simms's nails, I thought. There was no way that Redding could know about that—and yet,

I was aware that there were two layers to this conversation: the obvious and what lay underneath.

Agent Briggs put a hand on my shoulder, and I turned my attention to the list of questions in front of me—Agent Sterling's list.

"I have some questions," I said. "If I ask them, will you answer them?"

"I'll do you one better," Redding told me. "I'll tell you the truth."

We'd see about that. Or, more specifically, *Lia* would see about that from her position behind the two-way mirror.

"Let's talk about your partner," I said.

"*Partner* isn't the word I would have chosen."

I knew that—and I'd used it on purpose. Agent Sterling had suggested that it was to our benefit if Redding thought he was in charge. Let him think me an ordinary girl, not an adversary.

"What word would you use?"

"Let's go with *apprentice*."

"Is your apprentice a college student?" I asked.

Redding didn't hesitate, not even for a second. "Yes."

"Is your apprentice someone who's never been to college?"

If Redding thought it odd that I was asking two versions of the same question, he gave no indication of it. "Yes."

"Is your apprentice under the age of twenty-one?"

"Yes."

"Is your apprentice over the age of twenty-one?"

He smiled. "Yes."

"Is your apprentice someone you met through the mail?"

"Yes."

"Is your apprentice someone you met in person?"

"Yes."

There were more questions. I asked them. He answered in similar fashion. When I reached the end of Sterling's questions, I spent a second hoping that Lia would be able to tell us which answer in each pair had been true and which had been the lie.

"Any other questions?" Redding asked.

I swallowed. I was supposed to say no. I was supposed to get up and walk out of this room, but I couldn't. "Are you trying to replace Dean?" I asked. It was hard to look at him and not see Locke and the way she'd fixated on me.

"No. A man does not simply *replace* his finest work." Redding smiled. "My turn: do you care for my son?"

"Yes." I kept my answer short. "Why did you want me to come here?"

"Because if you're a part of Dean's life, you're a part of mine." There was something about the look in Redding's eyes that was chilling. "Do you know what he's done? What he is?"

I could feel Dean stiffening behind me, but I didn't give in to the urge to turn around. "I know about Veronica Sterling. I know about Gloria, and all the others."

That wasn't quite true—but I let Redding think that Dean had told me everything.

"And you don't care?" Redding said, tilting his head to one side and staring at me, *into* me. "You're drawn to darkness."

"No," I said. "I'm drawn to Dean, and I do care, because I care about him. My turn—and you owe me two questions."

"Ask away."

My instincts were telling me that Briggs wouldn't let this go on for much longer. I had to choose my questions carefully.

"How do you choose who dies?" I asked.

Redding put his palms flat on the table. "I don't."

He was lying. He had to be. The only connection between Trina Simms and Emerson Cole was that they both had a connection to Redding.

"I believe I owe you one more answer."

"Fine," I said. "Tell me something I don't know."

Redding chuckled. "I like you," he said. "I do."

I waited. *Give him enough rope,* I thought, *and he'll hang himself.*

"Something you don't know," Redding mused. "Okay. Let's try this one: you will never find the man who murdered your mother."

I couldn't reply. I couldn't breathe. My mouth was cotton-dry. My mother? What did he know about my mother?

"That's enough," Dean said sharply.

"Oh, but we're having such a nice little chat," Redding said. "We prisoners do a lot of that, you know. Chatting."

He wanted me to believe that he'd heard something through the prison grapevine about what had happened to my mother. That meant that he knew who I was—or at least, knew enough about me to know that I had a mother who was missing, presumed dead.

Despite the way my heart pounded in my chest, I was suddenly possessed of an unnatural calm. "Tell me something I don't know about this case," I said.

"Allow me to share my master plan," Redding said wryly. His tone was joking, but his eyes were dead. "I'm going to sit in my cell and wait, and while I wait, two more people are going to die. Agent Briggs will get the call about one of them any minute, and the other is going to die sometime tomorrow. Then the victims will start piling up. Body after body after body, because Briggs and Sterling aren't good enough." Redding lifted his gaze from my face to Briggs's. "Because you aren't smart enough." He let his eyes travel to Dean. "Because you're weak."

I pushed my chair back from the table, bumping into Dean as I did. He kept his balance, and I stood up.

We're done here, I thought, but I didn't say it out loud. Single file, Briggs, Dean, and I walked out of the room, leaving Dean's father chained to the table alone.

CHAPTER 40

We joined the rest of the team in the observation room. Sloane was sitting cross-legged on top of a nearby desk, her blond hair barely contained in a messy ponytail, her posture unnaturally straight. Agent Sterling stood beside her, a few feet behind Lia, who was still staring at Redding through the two-way mirror, her arms crossed over her chest, painted fingernails resting on her elbows. On the other side of the mirror, Agent Vance entered to transfer the prisoner back to his cell.

A hand grazed my shoulder, and I turned. Michael didn't say anything—he just studied my face.

I couldn't turn my face away from his. I didn't tell him I was fine or that Redding hadn't gotten under my skin—whatever I was or wasn't, Michael already knew. There was no use belaboring the point.

"Are you okay?" Agent Sterling actually verbalized the question. I wasn't sure if she was talking to me or to Dean.

I sidestepped the question for both of us. "Ignore the bit about my mother," I told Lia. "Focus on the case. How much of what Redding told me in there was true?"

Lia finally managed to pull her eyes away from the mirror. For a few seconds, I thought she would ignore my instructions. I willed her not to. She'd said it herself: the best liars were magicians. Whether Dean's father had been lying or telling the truth when he'd said I would never find my mother's killer, I didn't want to know. *Misdirection.* My mother's case was five years old. Our UNSUB was out there killing *now*.

"Well?" I said. "What was everyone's favorite psychopath lying about?"

Lia crossed the room and flopped down into an office chair, flinging a hand to each side. "Nothing."

"Nothing?" I repeated.

Lia slammed her palm into the side of the chair. "Nothing. I don't even know how he's doing this." She shot to her feet again, vibrating with anger and too restless to stay still. "There were two versions of every question. I was supposed to be able to contrast his responses. That should have made things easy, but I would *swear* that every single answer was true." She cursed—creatively and with impressive verve. "What is *wrong* with me?"

"Hey." Dean reached out and grabbed her arm as she paced by him. "It's not your fault."

She jerked out of his grasp. "Then whose fault is it? The other deception reader in the room who is apparently *completely useless*?"

"What if you're not?" Sloane interjected. Her eyes weren't quite focused on the here and now. I could practically hear the gears in her head turning. "Not useless, I mean," she said, haphazardly pushing white-blond bangs out of her eyes with the heel of her hand. "What if he *was* telling the truth, every single time?"

Lia shook her head hard enough to send her ponytail swishing. "That's not possible."

"It is," Sloane said, "if there's more than one apprentice."

Is your apprentice a college student?

Is your apprentice someone who's never been to college?

Is your apprentice over the age of twenty-one?

Is your apprentice under the age of twenty-one?

Oh, God.

Sloane was right. Redding could have answered every single question truthfully if he was working with *two* people on the outside—very different people on paper, but equally easy for Redding to manipulate, with equal tastes for violence and control.

Briggs weighed the possibility. "So Redding gives us answers specifically designed to make us think he's just jerking us around, when in reality, he's telling us exactly why this case has never added up."

Why Emerson Cole's murder had appeared to be the work of a primarily organized, extremely precise offender who left behind no evidence, while Trina Simms's killer had killed her within earshot of her neighbors and left his DNA at the scene.

Briggs's phone rang. The rest of us fell into silence. Redding's promise that the bodies were going to start piling up echoed in my mind. *Agent Briggs will get the call about one of them any minute.*

Beside me, Michael watched Briggs out of the side of his eye, until the older man turned his back to us. I raised an eyebrow at Michael. He shook his head.

Whatever Briggs was feeling, it wasn't good.

Keeping his voice low, Briggs stepped out into the hallway, allowing the door to slam shut behind him. In the silence that followed, none of us wanted to put the likely into words.

There's been another murder.

I couldn't just stand there, waiting for Briggs to come back and tell us that someone else was dead. I kept picturing the victims' faces—Emerson's lifeless eyes, Trina's widening when she realized who Dean was.

Two killers, I thought, focusing on the UNSUBs and not the victims. I let the thought take hold. *One killer who left evidence. One who didn't. Both under Redding's control.*

Briggs came back into the room. He must have hung up, but he still had a death grip on his phone. "We have another body."

"Where?" Agent Sterling asked.

The expression on Briggs's face was grim. "Colonial University."

My mind went straight to the people we'd met there, the others in Professor Fogle's class.

"Anyone we know?" Michael managed to keep his tone neutral.

"The victim was nineteen." Briggs was in full-on FBI mode—all business. "Male. According to his roommate, who discovered the body, his name was Gary Clarkson."

A breath caught in my throat. Lia slumped back against the mirror.

Clark.

Briggs and Sterling didn't take us to the crime scene. They dropped us off at the house, then went themselves. No matter how many lines they crossed, there were still limits. They wouldn't risk anyone—including the killer—seeing us at the crime scene. Not when they could, at least theoretically, bring us pictures that would work just as well.

We waited. By the time Briggs and Sterling got back, a restless pallor had settled over the house.

They didn't come bearing pictures. They came with news.

"Forensics is still processing the evidence, but they won't find any trace of the killer," Agent Sterling said. "This UNSUB bludgeoned the victim with an iron brand, but followed the rest of Redding's MO down to the tiniest detail. He was confident, not frantic. He enjoyed himself."

He's learning, I thought.

"It sounds more like the UNSUB who killed Emerson Cole than the one who killed Trina Simms," I said out loud, my mind flipping into high gear. *Two UNSUBs. UNSUB 1 was organized. He'd killed Emerson and Clark—and quite possibly the professor. UNSUB 2 was disorganized. He'd murdered Trina Simms right after we'd gone to visit her.*

"What's the connection?" Dean asked. "How does someone go from targeting Emerson to targeting Clark?"

"They were in the same group in Fogle's class," Lia offered. "Clark was head over heels for the girl."

"His dorm room was full of pictures of her," Briggs confirmed. "Thousands of them, under his bed."

"What about the other two people in their group?" I asked. "Derek and Bryce. Think UNSUB 1 could be going after them next?"

First Emerson. Then Clark. Meanwhile, UNSUB 2 kills Trina Simms. . . .

My thoughts were interrupted by the ding of incoming texts—one from Sterling's phone and one from Briggs's.

"Forensics?" Michael guessed.

Sloane naysayed him. "It's too soon. Even if results are being rushed, they can't have run more than one or two tests—"

"The tests *were* rushed," Briggs interrupted. "But the only thing they've managed to do so far is take a sample of our victim's DNA."

"Why did that merit simultaneous texting?" Lia asked suspiciously.

"Because a match came up in the system." Briggs shrugged off his suit jacket and folded it neatly over one arm. It was a restrained action, one that didn't match the look in his eyes in the least. "Clark's DNA matches the sample found under Trina Simms's fingernails."

I took a moment to process the implication. Sloane was obliging enough to put it into words.

"So what you're saying," she replied, "is that Gary Clarkson isn't just victim number four. He's also our second UNSUB."

YOU

You can still see the look in that pudgy, pathetic little hanger-on's eyes when you dug the point of the knife into his chest.

"This is how you're supposed to do it," you'd told him, zigging and zagging your way down his abundant flesh. "Every moment, perfect control. No evidence. No chances."

After you'd received word that Trina Simms was dead, you'd imagined how it should have gone down. You'd pictured every detail—how you would have done it. The pleasure you would have gotten from hearing her scream.

But this imitation, this pretender—he'd done it wrong.

He'd had to pay.

Sweat and tears had mingled on his face. He'd struggled, but you took your time. You were patient. You explained to him that you were acquainted with Trina Simms and that she deserved better.

Or worse, depending on your perspective.

You'd showed that pale imitation, that copy of a copy, what patience really was. The only shame was that you had to gag him—couldn't risk Joe College next door coming over to see what the little pig was squealing about.

You smile in memory as you clean the tools of your trade. Redding didn't tell you to kill the pretender. He didn't have to. You're a species apart, you and the boy you just dispatched to hell.

He was weak.

You're strong.

He was painting by numbers and still couldn't manage to stay in the lines.

You're a developing artist. Improvisation. Innovation. A rush of power works its way through your body just thinking about it. You thought you wanted to be like Redding. To be Redding.

But now you're starting to see—you could be so much more.

"Not yet," you whisper. There's one more person who has to go first. You hum a song and close your eyes.

What will be will be—even if you have to help it along.

CHAPTER 41

f the evidence was to be believed, Clark was a killer—
and Redding's other apprentice had killed him.

Sibling rivalry. The thought was misplaced, but I couldn't shake it. Two young men who idolized Redding, who had somehow developed relationships with him—how much had they known about each other?

Enough for our remaining UNSUB to kill Clark.

"Clark killed Trina?" Michael couldn't hide the disbelief in his voice. "I knew there was anger there—about Emerson, about the professor, but still."

I tried to picture it. Had Clark forced his way into Trina's house? Did she let him in? Had he mentioned Redding?

"Clark was a loner," I said, thinking out loud. "He never fit in. He wasn't aggressive, but he wasn't the kind of person you wanted to be around, either."

Dean shot a sideways glance at Agent Sterling. "Just how disorganized was Trina Simms's murder?"

I saw the logic to Dean's question immediately: Clark fit the profile for a disorganized killer almost exactly.

"He followed the MO," Agent Sterling said. "He just didn't do it well."

That's why you killed him, I thought, addressing the words to our remaining UNSUB. *You were both playing at the same game, but he messed up. He was going to get himself caught. Maybe he was going to get you caught, too.*

"Did they know each other?" I asked. "Clark and our UNSUB—I'm betting they knew *about* each other, but had they actually met?"

"He'd want to keep them as separate as possible." Dean didn't specify who *he* was. Under the circumstances, he didn't have to. "The less interaction they have with each other, the more control he has over the situation. This is his game, not theirs."

It wasn't enough to profile Clark or our UNSUB. At the end of the day, this all came back to Redding. I pictured him sitting across the table from me. I heard myself asking the questions, heard his replies. I walked through them, step by step, thinking all the while that I was missing something.

You sent Clark after Trina, I thought. *Who did you send after Emerson?*

The nagging feeling that there was something I wasn't seeing intensified. I sat very still, and then suddenly, all the inconsequential details melted away until there was only one thing left. One detail.

One question.

"Lia," I said urgently, "you're sure that Redding didn't lie in response to any of my questions?"

She inclined her head slightly—clearly, she didn't think the question merited a verbal response.

"I asked him how he chose the victims." I looked around the room to see if anyone's mind would take the same path mine had. "I said, *how do you choose who dies*, and do you remember what he said?"

"He said *I don't*." Dean was the one who answered. I doubted he'd forgotten a single word his father had uttered in that meeting—in any of their meetings.

"If he doesn't choose the victims," I said, looking from Dean to Sterling to Briggs, "who does?"

There was a beat of silence.

"They do."

I hadn't expected the answer to come from Michael, but maybe I should have. He and Lia had met Clark, and he was the one who'd recognized the anger in the other boy.

She wasn't like that, Clark had said when it had come out that Emerson had been sleeping with their professor— but he hadn't believed the words he was saying. And that meant that he had believed that Emerson *was* like that. That she was less and worthy of scorn. That she deserved to be degraded.

He'd had pictures of her hidden under his bed.

Clark had been obsessed with Emerson. He'd loved her, and he'd hated her, and she'd turned up dead. The only reason he hadn't been a viable suspect in her murder was that he had an alibi.

"Redding had the UNSUBs choose victims for each other." Michael was still talking—and his thoughts were in sync with mine. "Clark chose Emerson, but someone else killed her. It's *Strangers on a Train*."

"Alfred Hitchcock," Sloane chimed in. "1951 film. One hour and forty-one minutes long. The movie postulates that the most foolproof way to get away with murder is for two strangers to take out each other's targets."

"That way," Briggs said softly, "each killer has an alibi when their target dies."

Like Clark had been in a room with hundreds of others taking a test when Emerson had been killed.

The dominoes fell, one by one in my head.

Like Christopher Simms was in a meeting with Briggs when someone killed his mother.

I sat on the stairs, waiting. The FBI had been attempting to locate Christopher Simms for the past fourteen hours. Daniel Redding had promised us another body today, and all I could do was wait—to see if we were right, to see if they caught him in time. I couldn't go up the stairs. I couldn't go down them. I couldn't do anything but sit there, halfway in between, obsessing over the evidence and praying that when the phone rang, it would be to tell us they had apprehended the suspect, not to inform us that we had a fifth victim.

No matter how many times I went over the case, the details stayed the same. Clark had chosen Emerson, and someone else had killed her at a time when Clark's alibi was ironclad. That person had then chosen a victim—Trina Simms.

I could still see the look in Christopher's eyes when he'd grabbed my arm and wrenched me off the couch. He was sick of being under his mother's thumb. What better pay-back than to see her killed—in a roundabout way—by the man she fancied herself in love with?

It all came back to Daniel Redding. Christopher may have chosen Trina to die, but Redding had been the one to choose Christopher as an apprentice. Dean's father had probably used Trina to get to her son. He'd almost certainly told Clark to hold off on killing Trina until she'd received a visit from Dean.

How long has he been planning this? How many moving parts did he set in motion before Emerson's body was found on that lawn? I turned to my left and glanced at the wall. The stairway was lined with portraits—serial killers decorating our walls like they were family.

The irony did not escape me.

In my hand, I held the Rose Red lipstick. I took the cap off and turned the bottom of the tube until the dark red color peeked over the edge of the plastic casing.

You will never find the man who murdered your mother. Redding's words were there in the back of my mind, mock-ing me.

"Mind if I keep you company while we wait?"

I glanced back over my shoulder at Dean, who was stand-ing near the top of the stairs.

"Grab a seat," I told him. Instead of sitting on one of the steps above me, he walked until he reached my step and lowered himself down next to me. The staircase was wide enough that there was still space between us, but narrow enough that there wasn't much. His eyes fell on the tube of lipstick in my hands.

He knows, I thought. *He knows this was Locke's, and he knows why I kept it.*

"I can't stop thinking about them," Dean said after a moment. "Gary Clarkson. Christopher Simms. They were never my father's endgame."

I lowered the lipstick back into the tube and capped it. "You were," I said, knowing it was true, knowing that somehow, this had always been about Dean.

Dean closed his eyes. I could feel him next to me, feel each breath in and each breath out. "I can't decide if my father engineered this whole thing just so I'd be forced to go see him, or if he was banking on one of his students eventually trying to prove himself the better man by killing me."

Dean's eyelids lifted, and I thought through his words. Emerson's murderer had killed Clark. That was the work of an UNSUB who wanted to be Redding's only apprentice. His only heir. His only *son.*

"Your father doesn't want you dead," I told Dean. For Redding, that would be a last resort. He'd kill Dean only if he believed he'd truly lost him—and Daniel Redding was incapable of ever believing he'd truly lost.

"No," Dean agreed, "he doesn't want me dead, but if one of the UNSUBs had escalated, if one of them had come here to kill me, I would have defended myself."

Maybe, in Redding's mind, that was the way this was supposed to end, with Dean killing the others. Redding saw

Dean as an extension of himself. Of course he thought Dean would win—and if Dean didn't, well, then maybe Daniel Redding believed that he deserved to die. For being weak.

For not being his father's son.

The phone rang. My muscles tensed. I was frozen, unable to move, unable to breathe. Two seconds later, the phone stopped ringing. Someone had answered.

Please let them have found him in time. Please let them have found him in time.

"Dean." I managed to force his name out of my suddenly dry mouth. He sat, just as immobile, beside me. "Last summer, after everything that happened, Michael told me to figure out how I felt. About you."

I didn't know why I was saying this now—but I *needed* to. Any second, someone would come in with news. Any second, things could change. I felt like a train hurtling toward a tunnel.

Please don't let there be another body.

"Townsend, he means something to you," Dean said, his own voice as hoarse as mine. "He makes you smile." *And you deserve to smile.* I could practically hear him thinking it, could feel him fighting against the words he said next, unable to keep them back. "What did you figure out?"

He was asking. And if he was asking, that meant that he wanted to know, that the answer *mattered* to him. I swallowed. "Do you—Dean, I need to know what you feel. For me."

Any second, things could change.

"I feel . . . *something.*" Dean's words came unevenly. He turned toward me, his leg brushing against mine. "But I don't know if I can—I don't know if it's enough." He closed my hand around the tube of lipstick I was holding, his hand covering mine. "I don't know if I *can.* . . ."

Can what? Open up? Let go? Risk letting something matter so much that losing it could push you off the edge?

Michael appeared at the bottom of the stairs. Dean let go of my hand.

"They found him," Michael said, coming to a standstill and looking up at us. "Briggs's team found Christopher Simms."

They apprehended Christopher Simms outside of a coffee shop, waiting for a girl. In his truck, they'd found zip ties, a hunting knife, a cattle brand, and black nylon rope.

Body after body after body, Redding had promised. *Because you aren't smart enough. Because you're weak.*

But we weren't, and this time, we'd won. That hunting knife wouldn't slice into another girl's skin. Her hands wouldn't be bound behind her back. She wouldn't feel burning metal melting through her flesh.

We'd saved that girl at the coffee shop, the same way we'd saved little Mackenzie McBride. Another victim would be dead right now if I hadn't sat down across the table from Daniel Redding. If Sterling hadn't wound him up enough to bait him into torturing us with the truth. If Lia hadn't been there behind the mirror, reading Redding for deception and finding none. If Sloane hadn't realized that Lia's ability *wasn't* on the fritz.

If Michael and I had never met Clark, if Dean hadn't gone out to visit Trina, how would this have played out?

Dean was off dealing with the news in his own way. Michael had retreated to working on his car. I was standing in the backyard, eyeing the trash can, the Rose Red lipstick in my hand.

I'd joined the Naturals program in hopes that I might be able to save some other little girl from coming back to a blood-drenched room. That was what we were doing. We were saving people. And still, I couldn't throw away the lipstick, I couldn't shut the door on my past.

You will never find the man who murdered your mother. How could Redding possibly know that? He couldn't. But still, I couldn't push down the part of my brain that thought, *Prisoners chat.* How had Dean's father even known that I had a dead mother?

"Don't." Michael came up behind me. I closed my fingers around the lipstick and slipped it into the front pocket of my jeans.

"Don't what?" I asked.

"Don't think about something that makes you feel small and scared and like you're stuck in a tunnel with no light at the end."

"You're standing behind me," I said without turning around. "How could you possibly get a read on my emotions from there?"

Michael crossed to stand in front of me. "I could tell you," he intoned, "but then I'd have to kill you." He paused. "Too soon?"

"To be making jokes about killing me?" I asked dryly. "Never."

Michael reached out and brushed a strand of hair out of my face. I froze.

"I know," he said. "I know that you care about him. I know that you're attracted to him. I know that when he hurts, it hurts you. I know that he never looks at you the way he looks at Lia, that you're not a *sister* to him. I know that he wants you. He's in over his head with you. But I also know that half the time, he *hates* that he wants you."

I thought of Dean on the stairs, telling me that he felt something, but unsure that it was *enough*.

"That's the difference between the two of us," Michael told me. "I don't just want you." Now both of his hands were on my face. "I *want* to want you."

Michael wasn't a person who let himself want things. He certainly didn't admit to wanting them. He didn't let anything under his skin. He expected to be disappointed.

"I'm here, Cassie. I know what I feel, and I know that when you let your guard down, when you let yourself, you feel it, too." He ran his fingers lightly over the back of my neck. "I know that you're scared."

My heart pounded so hard, I could feel it in my stomach. A mishmash of memories rushed through my head, like water exploding out of a broken faucet.

Michael walking into the diner where I'd worked in Colorado. Michael in the swimming pool, bringing his lips to meet mine during a midnight swim. Michael easing himself down next to me on the couch. Michael dancing with me on the lawn. Michael working on that death trap of a car.

Michael taking a step back and trying to be the good guy. For me.

But it wasn't just Michael in my head; it was also Dean.

Dean sitting next to me on the steps, his knee brushing against mine. My hand, bathing his bloody knuckles. The secrets we'd traded. Kneeling in the dirt next to the beat-up picket fence at his old house.

Michael was right. I *was* scared. I was scared of my own emotions, scared of wanting and longing and *loving*. Scared of hurting either one of them.

Scared of losing someone I cared about when I'd already lost so much.

But Michael was there, telling me how *he* felt. He was leveling the playing field. He was asking me to choose.

He was saying *Pick me.*

Michael didn't pull me toward him. He didn't lean forward. This was my decision, but he was so close, and slowly, my hands found their way to his shoulders.

His face.

And still, he waited—for me to say the words, or for me to close the space between my mouth and his. I shut my eyes.

The next time my lips touch yours, I thought, remembering

his words, *the only person you're going to be thinking about is me*.

The rush in my head went silent. I opened my eyes, and—

Mariachi music started blaring all around us. I jumped a foot and a half in the air, and Michael nearly lost his balance on his bad leg. We turned in unison to see Lia toying with a set of speakers.

"Hope I'm not interrupting anything," she called over the sound of the music.

"'Feliz Navidad'?" Michael said. "Really, Lia? *Really?*"

"You're right," she said, sounding as sedate and chastened as a person could while yelling to be heard over the sounds of an extremely inappropriately timed Christmas carol. "It's barely even October. I'll change the song."

Sloane stuck her head out of the back door. "Hey, guys," she said, sounding more chipper than she had in days. "Did you know that a power saw produces noise at one hundred and ten decibels?"

There was murder on Michael's face, but even he didn't have the heart to glare at Sloane. "No," he said, sighing. "I didn't."

"A motorcycle is closer to a hundred," Sloane prattled on happily at high volume. "I'm betting this music is at one hundred and three. And a half. One hundred and three and a half."

Lia finally switched the song to one of her dance tracks. "Come on," she said, chancing coming within throttling range to take me by one hand and Sloane by another. "We caught the bad guy." She pulled the two of us out onto the lawn, her hips swaying to the beat of the music, her eyes daring me to object. "I think this calls for a celebration. Don't you?"

CHAPTER 43

woke up in a cold sweat in the middle of the night. I should have expected the nightmares. They'd plagued me on and off for five years. Of course Redding's mind games had brought them back.

It's not just that, I thought in a moment of brutal honesty with myself. *They come back when I'm stressed. When things are changing.*

This wasn't just about Redding. It was about Michael and Dean, but most of all, it was about me. Sloane had asked me once, in a game of Truth or Dare, how many people I loved. Not just romantic love—any kind of love. At the time, I'd wondered if growing up with only my mother for company—and then losing her the way I had—had cut my ability to love other people off at the knees.

My answer had been *one.*

But now . . .

You want to know why you, in particular, concern me, Cassie? Agent Sterling's words rang in my ears. *You're the one who really feels things. You won't ever be able to stop caring. It will always be personal.*

I cared about the victims we fought for—the Mackenzie McBrides and the nameless girls at coffee shops. I cared about the people in this house—not just Michael and Dean, but Sloane and Lia. Lia, who would have thrown herself on an open flame for Dean.

Lia, who'd flung herself in the middle of my moment with Michael with that same determination.

I tried to lull my mind into silence and myself back to sleep.

Mackenzie McBride. The girl in the coffee shop. My thoughts circled back. *Why?* I turned my head to the side on my pillow. My chest rose and fell with steady, even breaths.

The FBI had gotten Mackenzie McBride's case wrong. They'd missed the villain hiding in plain sight. But we hadn't missed anything on this case. Christopher Simms *was* the villain. They'd caught him in the act. He'd had supplies in his truck—bindings for the girl's ankles and wrists, a knife, the brand.

The girl in the coffee shop. That was what I kept coming back to. Who was Christopher's intended victim? Redding had known that someone was scheduled to die. He'd told us to expect it.

How do you choose who dies?

I don't.

Clark had chosen Emerson.

Christopher had chosen his mother.

Fogle had been nothing but a complication that needed to be dealt with.

So who chose the girl?

There was no getting away from that question. Maybe it was nothing, but I slipped out of my bed, out of the room. The house was silent, but for the sound of my own light footsteps as I made my way down the stairs. The door to the study—Agent Sterling's temporary lodging—was open a crack. The faint glow of lamplight from inside the room told me that she wasn't asleep, either.

I hovered at the door. I couldn't quite bring myself to knock. Suddenly, the door flew inward. Agent Sterling stood on the other side, her brown hair loose and messy, her face free of makeup, and her gun at the ready. When she saw me, she let out a breath and lowered the weapon.

"Cassie," she said. "What are you doing here?"

"I live here," I responded automatically.

"You live directly outside my door?"

"You're on edge, too," I told her, reading that much in her behavior, the fact that she'd answered the door with a gun. "You can't sleep. Neither can I."

She shook her head in chagrin—though whether that emotion was directed at herself or at me, I couldn't tell—and then she took a step back, inviting me into the room.

I crossed the threshold, and she shut the door behind me, flipping on the overhead light.

I'd forgotten that Briggs's study was full of taxidermy— predators, posed seconds before they struck. "No wonder you can't sleep," I told her.

She bit back a smile. "He's always had a flair for the dramatic." She sat down on the end of the folded-out couch. With her hair loose, she looked younger. "Why can't you sleep?" she asked. "Ankle tracker giving you problems?"

I glanced down at my feet, bewildered, as if they had only just appeared on my body. The constant weight on my right ankle should have been more bothersome than it was, but there'd been so much going on the past few days, I'd barely even noticed it.

"No," I said. "I mean, yes, I'd love for you to take it off, but that's not why I'm up. It's about the girl, the one that Christopher Simms was meeting at the coffee shop. The one he was planning to abduct."

I didn't specify what else Christopher had been planning on doing to that girl, but I knew Agent Sterling well enough by now to know that her mind would go there, the same as mine.

"What about her?" Sterling's voice was slightly hoarse. I wondered how many nights she'd spent like this one, unable to sleep.

"Who was she?" I asked. "Why was she meeting Christopher?"

"She worked at the coffee shop," Sterling replied. "She'd been conversing with someone on an online dating site. He used a fake name and only accessed the account from public computers, but it stands to reason that it was Christopher, taking things to the next level with victim selection. His mother was dead. He'd killed Emerson—that could have given him a taste for college-aged girls."

Strangers on a train, I thought. "Christopher had an alibi for his mother's murder. Clark had one for Emerson's." I swallowed. My mouth had gone so dry, I had to work to push out the next words. "Maybe that was it. Maybe now that Clark's dead, Christopher was on his own—but Redding knew that someone was going to die soon, besides Clark. It was *planned*. And if it was part of the plan . . ."

I sat down next to Agent Sterling, willing her to understand what I was saying, even though I wasn't sure I was making any kind of objective sense.

"What if Christopher wasn't the one communicating with this girl online? What if *he* didn't choose her?"

Clark chose Emerson.

Christopher chose his mother.

They both had ironclad alibis for the murders of the women they had chosen. What if they weren't the only ones?

"You think there's a third." Sterling put the possibility into words. That made it real. I braced the heels of my hands against the edge of the bed, steadying myself.

"Did Christopher confess to Emerson's murder?" I asked. "Is there *any* physical evidence tying him to the scene? Any circumstantial evidence? Anything, other than the fact that he was planning to kill another girl?"

Agent Sterling's phone rang. The sound was garish, jarring in contrast with my quiet questions. Phone calls at two in the morning never brought good news.

"Sterling." Her posture changed when she answered the phone. This wasn't the woman with tousled hair, sitting on the edge of her bed. This was the agent. "What do you mean, 'he's dead'?" Short pause. "I know the literal meaning of the word, Dad. What happened? When did you get the call?"

Someone was dead. That knowledge weighed me down and set my heart to beating a vicious rhythm against my rib cage. *The way she's talking means it's someone we know.* As that realization occurred to me, a plea wrenched its way through me, taking over my thoughts, silencing everything else in its wake. *Please don't let it be Briggs.*

"No, this isn't a blessing," Agent Sterling said sharply. "This case isn't closed."

Not Briggs, I thought. Director Sterling would never have referred to the death of his former son-in-law as a *blessing.*

"Are you listening to me, Dad? *Director,* we think there might be—" She cut off. "'Who's *we?*' Does it matter who *we* is? I'm telling you—"

She wasn't telling him anything, because he wasn't listening.

"I know it would be to your advantage, politically, if this case was closed, if it never had to go to trial because our first killer took out our second killer and then strung himself up by the bedsheets once he was caught. That's neat, and it's tidy. It's *convenient*. Director?" She paused. "Director? *Dad?*" She punched her thumb viciously onto her touch screen and threw down her phone.

"He hung up on me," she said. "He told me that he'd gotten a call from the prison, that Christopher Simms had been found dead in his cell. He hung himself—or at least, that's the going theory."

I read the implication in those words: Agent Sterling thought that there was at least a chance—and possibly a good one—that Christopher Simms had met with foul play. Had Redding somehow managed to have him killed?

Or had the person who had killed Emerson Cole—and maybe even Clark—come back to finish the job?

Three UNSUBs. Two of them are dead.

If there was a third, if someone was still out there . . .

Agent Sterling slammed her suitcase open.

"What are you doing?" I asked.

"Getting dressed," she said tautly. "If there's even a sliver of a chance that this case isn't over, I'm working it."

"I'll go with you."

She didn't even look up at the offer. "Thank you, but no. I still have a few scruples. If there's a killer still out there, I'm not putting your life on the line."

But it's okay to risk yours? I wanted to ask, but I didn't. Instead, I went upstairs and changed clothes myself. I caught Agent Sterling in the driveway, headed toward her car.

"At least have Briggs meet you there," I called after her, running to catch up. "Wherever *there* is."

She hit the unlock button on the car. The headlights flashed once, then darkness set back in.

"It's two o'clock in the morning," Agent Sterling said, clipping the words. "Just go to bed."

A week ago, I would have argued with her. I would have resented her for shoving me onto the sidelines. But somehow, a part of me understood—even after everything she'd had us do, her first instinct was still to protect me. She'd take risks with her own life, but not with mine.

Who's going to protect you? I thought.

"Call Briggs, and I'll go to bed," I promised.

Even in the dark, I could make out the annoyance on her face. "Fine," she said finally, pulling out her phone and waving it at me. "I'll call him."

"No," a voice said, directly behind me. "You won't."

I didn't have time to turn, to think, to process the words. An arm locked around my throat, cutting off my air supply and jerking me to the tips of my toes. My body was pulled flat against my assailant's. I clawed at the arm around my neck. It tightened.

I couldn't breathe.

Something metal and cool grazed my cheek and came to rest at my temple.

"Put your gun on the ground. *Now.*" It took me a moment to realize that those words were aimed at Agent Sterling. A second after that, I realized that I had a gun at my head, that Sterling was doing exactly as she'd been instructed.

She'd risk her life, but she wouldn't risk mine.

"Stop struggling," the silky voice whispered in my ear. He pressed the gun harder into my temple. My whole body hurt. I couldn't breathe. I couldn't stop struggling.

"I'm doing what you asked. Let the girl go." Sterling sounded so calm. *So far away.*

It was dark outside, but things were getting darker as my vision blurred and inky blackness began to close in on me.

"Take me. That's what you came here for. *I'm* the one who got away from Redding. Proving you're better than his other apprentices, killing them isn't enough. You want to prove you're better than *him*. To show *him*."

The grip on my neck relaxed, but the gun never wavered. I sucked air into my burning lungs, gasping for just one breath, then two.

"Eyes on me, Cassie." Sterling shifted her focus from the UNSUB to me just long enough to issue that instruction. It took me a moment to realize why.

She doesn't want me to see him.

"Knock her out. Leave her here. She wasn't part of the plan. *Your* plan." Sterling's voice was steady, but her hands were shaking. She was playing a dangerous game. One wrong word and the UNSUB could kill me as easily as he could knock me out. "She can't identify you. By the time she wakes up, you'll be long gone, and I'll be yours. You won't lose me, the way Redding did. You'll take your time. You'll do it your way, but they won't find *you*. They won't find *me* if you stick to the plan."

Sterling was targeting her words at the UNSUB, playing on his fears, his desires, but I heard what she was saying, too, and the real kicker was, I believed her. If I couldn't identify the UNSUB, if he took her, if they left me in the driveway unconscious, by the time I woke up, it would be too late.

He'd have too much of a head start.

But there was one way to make sure that Briggs knew immediately that something was amiss. One way to make sure that he could find her.

The UNSUB let go of my neck.

"Look here, Cassie. Look right here." I could hear the desperation in Agent Sterling's voice. She needed this, needed me to keep looking right at her.

I turned around. Even in the dark, I was close enough to make out the features of the UNSUB's face. He was young, early twenties. Tall and built like a runner. I recognized him.

The guard from the prison. Webber. The one who'd been disgusted by Dean's very existence, who had a problem with female FBI agents. The one who'd refused to allow us to stay in the car.

The pieces fell into place in a single, horrible moment: *why* the man hadn't let us stay in the car, how Redding had known I existed, how our third UNSUB had been able to kill Christopher Simms in prison.

"Redding would take me, too. He'd *kill me*, too." My voice

was scratchy and barely audible. "You work at the prison. You know he asked for me. You're probably even the one who delivered the message."

He could shoot me. Right now, he could shoot me. Or my gamble could pay off.

All I saw was a flash of movement, the glint of metal. And then everything went black.

YOU

The gun cracks against her skull with a sickening thwack.

It doesn't sicken you.

The girl's body crumples to the ground. You aim your gun at the pretty FBI agent. She looked down her nose at you when she visited Redding. She dared to tell you what to do.

She probably laughs at boys rejected from the FBI Academy, let alone the local police force.

"Pick her up," you say.

She hesitates. You aim the gun at the girl. "Either you pick her up, or I shoot her. Your choice."

Your heart is thudding in your ears. Your breaths are coming faster. There's a taste to the night air—almost metallic. You could run a marathon right now. You could dive off Niagara Falls.

The FBI agent picks up the girl. You pocket her gun. They're yours. You're taking them both. And that's when you know.

You're not going to hang them. You're not going to brand them. You're not going to cut them.

You have the One Who Got Away. You have his useless little son's girl. This time, *you think*, we're doing it my way.

You make the FBI agent put the girl in your trunk, climb in herself. You knock her out—and oh, it feels good. It feels right.

You slam the trunk. You climb into the car. You drive away.

The student has become the master.

onsciousness came slowly. The pain came all at once. The entire right side of my face was white-hot agony: throbbing, aching, needles jabbing down to the bone. My left eyelid fluttered, but my right eye was swollen shut. Bits and pieces of the world came into focus—rotted floorboards, heavy rope encircling my body, the post I was tied to.

"You're awake."

My good eye searched for the source of the voice and found Agent Sterling. There was blood crusted to her temple.

"Where are we?" I asked. My arms were bound behind my back. I twisted my neck, trying to catch a glimpse of them. The zip ties digging into my flesh looked uncomfortably tight, but I couldn't feel anything beyond the blinding pain radiating out from my cheekbone.

"He hit you with his gun, knocked you out. How's your head?"

The fact that she'd ignored my question did not go

unnoticed. A moan escaped my lips, but I covered it as best I could. "How's yours?"

Her dry lips parted into a tiny, broken smile. "I woke up in the trunk of his car," she said after a few seconds. "He didn't get as good a hit in on me. I pretended I was unconscious when he brought us in here. As best I can tell, we're in an abandoned cabin of some type. The surrounding area is completely wooded."

I wet my lips. "How long ago did he leave?"

"Not long." Sterling's hair hung in her face. She was bound the same way I was: hands behind her back, tied to a wooden post that stretched from ceiling to floor. "Long enough for me to know I can't get out of these knots. Long enough for me to know that you won't be able to, either. *Why*, Cassie?" Her voice broke, but she didn't stop talking. "*Why couldn't you just do what I asked?* Why did you make him bring you, too?"

The anger drained out of her voice from one sentence to the next until all that was left was a terrible, hollow hopelessness.

"Because," I said, nodding toward my right foot and wincing when my head protested, "I'm wearing a GPS tracking anklet."

Sterling's head was bowed, but her eyes found their way to mine.

"The minute I left the property, Briggs got a text message," I said. "It won't take him long to realize that you're missing, too. He'll pull up the data from my tracker. He'll find us. If I'd let you go alone . . ." I didn't finish that sentence. "Briggs will find us."

Sterling lifted her head to the ceiling. At first, I thought she was smiling, but then I realized she was crying, her mouth stretched tight enough to clamp down on any sounds trying to escape her mouth.

Those don't look like tears of relief.

Sterling's lips parted, and an odd, dry laugh escaped. "Oh, God. Cassie."

How long had we been here? Why hadn't Briggs already come bursting through that door?

"I never activated the tracker. I thought wearing it was deterrent enough."

The tracker was supposed to go off. It was supposed to lead Briggs right to us.

It had never occurred to me that she might have lied to me. I'd known I was taking a risk, but I'd thought I was putting my life on the line to help save hers.

The tracker was supposed to go off. It was supposed to lead Briggs straight to us.

"You were right about Emerson's killer." Those were the only words my lips would make, all there was left to say. The killer would be back. No one was coming to save us.

"How so?"

I could tell by the look in Sterling's eyes that she was keeping the conversation up for my benefit, not hers. Mentally, she was probably berating herself—for not finding the killer, for agreeing to live in our house and dealing us in on this case, for letting me in when I'd knocked on her door.

For not activating the tracker. For letting me believe that she had.

"You said that Emerson's killer was between the ages of twenty-three and twenty-eight, above average intelligence, but not necessarily educated." I paused. "Though if he stuffed us in his trunk, that seems to suggest that he doesn't drive a truck or SUV."

Sterling managed a wry grin. "Ten bucks says that wasn't his car."

My lips tilted slightly upward on one side, and I winced.

"Try not to move," Sterling told me. "You're going to need to conserve your energy, because when he gets back here, I'm going to distract him, and you're going to run."

"My hands are bound, and I'm tied to a post. I'm not going anywhere."

"I'll get him to untie you, to untie me. I'll distract him." There was a thread of quiet determination in her voice, but there was also desperation—a desperate need to believe that what she was saying could happen. "Once he's distracted, you run," she said fiercely.

I nodded, even though I knew he had a gun, knew I wouldn't even make it out the front door. I lied to her, and she accepted the lie, even though she *knew* as well as I did that a distraction wasn't going to be enough.

There was no enough.

There was nothing but him and us and the certainty that

we were going to die in this damp, rotting cabin, screaming with no one but each other to hear.

Oh, God.

"He broke from Redding's pattern." Now Sterling was the one trying to distract me. "He's broken away from him altogether."

So maybe we wouldn't die the way Emerson Cole had, the way the dozen women Daniel Redding had murdered before being caught had.

This isn't Redding's fantasy anymore. It's yours. You enjoyed squeezing the life out of me. Did you enjoy hitting me with that gun? Are you going to beat us to death? I forced myself to keep breathing—quick, shallow breaths. *Will you display our broken bodies in public, the way you laid Emerson out on the hood of her car? Will we be trophies, testaments to your control, your power?*

"Cassie."

Sterling's voice brought me back.

"Is it sick if I wish I was normal?" I asked. "Not because I wouldn't be here—I wouldn't trade my life for the lives that I've helped save—but because if I were *normal*, I wouldn't be sitting here climbing into his head, seeing us the way he sees us, knowing how this is going to end."

"It ends with you running," Sterling reminded me. "You get away. You escape, because you're a survivor. Because someone else thought you were worth saving."

I closed my eyes. Now she was just telling me a story—a fairy tale, with a happily ever after.

"I knew a girl growing up who used to plot her escapes from all kinds of nasty situations. She was a living, breathing guide to surviving the most unlikely worst-case scenarios you could possibly think of."

I let Sterling's voice wash over me. I let her words banish all the things I didn't want to think.

"'You've been buried alive in a glass coffin with a sleeping cobra on your chest. Oxygen is running out. If you try to break the coffin, you'll wake the cobra. What do you do?'"

I opened my good eye. "What *do* you do?"

"I don't even remember, but she always had an answer. She always had a way out, and she was so darn cheerful about it all." Sterling shook her head. "Sloane reminds me of her sometimes. When we grew up, she worked in the FBI laboratory. She always was better with facts than with people. Most second graders don't appreciate a classmate who's constantly putting their lives in theoretical peril."

"But you did," I said. Sterling nodded. "Her name was Scarlett, wasn't it?" I asked. "She was Judd's daughter. Your best friend. I'm not sure what she was to Briggs."

Sterling stared at me for a few seconds. "You're eerie," she said. "You know that, right?"

I shrugged as well as I could under the circumstances.

"She was Briggs's best friend, too. They met in college. I'd known her since kindergarten. She introduced us. We all joined the FBI together."

"She died." I said it so that Sterling didn't have to, but she repeated the words anyway.

"She died."

The sound of a door opening ended our conversation. Ancient hinges creaked in protest. I fought the urge to turn toward the door. It wouldn't be worth the bolts of pain the movement would send through my face and neck.

You're standing there. You're looking at us.

Heavy footsteps told me he was coming close. Soon, the man who'd killed the professor and Emerson, Clark, and—in all likelihood—Christopher, was standing directly between Sterling and me.

He was holding a hunting rifle.

YOU

Guns and neat little bullet holes and the glory of being the one to pull the trigger.

They're yours. This time, you're doing it your way.

The little red-haired one who practically begged *you to take her isn't looking so good. She'll be the first to fall. Her face is already a mottle of bruises. You did that. You. The FBI agent's face is marred with obvious tear tracks. You rest the rifle to one side and reach out and drag your thumb over her face.*

She jerks back, but she can't fight you. Neither of them can.

"I'm going to untie you," you say, just to watch the surprise flicker through their eyes. "You're going to run. I'll even give you a two-minute head start."

Take them. Free them. Track them. Kill them.

"Now . . ." You draw the word out and tap the butt of the rifle thoughtfully against the ground. "Who's first?"

Adrenaline is already starting to pump through your body. You are powerful. You are the hunter. They are the prey.

"Me." The FBI agent is the one who speaks. Doesn't she realize she's nothing but a deer in your target?

You're *the hunter.*

She's *the prey.*

You grab the younger one by the elbow. "You." You breathe the word directly into her face. Let her shrink back from it, from you. "You're first." The smell of fear is tantalizing. You smile. "I hope you can run."

CHAPTER 45

He pulled a knife out of his boot. I pictured it coming toward me. I *felt* it slicing through skin and muscle, peeling the flesh from my bone. But instead, our captor knelt. He trailed the flat of the blade down the side of my cheek. He paused at my neck, then moved slowly down toward my wrists. The blade hovered over my arm for a moment. He traced the tip lightly over a vein, but didn't press down hard enough to cut.

With one slash, my hands were free.

He returned the knife to his boot and untied the rope around my torso by hand. He relished the task, drinking it in, savoring it. His hands brushed against my stomach, my side, my back.

Soon, I was free. I glanced over at Agent Sterling. She'd wanted to go first, wanted to buy me time—but for what? *This* was the only way out. If he really gave me a head start, if I ran hard enough . . .

You want me to think I have a chance, don't you?

Even knowing that, I still clung to the hope that two minutes might be enough time to disappear in the woods outside.

There was a way out of this—I had to believe that. I had to fight.

He put a hand in the middle of my back and pushed me roughly toward the door.

"Cassie." Agent Sterling's voice broke as she said my name. "You've been buried alive in a glass coffin with a sleeping cobra on your chest. There's a way out. There's *always* a way."

Our captor didn't give me the chance to turn around. To say good-bye. An instant later, I was on the porch. Sterling's earlier description was spot-on—we were completely surrounded by woods, but at its closest point, the edge of the woods was about fifteen yards off. The trees were denser farther in. I'd need the cover.

I needed a plan.

"Two minutes. Starting now."

He shoved me off the porch. I stumbled. My face throbbed. I ran.

I ran as hard as I could, as fast as I could, for the densest trees I could find. I reached cover in seconds—less than ten, more than five. I tore my way through the brush until my lungs started to burn. I looked back. I couldn't see him through the forest, which meant he couldn't see me.

How much time had passed? How much did I have left?

There's always a way out.

Running wasn't a solution. The man hunting me had a longer stride than I did. He had a runner's build, and he didn't need to catch me—he just needed to get me in his sights.

Two minutes is nothing.

My only hope was losing him, sending him one way while I was going the other. It went against every instinct I had, but I backtracked. I split off from the trail I'd laid the first time, stepping lightly and staying low, ducking into heavy brush and hoping to God he'd follow my original path and not this one.

A twig snapped somewhere nearby. I went deathly still.

Please don't see me. Please don't see me. Please don't see me.

Another snap. Another footstep.

Moving away from me. He's moving away.

I didn't have much time before he'd realize his mistake. I didn't have anywhere to go. I couldn't keep running. Could I climb? Bury myself in brush? I crossed a small stream, wishing it were a river. *I'd toss myself in.* I heard a yell—almost inhuman-sounding.

He must have hit the end of my original trail, discovered my little trick. He'd be moving fast now, determined to recover lost ground.

You're not angry. Not really. This is the game. You know you'll find me. You know I won't escape. There's probably nothing to escape to.

I had no idea where we were—all I knew was that I had

to do *something*. I knelt down and grabbed a rock. It barely fit in my hand. With my other hand, I reached for a branch overhead and gritted my teeth—which made the pain worse, not better.

No time. No time for pain. Climb. Climb. Climb.

I could only grip with one hand, but I made use of the other arm, hooking it around branches, ignoring the way the bark tore at tender skin. I went as high as I could before the branches became too thin to support my weight and the leaves too sparse to cover me. I transferred the rock from my left hand to my right and used the left to steady myself.

Please don't see me. Please don't see me. Please don't see me.

I heard him—fifty yards away. Forty. Thirty. I saw him when he stepped into view, crossing the stream.

Please don't see me. Please don't see me. Please don't see me.

His eyes were on the ground. *Tracks.* I'd left tracks—and they stopped right under this tree. I knew the second he was going to look up. I only had time for one thought, one silent plea.

Don't miss.

My arm whipped the rock at him so hard, I nearly knocked myself out of the tree. He looked up.

I didn't miss.

The rock caught him just above the eye. He went down, but didn't stay down, and as he climbed from his knees to his feet, bleeding and dazed, but very much alive, I felt the adrenaline that had pushed me to this point evaporate. There would be no superhuman feats of strength or speed. This was it: him aiming the rifle into the tree, and me clinging to a branch fifteen feet up in the air, shaking and bleeding, with nothing left to throw.

"Out of tricks?" he called up, his finger toying with the trigger.

I thought of Agent Sterling back in the cabin. He'd go for her next, run her through this sick little game.

No.

I did the only thing there was left to do. I jumped.

The gun went off. The shot went wide, and I crashed into him, feet first. We both went down in a tangle of limbs. He kept hold of the rifle, but I was too close for him to point it at me.

Three seconds.

That was how long it took for him to get the upper hand, to wrestle me to the ground. He pinned me with one hand, then rose to a crouch and slammed a foot into my chest, replacing his hand. Head wound bleeding heavily, he stood. From my position on the ground, he looked impossibly tall. *Invincible.*

He brought the gun to his shoulder. The tip of the barrel was less than three feet away from my body. It hovered over my midsection for a few seconds, then settled just over my forehead.

I closed my eyes.

"Take them. Free them. Track them. Kill—" He cut off, suddenly and without warning. It was only later that my brain processed the sound of gunfire, the rush of footsteps coming toward me.

"Cassie. *Cassie.*"

I didn't want to open my eyes. If I opened my eyes, it might not be real. The gun might still be there. *He* might still be there.

"Cassandra." There was only one man in the universe who could say my full name in exactly that tone.

I opened my eyes. "Briggs."

"Webber's dead." He clarified that point before asking me if I was okay.

"Webber?" I croaked. I knew the name, but my mind couldn't process it, couldn't process the fact that the man who'd done this to me even *had* a name.

"Anthony Webber," Briggs confirmed, doing a cursory check of my injuries, tallying them, down to every last detail.

"Sterling?" I managed to ask.

"She's safe."

"How did you—"

Briggs held up a hand and dug his phone out with the other. The call he made was brief and to the point: "I've got her. She's fine." Then he turned his attention back to me and answered the question I hadn't even finished asking. "Once we realized the two of you were missing and unaccounted for, the director threw the entire agency behind finding you. He kept saying that Veronica had tried to tell him something was off about this case."

"But how did you—"

"Your ankle tracker."

"Agent Sterling said she hadn't activated it."

Briggs smiled wryly. "She hadn't, but since she was on a playing-by-the-rules kick when she checked it out, she filled out all the paperwork. *I*'s were dotted. *T*'s were crossed. We had the serial number and were able to activate it remotely."

It was ironic—I'd saved Agent Sterling's life by breaking the rules, and she'd saved mine by following them.

Briggs helped me to my feet. "My team's on their way in," he said. "We left straight from the house, so we had a head start."

We?

"Cassie." Dean broke through the brush.

"I told him to wait at the cabin," Briggs said to me. "I told you to wait at the cabin," he reiterated to Dean, annoyance creeping into his voice. But he didn't stop me from taking three steps toward Dean, or Dean from crossing the remaining space between us in a heartbeat. The next second, he had a hand on each of my shoulders, touching me, confirming that I was okay, that I was here, that I was *real*.

"What are you doing here?" I asked him.

His hands went from my shoulders to my face. His right hand cupped the left side. His left gently bypassed my injuries, burying itself in my hair and holding my head up for me, like he thought my neck might not be able to do the job.

"Activating the tracker was Sloane's idea. Everyone else forgot about it. Briggs was at our place when we got the coordinates. I may have arranged it so that I was in his car when he went to leave."

Briggs wouldn't have wasted even a second trying to kick him out.

"What happened?" Dean asked me, his voice thick with emotions I couldn't quite identify. I knew he was probably asking about the abduction, about my face, about being tied up in the cabin and scrambling for my life, but I chose to interpret the question slightly differently.

"I hit him in the head with a rock. Then I jumped on him from up in that tree." I gestured vaguely with one hand. Dean stared at me, his expression unreadable until the ends of his lips began to turn slowly upward.

"I was wrong," he said, "when I said I just felt *something*." He was breathing heavily. I couldn't breathe at all. "When I said I wasn't sure it was enough."

He was scared, like me. But he felt it, and I felt it, and *he was there*. I'd spent so long trying *not* to choose, trying *not* to feel, and in an instant, I felt something inside of me break, like floodwaters bursting through a dam.

Dean pulled me gently toward him. His lips brushed lightly over mine. The action was hesitant, uncertain. My hands settled on the back of his neck, pulling *him* closer.

Maybe this was a mistake. Maybe when the smoke cleared, things would look different. But I couldn't stop it, couldn't keep living my life on maybes if I wanted to *live*.

I rose up on my toes, my body pressed against his, and returned the kiss, the pain in my face fading, washed away with the rest of the world, until there was only *this* moment—one that I hadn't thought I'd live to see.

CHAPTER 46

I spent the night at the hospital. I had a concussion, bruising on my neck from nearly being strangled, and countless cuts and abrasions on my hands and legs. They had to pry Dean away from me.

I was alive.

The next morning, the doctors released me into Agent Briggs's custody. We were halfway to his car before I realized that he was being too quiet.

"Where's Agent Sterling?" I asked.

"Gone." We climbed into the car. I gingerly pulled on my seat belt. Briggs pulled out onto the road. "Her injuries were minimal, but she's on a mandated leave until a Bureau psychologist gives her the green light for fieldwork."

"Is she coming back?" My eyes stung as I asked the question. A week ago, I would have been glad to be rid of her, but now . . .

"I don't know," Briggs said, a muscle in his jaw ticking. He was the kind of person who hated admitting uncertainty. "After Redding captured her—after Dean helped her escape—she fought to get back to active duty. She threw herself into work."

That was then. This was now. I'd thought Agent Sterling was coming around to the idea of the program, but I couldn't stop thinking about the look on her face when she'd asked me *why*. Why hadn't I listened to her? Why had I made the madman take me, too?

All she'd wanted, in those last moments, was to believe that I would make it out of that hellhole alive.

"She blames herself?" I asked—but it wasn't really a question.

"Herself. Her father. Me." Something in Briggs's tone told me that Agent Sterling wasn't the only one shouldering that guilt. "You were never supposed to be in the field," he told me. "None of your lives were ever supposed to be on the line."

If the Naturals hadn't worked this case, Christopher Simms would have killed that girl. If I hadn't gone with Agent Sterling, she'd be dead. No matter how much what I'd been through haunted Agent Briggs, I knew in my gut that at the end of the day, he would be able to live with the risks of this program. I wasn't sure that Agent Sterling could.

"Where are we going?" I asked when Briggs drove past our exit on the highway.

He didn't say anything for several minutes. Mile blurred

into mile. We ended up at an apartment complex across the street from the prison.

"There's something I want you to see."

Webber's apartment had two bedrooms. His life was highly segmented. He slept in one room—hospital corners on his bed, blackout curtains on the windows—and he worked in the other.

Briggs's team was cataloging evidence when we walked in: notebooks and photographs, weapons, a computer. Hundreds—if not thousands—of evidence bags told the story of Webber's life.

The story of his relationship with Daniel Redding.

"Go ahead," Briggs told me, nodding toward the carefully documented bags. "Just wear gloves."

He hadn't brought Dean to this crime scene. He hadn't brought Michael or Lia or Sloane.

"What am I looking for?" I asked, slipping on a pair of gloves.

"Nothing," Briggs said simply.

You brought me here to look at this, I thought, slipping back into profiling mode without even thinking about it. *Why?*

Because this wasn't about processing evidence. It was about me and what I'd been through out in the woods. I would always have questions about Locke, the way that Dean would always have questions about his father, but this UNSUB—this man who'd tried to snuff out my life—didn't have to be some larger-than-life figure, another ghost to haunt my dreams.

Hospital corners and hunting rifles.

Briggs had brought me here so that I could understand—and move on, as much as a person *could* move on after something like this.

It took me hours to go through it all. There was a picture of Emerson Cole tucked into the side of a journal. Webber's writing—*all capital letters, angled to one side*—marked the pages, telling me his story in horrific, nauseating detail. I read it, sifting through those details, absorbing them and building a profile.

Six months ago, you transferred onto Redding's cell block. You were fascinated with him, mesmerized by the way he played the other prisoners, the guards. The prison was the only place you had any power, any control, and when another rejection came in from the police academy, that wasn't enough anymore.

You wanted a different kind of power. Intangible. Undeniable. Eternal.

Webber had become obsessed with Redding. He'd thought he was successfully hiding that obsession until Redding had offered him a very special job.

He recognized your potential. You needed to prove yourself—to prove that you were smarter and better and more than everyone who looked down on you, rejected you, and shoved you to the side.

Redding had asked Webber to do two things: keep tabs

on Agent Briggs and find Dean. Webber had proven himself on both fronts. He'd followed Agent Briggs. He'd found the house where Dean was living. He'd reported back.

That was the turning point. That was the moment when you knew that to eclipse that mewling little brat in Redding's eyes, you'd have to do more.

There was a newspaper article folded up and stuck between two of the pages in the journal—an article Webber had given Daniel Redding to read, then hidden away in his work room.

An article about FBI Special Agent Lacey Locke. A wolf in sheep's clothing. A killer who was one of the Bureau's own.

Shortly after that, Redding had said that you were ready. You were his student. He was your master. And if there were others competing for your role, well, you'd take care of them in time.

I flipped from one page to the next and back again, rereading, building a time line in my mind. Redding had begun laying the groundwork for this series of "tests" for his apprentices—or, as Webber liked to refer to it, *what would be*—the day after he'd read the article about the Locke murders.

Don't you think it's weird? I'd asked what seemed like an eternity ago. *Six weeks ago, Locke was reenacting my mother's murder, and now someone's out there playing copycat to Dean's dad?*

Sitting there, re-creating the series of events that had led to the murder of Emerson Cole, I realized that it wasn't weird. It wasn't a coincidence.

Daniel Redding had started this *after* reading about the Locke murders. Dean understood killers because of his father; it went without saying that Daniel Redding understood them, too. And if he understood Locke—what drove her, what motivated her, what she wanted—if he'd had Webber keeping tabs on Dean, if he knew who I was and what had happened to my mother . . .

Locke killed those women for me, and Redding stepped up to the challenge.

There were still so many questions: how Redding had known who I was; how he'd drawn the connections he must have drawn to figure out what had happened with Locke; what—if anything—he knew about my mother's murder. But Webber's journal didn't hold those answers.

Once the *test* started, Webber's writing became less focused on Redding.

You worshipped him—but then you became him. No, you became something better. Something new.

Five people were dead. By his own confession in these pages, Webber had killed four of them: Emerson, the professor, and both of his competitors. The original plan—laid out by Redding to each of the three, with Webber enabling the communication—had been for each of the three to choose one victim and kill one of the others'.

In your mind, there was never room for any others.

There were pages in this journal describing Webber's

fantasies of what it would have been like if he'd been the one to kill Trina Simms. He'd pictured it, he'd imagined it, and Clark had died for the sin of not *doing it right*. Christopher's days were numbered the second he got caught.

And then there was one.

"Cassie?" Briggs said my name, and I looked up at him from my spot on the floor. "You okay?"

I'd been here for hours. Briggs had achieved his objective: when I closed my eyes, I wasn't caught back up in the horror of being hunted like an animal. I didn't feel Webber looming over me, or his arm cutting off the air in my throat. Those memories weren't gone. They would never be gone. But for minutes, hours, maybe even days at a time, I could forget.

"Yeah," I said, closing the journal and tearing the gloves off first one hand and then the other. "I'm good."

By the time we got back to the house, it was almost dark. Lia, Dean, and Sloane were sitting on the front porch, waiting for me. Michael was taking a sledgehammer to the cracked windows of the junkyard car.

Every time he took a swing, every piece of glass he shattered, I felt something shattering inside me.

He knew.

From the moment Dean had come back to the house, from the moment Michael had laid eyes on him, he knew.

I didn't mean for this to happen. I didn't plan it.

Michael looked up and caught sight of me, as if my

thoughts had somehow made their way from my mind to his. He studied me, the way he had the first day we'd met, before I'd known what he could do.

"That's it, then?" he asked me.

I didn't answer. I couldn't. My eyes darted toward the porch. Toward Dean.

Michael gave me a careless smile. "You win some, you lose some," he said with a shrug. Like I'd never been anything more than a game. Like I didn't matter.

Because he wouldn't *let* me matter anymore.

"It's just as well," he continued, each word a calculated shot to my heart. "Maybe if Redding's getting some, he'll finally loosen up."

I knew, objectively, what this was. *If you can't keep them from hitting you, you* make *them hit you.* That didn't stop his words from cutting into me. The bruises and scrapes, the pounding in my head—it all faded away under Michael's casual cruelty, his utter indifference.

I'd known that choosing would mean losing one of them. I just hadn't imagined losing Michael like this.

I turned back to the house, willing myself not to cry. Dean stood. His eyes met mine, and I allowed myself to go back to the moment in the woods—and all of the moments that had led up to it. *Holding his hand, tracing my fingertips along his jawline. The secrets we'd traded. The things that no one else—Natural or not, profiler or not—would ever understand.*

If I'd chosen Michael, Dean would have understood.

I started walking toward the porch, toward Dean, my pace gaining with each step. Michael's voice called after me.

"Cassie?"

There was a hint of genuine emotion in his voice—just a hint of something, but I couldn't tell what. I looked back over my shoulder, but didn't turn around.

"Yes?"

Michael stared at me, his hazel eyes holding a mixture of emotions I couldn't quite parse. "If it had been me in the woods, if I'd been the one to go with Briggs, if I'd been the one you saw at the exact second . . ."

Would it have been me? He didn't finish the question, and I didn't answer it. As I turned back toward the house, he went back to knocking the windows out of that broken, battered car.

"Yeah," he said, his voice carrying on the wind. "That's what I thought."

T
he day the last of my bruises disappeared was the day that we took the GED. It was also the day that Agent Sterling moved back into the house.

When the five of us arrived back from taking the exam, she was directing movers, her own arms loaded down with a large box. Her hair was pulled into a loose ponytail at the base of her neck, stray hairs plastered to her forehead with sweat. She was wearing jeans.

I took in the changes in her appearance and the fact that Briggs's possessions were being carted out of his study. Something had shifted. Whatever soul-searching she'd been doing, whatever memories our captivity had stirred up, she'd reached some kind of resolution. Something she could live with.

Beside me, Dean stared after Sterling as she disappeared into her room. I wondered if he was thinking about the woman he'd known five years ago. I wondered what relationship she bore to the woman in front of us now.

"Think it's therapeutic to have all her ex-husband's stuff hauled out of this house?" Michael asked as a pair of movers walked by with Briggs's desk.

"One way to find out." Lia strolled in the direction Sterling had gone. A split second later, the rest of us followed.

Almost all traces of Briggs had been removed from the room, which now boasted an actual bed in place of the fold-out couch. Sterling's back was to us as she placed the box on the bed and began opening it. "How did the test go?" she asked without turning around.

"Splendidly," Lia replied. She twirled a strand of dark hair around her index finger. "How was federally mandated psychological evaluation?"

"So-so." Sterling turned to face us. "How are you doing, Cassie?" she asked. Something in her tone told me that she knew the answer.

Some people said that broken bones grew back stronger. On the good days, I told myself that was true, that each time the world tried to break me, I became a little less breakable. On the bad days, I suspected that I would always be broken, that parts of me would never be quite right—and that those were the parts that made me good at the job.

Those were the parts that made this house and the people in it *home*.

"I'm okay," I said. Lia refrained from commenting on my

answer to Agent Sterling's question. Beside us, Sloane tilted her head to one side, staring at Sterling with a perplexed look on her face.

"You came back," Sloane told the agent, her forehead crinkling. "The probability of your return was quite low."

Agent Sterling turned back to the boxes on her bed. "When the odds are bad," she said, removing something from one of them, "you change the rules."

The look on Sloane's face left very little doubt that she found that statement to be somewhat dubious. I was too busy wondering what Sterling meant when she referenced changing the rules to spare a moment's thought to probabilities or odds.

You've been buried alive in a glass coffin with a sleeping cobra on your chest. I thought of the game Sterling had played with Scarlett Hawkins. Impossible situations required impossible solutions. Veronica Sterling had come here largely intending to disband this program, and now she was moving in.

What was I missing?

"This mean you're done running?"

I turned to see Judd standing in the doorway behind us. I wondered how long he'd been there and turned the question over in my mind. He'd watched Agent Sterling grow up. When she'd left the FBI and turned her back on this program, she'd put distance between them, too.

"I'm not going anywhere," Sterling told him. She walked over to her nightstand and unwrapped the object in her hand, discarding the tissue paper.

A *picture frame.*

I knew, before attempting to get a closer look, what I would see in the frame.

Two little girls, one dark-haired, one light. Both of them beamed at the camera. The smaller one—Scarlett—was missing her two front teeth.

"I'm not going anywhere," Sterling said a second time.

I glanced at Dean, knowing instinctively, even before our eyes met, that his thoughts would be operating in tandem with mine. Sterling had spent a long time keeping her emotions on lockdown. She'd spent a long time trying not to care, trying to keep the person she used to be in check.

"Not to interrupt a touching moment," Michael said, his voice lined with enough bite to make me think he wasn't talking just about the moment between Sterling and Judd—he was referring to the synchrony between Dean and me. "But I detect a hint of tension in your jaw, Agent." Michael's eyes flitted left and right, up and down, cataloging everything about Sterling's posture and expression. "Not stress so much as . . . anticipation."

The doorbell rang then, and Sterling straightened, looking slightly more formidable than she had a moment before. "Visitors," she told Judd briefly. "Plural."

Briggs arrived first, followed by Director Sterling. I'd assumed that was it, but it quickly became clear that they were waiting for someone else.

Someone important.

Minutes later, a dark-colored sedan pulled up. A man

exited the car. He was wearing an expensive suit and a red tie. He walked with purpose, like each step was an integral part of a greater plan.

Once we were all settled in the living room, Agent Sterling introduced him as the director of National Intelligence.

"Principle advisor of the National Security Council," Sloane rattled off. "Reports directly to the president. Head of the Intelligence Community, which encompasses seventeen elements, including the CIA, the NSA, the DEA—"

"And the FBI?" Lia suggested dryly before Sloane could list off all seventeen agencies the man in front of us oversaw.

"Until last week," the man in the red tie said, "I had no idea this program existed."

The purpose of this meeting soon became clear. *When the odds are bad, you change the rules.* Agent Sterling had blown the whistle on the Naturals program.

"I've given a great deal of thought to your report," the director of National Intelligence told Agent Sterling. "The pros and cons of this program. Its strengths. Its weaknesses."

He lingered on the word *weaknesses.* Director Sterling's face was still. This man was his boss. He could disband the program. From the FBI director's perspective, the director of National Intelligence could probably do worse. How many laws had Agent Sterling's father broken, keeping this program off the books?

Agent Sterling is moving in. I clung to that fact. Surely that meant that her father's boss wasn't here to pull the plug. *Surely.*

Sensing that Director Sterling wasn't the only one dis-comfited by his words, the man at the head of National Intelligence addressed the rest of us. "Agent Sterling seems to believe that this program saves lives—and that if you were allowed to participate in active investigations, you could save many more." The intelligence director paused. "She also believes that you can't be trusted to watch out for yourselves, and that no agent involved in an active case, no matter how well-intentioned, can be counted on to put your physical and psychological well-being first."

I glanced at Agent Sterling. That wasn't just an indict-ment of the program—it was an indictment of what *she'd* allowed us to do.

What if they're letting us stay, but won't let us near real cases? Before I'd come here, training to profile people might have been enough, but it wasn't, not now. I needed what I had been through to mean something, I needed a purpose. I needed to *help*.

"Based on Agent Sterling's assessment of the risks inher-ent in this program," the director of National Intelligence continued, "it is her recommendation that this program be restructured, that one Judd Hawkins be appointed as an advocate in your stead, and that any and all deviations from protocol be approved by said advocate, irrespective of the potential benefit to the case."

Restructured. I processed that word. Across from me, Director Sterling's jaw clenched slightly, but the rest of his face remained impassive. If his daughter's recommendation was accepted, that would make Judd the final authority on what we could and could not do.

Judd, not Director Sterling.

"You'll all turn eighteen within the year?" the man who'd come here to decide our future asked. Coming from someone who reported directly to the president, it sounded more like an order than a question.

"Two hundred and forty-three days to go," Sloane confirmed. The rest of us settled for nods.

"They stay behind the scenes." He fixed his casually weighty stare on the director. "Those are the rules."

"Agreed."

"Agents Sterling and Briggs will supervise their participation on all cases, subject to the approval of Major Hawkins. When it comes to what does and does not fall within the purview of this program, his word is final—even for you."

The director stiffened, but didn't hesitate in his reply. "Agreed."

"And the next time you decide to fund an innovative program *off* the books—don't."

The director of National Intelligence didn't give Director Sterling the chance to respond. He just nodded once at us and left.

"I believe I speak for everyone," Michael said, "when I ask *what just happened here?*"

The rules just changed, I thought.

"The Naturals program just got some oversight," Agent Sterling replied. "There are going to be some new regulations.

374

New protocols. And they'll mean something. No more special exceptions—not even from me." Her expression was stern, but Michael must have seen something I didn't, because he broke into a grin. Agent Sterling smiled, too—directly at me.

"We're going to need those regulations," she added, "because as of tomorrow, the five of you are cleared to consult on active cases."

They weren't shutting us out. They were letting us in. Instead of taking away my purpose, they'd given it new life.

This was a whole new world.

ACKNOWLEDGMENTS

Much like catching a killer, writing a book is a team effort, and I feel incredibly lucky to work with such wonderful people. Thanks go first and foremost to the two lovely editors who shepherded this book from its first stages to its last: Catherine Onder and Lisa Yoskowitz. I cannot begin to express how fortunate I feel to be in such good hands or how much better this book is because of their insights and dedication. I would also like to thank Niamh Mulvey, who has been my *Naturals* champion in the UK, as well as the wonderful teams at Hyperion and Quercus, for helping this series find its readers. So much of what goes into a book is done behind the scenes, and I am grateful for all of the work that has gone into this one!

Thanks, too, go to Elizabeth Harding, Ginger Clark, Holly Frederick, and Jonathan Lyons—incredible agents, all! Much like the Naturals' knacks, their abilities border on the uncanny. As with the first book, thanks also go out to everyone at the Dino De Laurentiis Company, especially Martha De Laurentiis and Lorenzo De Maio (who once asked me what case haunted Briggs as "the one that got away").

Finally, I owe a major debt to all of the people in my life who keep me sane when writing is crazy: my wonderful family, NLPT & Ti30, everyone at the University of Oklahoma, and the wonderful and supportive YA writing community. Thanks to Rachel Vincent for writing company and sharing my id, and to Ally Carter, who not only helps me brainstorm, but also locks me in her closet when I am on deadline, which is the sign of a true and wonderful friend. I'm also grateful to Melissa de la Cruz, Carrie Ryan, and Rose Brock, for writing vacations, Rose Fest, and adventure! This book was revised in Cornwall, where Sarah Rees Brennan, Maureen Johnson, Cassandra Clare, Joshua Lewis, and Kelly Link provided both moral and creative support—not to mention a whole lot of fun. I am so grateful both to and for you all.

Finally, I would like to thank all of the readers who have championed the first book—and looked forward to the second. I can't wait for you all to see what's in store for Cassie and the others next.

ALL IN

JENNIFER LYNN BARNES

A NATURALS NOVEL

TURN THE PAGE FOR A SNEAK PEEK

at the next case for the Naturals

YOU

Anything can be counted. The hairs on her head. The words she's spoken to you. The number of breaths she has left.

It's beautiful, really. The numbers. The girl. The things you have planned.

The thing you're destined to become.

New Year's Eve fell on a Sunday. This would have been less problematic if my grandmother hadn't considered "Thou shalt gather thy family for Sunday dinner" an inviolable commandment, or if Uncle Rio had not appointed himself the pourer of wine.

There was a lot of wine.

By the time we were clearing away the plates, it was pretty clear that none of the adults would be driving themselves home anytime soon. Given that my father had seven siblings, all of them married, several with kids a decade or more my senior, there were a lot of "adults." As I carried a stack of plates into the kitchen, the dozen or so arguments brewing behind me were almost, but not quite, drowned out by the sound of boisterous laughter.

Viewed from the outside, it was chaos. But viewed with a profiler's eye, it was simple. Easy to understand. Easy to make sense of. This was a family. The *kind* of family, the individual personalities—those were there in the details: shirts tucked and un-tucked, dishes chipped but handled with love.

"Cassie." My great-uncle bestowed upon me a beatific, bleary-eyed smile as I came into the kitchen. "You miss your family, eh? You come back to visit your old Uncle Rio!"

As far as anyone in this house knew, I'd spent the past six months at a government-sponsored gifted program. Boarding school, more or less. Parts of that were true.

More or less.

"Bah." My grandmother made a dismissive noise in Uncle Rio's general direction as she took a stack of plates from my hands and transferred them to the sink. "Cassie did not come back for old fools who drink too much and talk too loud." Nonna rolled up her sleeves and turned on the faucet. "She came back to see her nonna. To make up for not calling like she should."

Two guilt trips, one stone. Uncle Rio remained largely unfazed. I, on the other hand, felt the intended twinge of guilt and joined Nonna at the sink. "Here," I said. "Let me."

Nonna harrumphed, but slid over. There was something comforting about the fact that she was exactly the same as she'd always been: part mother hen, part dictator, ruling her family with baked ziti and an iron fist.

But I'm not the same. I couldn't dodge that thought. *I've changed.* The new Cassandra Hobbes had more scars—figuratively and literally.

"This one gets cranky when she does not hear from you

for too many weeks," Uncle Rio told me, nodding at Nonna. "But perhaps you are busy?" His face lit up at the prospect, and he studied me for several seconds. "Heartbreaker!" he declared. "How many boyfriends you hide from us now?"

"I don't have a boyfriend."

Uncle Rio had been accusing me of hiding boyfriends from him for years. This was the first and only time he'd ever been right.

"You." Nonna pointed a spatula—which had appeared in her hand out of nowhere—at Uncle Rio. "Out."

He eyed the spatula warily, but held his ground.

"Out!"

Three seconds later, Nonna and I were alone in the kitchen. She stood there, watching me, her eyes shrewd, her expression softening slightly. "The boy who picked you up here last summer," she said, "the one with the fancy car . . . He is a good kisser?"

"Nonna!" I sputtered.

"I have eight children," Nonna told me. "I know about the kissing."

"No," I said quickly, scrubbing at the plates and trying not to read too much into that statement. "Michael and I aren't . . . We don't . . ."

"Ahh," Nonna said knowingly. "His kisses, not so good." She patted me consolingly on the shoulder. "He is young. Room for improvement!"

This conversation was mortifying on so many levels, not the least of which was the fact that *Michael* wasn't the one

I'd been kissing. But if Nonna wanted to think that the reason my phone calls home had been so few and far between was because I was caught in the throes of young romance, let her.

That was an easier pill to swallow than the truth: I'd been subsumed into a world of motives and victims, killers and corpses. I'd been held captive. Twice. I still woke up at night with memories of zip ties digging into my wrists and the sound of gunfire ringing in my ears. Sometimes, when I closed my eyes, I saw light reflected off of a bloody blade.

"You are happy at this school of yours?" Nonna made her best attempt at sounding casual. I wasn't fooled. I'd lived with my paternal grandmother for five years before I'd joined the Naturals program. She wanted me safe, and she wanted me happy. She wanted me *here*.

"I am," I told my grandmother. "Happy." That wasn't a lie. For the first time in my life, I felt like I belonged somewhere. With my fellow Naturals, I never had to pretend to be someone I wasn't. I couldn't have, even if I'd wanted to.

In a house full of people who saw things the rest of the world missed, it was impossible to hide.

"You look good," Nonna admitted grudgingly. "Better now that I have fed you for a week." She harrumphed again, then gently shoved me to the side and took over washing the dishes. "I will send food back with you," she declared. "That boy who picked you up, he is too skinny. Maybe he will kiss better with a little meat on his bones."

I sputtered.

"What's this about kissing?" a voice asked from the doorway. I turned, expecting to see one of my father's brothers. Instead, I saw my father. I froze. He was stationed overseas, and we weren't expecting him for another couple of days.

It had been over a year since the last time I'd seen him.

"Cassie." My father greeted me with a stiff smile, a shade or two off from the real deal.

My thoughts went to Michael. He would have known exactly how to read the tension in my father's face. In contrast, I was a profiler. I could take a collection of tiny details—the contents of a person's suitcase, the words they chose to say hello—and build the big picture: who they were, what they wanted, how they would behave in any given situation.

But the exact meaning of that not-quite-a-smile? The emotions my father was hiding? Whether he felt a spark of recognition or pride or anything fatherly at all when he looked at me?

That, I didn't know.

"Cassandra," Nonna chided, "say hello to your father." Before I had a chance to say anything, Nonna had latched her arms around him, squeezing tightly. She kissed him, then smacked him several times, then kissed him again.

"You are back early." Nonna finally pried herself away from the prodigal son. She gave him a look—probably the same look she'd given him when he'd tracked dirt in on her carpet as a little boy. "Why?"

My father's gaze flitted back to me. "I need to talk to Cassie."

Nonna's eyes narrowed. "And what is it you need to talk to our Cassie about?" Nonna poked him in the chest. Repeatedly. "She is happy at her new school, with her skinny boyfriend."

I barely registered that assertion. My attention was fully focused on my father. He was slightly disheveled. He looked like he hadn't slept at all the night before. He couldn't quite look me in the eye.

"What's wrong?" I asked.

"Nothing," Nonna said, with the force of a sheriff declaring martial law. "Nothing is wrong." She turned back to my father. "You tell her nothing is wrong," she ordered.

My father crossed the room and took my shoulders gently in his hands.

You're not normally this gentle.

My brain ran through everything I knew about him—our relationship, the type of person he was, the fact that he was here at all. My stomach felt like it had been lined with lead. I knew with sudden prescience what he was going to say. The knowledge paralyzed me. I couldn't breathe. I couldn't blink.

"Cassie," my father said softly. "It's about your mother."

CHAPTER 2

There was a difference between *presumed dead* and *dead*, a difference between coming back to a dressing room that was drenched in my mother's blood and being told that after five long years, there was a body.

When I was twelve, thirteen, fourteen years old, I had prayed every night that someone would find my mother, that the police would be proven wrong, that somehow, despite the evidence, despite the amount of blood she'd lost, she'd turn up. Alive.

Eventually, I had stopped hoping and started praying that the authorities would find my mother's body. I had imagined being called in to identify the remains. I'd imagined saying good-bye. I had imagined burying her.

I hadn't imagined this.

"They're sure it's her?" I asked, my voice small, but steady.

My father and I were sitting on opposite sides of a porch

swing, just the two of us, the closest thing to privacy Nonna's house could afford.

"The location's right." He didn't look at me as he replied, staring out into the night. "So is the timing. They're trying to match dental records, but you two moved around so much. . . ." He seemed to realize, then, that he was telling me something I already knew.

My mother's dental records would be hard to come by.

"They found this." My father held out a thin silver chain. A small red stone hung on the end.

My throat closed up.

Hers.

I swallowed, pushing the thought down, like I could unthink it by sheer force of will. My father tried to hand me the necklace. I shook my head.

Hers.

I'd known my mother was almost certainly dead. I'd *known* that. I'd believed it. But now, looking at the necklace she'd worn that night, I couldn't breathe.

"That's evidence." I forced the words out. "The police shouldn't have given it to you. It's evidence."

What were they thinking? I'd only been working with the FBI for six months. Almost all of that time had been spent behind the scenes, and even I knew you didn't break chain of evidence just so a halfway-orphaned girl could have something that belonged to her mother.

"There weren't any prints on it," my father assured me. "Or trace evidence."

"Tell them to keep it," I ground out, standing up and walking to the edge of the porch. "They may need it. For identification."

It had been five years. If they were looking for dental records, there probably wasn't anything left for me *to* identify. *Nothing but bones.*

"Cassie—"

I tuned out. I didn't want to listen to a man who'd barely known my mother telling me that the police had no leads, that they thought it was all right to compromise evidence, because none of them expected this case to be solved.

After five years, we had a body. That was a lead. *Notches in the bones. The way she was buried. The place her killer had laid her to rest.* There had to be *something.* Some hint of what had happened.

He came after you with a knife. I slipped into my mother's perspective, trying to work out what had happened that day, as I had so many times before. *He surprised you. You fought.*

"I want to see the scene." I turned back to my father. "The place where they found the body, I want to see it."

My father was the one who'd signed off on my enrolling in Agent Briggs's gifted program, but he had no idea what kind of "education" I was receiving. He didn't know what the program really was. He didn't know what I could do. Killers and victims, UNSUBs and bodies—this was my language. *Mine.* And what had happened to my mother?

That was mine, too.

"I don't think that's a good idea, Cassie."

It's not your decision. I thought the words, but didn't say them out loud. There was no point in arguing with him. If I wanted access—to the site, to pictures, to whatever scraps of evidence there might be—Vincent Battaglia wasn't the person to ask.

"Cassie?" My father stood and took a hesitant step toward me. "If you want to talk about this—"

I turned around and shook my head. "I'm fine," I said, cutting off his offer. I pushed down the lump rising in my throat. "I just want to go back to school."

"School" was overstating things. The Naturals program consisted of a grand total of five students, and our lessons had what you would call *practical applications*. We weren't just pupils. We were resources to be used.

An elite team.

Each of the five of us had a skill, an aptitude honed to perfection by the lives we'd lived growing up.

None of us had normal childhoods. Those were the words I kept thinking, over and over again, four days later as I stood at the end of my grandmother's drive, waiting for my ride to arrive. *If we had, we wouldn't be Naturals.*

Instead of thinking of the way I'd grown up, going from town to town with a mother who conned people into thinking she was psychic, I thought about the others—about Dean's psychopath of a father and the way Michael had learned to read emotions as a means of survival. About Sloane and Lia and the things I suspected about their childhoods.

Thinking about my fellow Naturals came with a particular brand of homesickness. I wanted them here—all of them, any of them—so badly that I almost couldn't breathe.

"Dance it off." I could hear my mother's voice in my memory. I could see her, wrapped in a royal blue scarf, her red hair damp from cold and snow as she flipped the car radio on and turned it up.

That had been our ritual. Every time we moved—from one town to the next, from one mark to the next, from one show to the next—she turned on the music, and we danced in our seats until we forgot about everything and everyone we'd left behind.

My mother wasn't a person who'd believed in missing anything for long.

"You're looking deep in thought." A low, no-nonsense voice brought me back to the present.

I pushed back against the memories—and the deluge of emotions that wanted to come with them. "Hey, Judd."

The man the FBI had hired to look after us studied me for a moment, then picked up my bag and swung it into the trunk. "You going to say good-bye?" he asked, nodding toward the porch.

I turned back to see Nonna standing there. She loved me. Fiercely. Determinedly. *From the moment you met me.* The least I owed her was a good-bye.

"Cassandra?" Nonna's tone was brisk as I approached. "You forget something?"

For years, I'd believed that I was broken, that my ability

to love—fiercely, determinedly, freely—had died with my mother.

The past few months had taught me I was wrong.

I wrapped my arms around my grandmother, and she latched hers around me and held on for dear life.

"I should go," I said after a moment.

She tapped my cheek with a little more oomph than necessary. "You call if you need anything," she ordered. "Anything."

I nodded.

She paused. "I am sorry," she said carefully. "About your mother."

Nonna had never met my mother. She didn't know the first thing about her. I'd never told my father's family about my mom's laugh, or the games she'd used to teach me to read people, or the way we'd said *no matter what* instead of *I love you*, because she didn't just love me—she loved me forever and ever, no matter what.

"Thanks," I told my grandmother. My voice came out slightly hoarse. I tamped down on the grief rising up inside me. Sooner or later, it would catch up to me.

I had always been better at compartmentalizing than ridding myself of unwanted emotions altogether.

As I turned away from Nonna's prying eyes and walked back to Judd and the car, I couldn't banish the memory of my mom's voice.

Dance it off.